A PROMISE IS FOR EVER

A Promise Is For Ever

by

Denise Robins

Magna Large Print Books
Long Preston, North Yorkshire,
BD23 4ND, England.

British Library Cataloguing in Publication Data.

Robins, Denise
    A promise is for ever.

    A catalogue record of this book is
    available from the British Library

    ISBN   0-7505-2111-2

First published in Great Britain 1961
by Hodder & Stoughton Ltd.

Published in Large Print 2003 by arrangement with
Patricia Clark for Executors of Denise Robins' Estate

Magna Large Print is an imprint of Library Magna Books Ltd.

Printed and bound in Great Britain by
T.J. (International) Ltd., Cornwall, PL28 8RW

For
Harriet Lemon,
our 'Nellie',
who is as good a cook
as the heroine in this story

1

When Fern first told her husband about the disaster that had just befallen her parents, it was for her a personal tragedy. It brought into her life that bitter thing that every woman, old or young, hopes to avoid: disillusionment. It was as though she had once put her arms around a pillar which she thought fine and strong, hung on to it for support, then suddenly the ground had crumbled under her feet. The pillar crumbled, too. After that, feeling dazed and bruised, she had nothing left to hang on to except her own unshaken faith in her father.

She would never forget that night.

Terry came home at seven o'clock. He had said he might be late because he was 'having a drink in the City with a fellow who might give him a job'. There was always somebody who might give Terry a job. It had been that way since he and Fern first got married, a year ago. No one seemed to want him. Fern couldn't understand it. Of course, she knew her darling Terry had no particular qualifications and that he was a bit on the lazy side. But she was so madly in love with him, she was quite sure he would eventually come out on top. She always believed in people until they proved themselves unworthy. Now, at last she was forced to remember a few of the remarks her father had made on the day she told him she had fixed the date of the wedding.

'I don't think he's really worthy of you, lovey. But if you want him so much – well, you must have him.'

Typical of Daddy, who had always spoiled her and tried to give her everything.

Mummy had put in her word.

'Of course, darling, I see things more from the woman's angle, and Terry is absolutely *charming*. I admit it. But I do wonder just at times what lies *under* that charm. You *must* make *sure*, darling!'

Fern had laughed and disregarded the warning. She *was* sure. Terry could do no wrong. It wasn't his fault that he had failed all those silly high-grade exams that other young men seemed to pass; or that he hated the idea of sitting in an office. She could understand it. He was fond of being out-of-doors, and particularly of driving (he was wonderful with cars). He had figured in one

12

or two small rallies and won a trophy. And it wasn't his fault either, she decided, if a year ago when he was twenty-three, his father – a widower – had died and left him penniless. Old Mr Barrett was a Civil Servant whose job and pension had died with him. He left Terry nothing.

Anyhow, what did money matter? *(What had it mattered to Fern at the time?)* Her own father was a partner in a large, successful firm of stockbrokers. She had been brought up in luxury. She had never had to bother her head about £.s.d. But because she liked cooking enormously she had taken a Cordon Bleu course and used often to cook for Mummy's big dinner parties.

Daddy was always so proud of his domesticated daughter. She wasn't a time-waster, he used to inform his friends. She was industrious; a girl of real character. He used to boast in the office (and at his Club) that just before his daughter met Terry, she had come of age, and he had offered her a mink jacket, but she had refused it.

'I'd rather have a model kitchen – it'll set you back a bit but I want it. Ours is right out of date,' she had laughed. They lived in one of those big old-fashioned houses in Hampstead. Mrs Wendell, Fern's mother, was the exact reverse of Fern. She loathed house-work and cooking. She thought Fern mad when she induced her father to spend all that money on kitchen units and a new fridge and cooker.

'But just see what a good wife I'll make with all this experience,' Fern had laughed.

During this last year that was what she believed she had been to Terry. A devoted wife keen on the cooking and housekeeping – taking an immense pride in their flat, which was at the top of a new block in Sloane Street. Nobody had ever, of course, suggested to Fern that Terry had married her as much for her money as for herself. She wasn't the sort of girl to make an analysis of an emotional affair. When she fell in love she fell in love whole-heartedly. That was that. Anyhow, she was sure that Terry loved *her* and that the difference in their positions didn't come into it.

Terry was always 'talking big'.

'I'll soon find the sort of job to suit me. I'm not going to chuck my talents away.' (Etc., etc.)

When he had turned down her father's offer to go into the firm and teach him stockbroking, Fern had loyally upheld him. It didn't really do (quoting Terry) to work for one's in-laws. A young man must stand on his own feet. This seemed to her sensible, but he had spent all that he had ever had and they were already living on Fern's allowance, although she never let anybody know it. She was confident that Terry would come back from one of his many appointments to tell her that he had really found a job this time.

Meanwhile Fern was happy. She was naturally of a happy disposition. She lived on faith and her passionate absorption in the man she had chosen for a husband. They got on very well and were physically right for each other, which is important in marriage.

Yesterday had been a lovely May day. The trees in the London parks were green with the new delicate leaves. Spring was in the air. Fern dreamed of a country cottage. Then Fate cut her dreams in two.

She was reeling under the first blow when her husband came home and dealt her the second.

He walked into the kitchen where she was preparing one of her special dishes for the evening meal and started to make his usual excuses.

'Bit of a sell, darling, but the ruddy fellow

offered me a salary I wouldn't dream of taking. I want to be able to keep my wife in the manner to which she is accustomed.'

He didn't look particularly upset. He grinned at her. Fern, who knew him now, could tell that he had been drinking. He was flushed, and his handsome hazel eyes were a little defiant. He was finishing a half-smoked cigar. Who had paid for it, she didn't mean to ask. She stood straight and silent while he put his arms around her and kissed her. Her heart was heavy. Deep woe – so new to her – had taken all the colour out of her small, determined face. Slowly, nervously, she wiped her hands on a tea-towel. For the first time in her life she did not respond to Terry's kiss. Usually she flung her arms around his neck and returned the kiss rapturously. Tonight she did not even hear half he said as he uttered the usual slick, meaningless excuses.

At last she turned from him.

'Come and sit down with me, darling, in the lounge. I've got some bad news to tell you and I need all your support.'

(That was before the pillar crumbled.)

In their delightful elegant lounge, Fern stood with her back to the fireplace, pale, unsmiling, smoking a cigarette, and told

16

him what had happened. Mummy and Daddy (which included herself, of course) were ruined.

'Sunk, darling,' she said, with an attempt to laugh, which ended in tears. 'Absolutely sunk.'

Terence Barrett blinked at her a little stupidly. He took the cigar from his mouth and held it between his fingers. He exclaimed:

'I say – what *do* you mean?'

She tried to speak but could not. She was trying not to cry. She looked rather like a schoolgirl courageously facing disgrace, in that short sleeveless cotton frock. She was boyishly slim. Her hair, short-cut, springing crisply up from a broad intelligent forehead, was the brown of autumn leaves – with a trace of gold and red in it. Her eyes were of a clear periwinkle blue, thickly lashed. Those exceptionally blue eyes, the delightful way her hair grew, and her large attractive mouth made Fern a most desirable young woman. Terence Barrett had found her very desirable indeed (from all aspects, including the social and financial). He, and he alone, knew that if he had not met Fern at that dance a year ago, he might now have been in pretty poor straits. He had spent the small sum his mother had left him on having a good time. He might have had to settle down to a really dull, hard job of work instead of going on being a play-boy. It would have been fatal to Terry if his good looks and his charm couldn't get him a rich man's daughter for a bride.

Now, as he heard Fern's story, he learned that he was no longer married to an heiress. She had nothing now, like himself. Except her furs, a few bits of jewellery which her parents had given her, and the contents of this flat.

Right before his shocked gaze, Terence saw his cosy, easy life vanishing. The handsome house of his in-laws, filled with valuable furniture and paintings, would have to be sold, Fern was telling him. And his father-in-law, Bernard Wendell, was a criminal, wanted by the police.

Fern did not actually use that word. It was in Terry's mind. Staunchly, she was defending the father she adored. He was an innocent dupe, she said. He had known nothing of what was going on. The senior partner of the firm, Mr Boyd-Gillingham, was the real criminal. Daddy's firm had been acting for some big Trust. The stockbrokers had used money that did not

18

belong to them in order to buy shares that had gone down instead of up. The original shareholders were demanding restitution. The firm was to be hammered. Boyd-Gillingham, himself, was now seriously ill at his home in Gerrards Cross. And Fern's father, Bernard Wendell, had disappeared.

'I've spent the whole day with Mummy,' Fern finished wearily. 'You know what she's like – terribly helpless, poor darling, even in ordinary times. She's quite prostrate over this. Fortunately Aunt Pam has come to spend tonight with her. Tomorrow you and I will have to look after her interests.'

'And where, may I ask, is Papa?' demanded Terence in a stiff, shocked voice.

'Nobody knows. He left Mummy a private note to say that he'd be safely out of the country before the storm broke and that he would do everything in his power to make amends, and that we must all believe in him.'

'But why didn't he face the music? I think he's acted most foolishly,' said Terence in a lordly way, as though he, personally, would have done better in similar circumstances.

Fern explained that Daddy had relatives – very wealthy ones – in America. Mummy believed that he had flown over to solicit their help, in order to clear his name. He would never have been able to do it here. He had sworn that he, personally, had absolutely nothing to do with the fraud. It had all been a ghastly shock to him.

'I *know* it's true,' Fern declared loyally, her eyes full of burning tears. 'Daddy's proved it by telling us to sell everything we possess, and to use every penny we have in the world to help pay back the shareholders who have lost their money in this disaster. He thought only of those poor people.'

'And what about his own family?' asked Terry, using the drawl that he liked to adopt when he wanted to be haughty.

'Well, he knows that Mummy has a few hundreds a year of her own and that she can live on that, even if it only means existing in some small hotel. And he knows that I've got *you*. He said how thankful he was that I was married.'

Then Terence laughed. It was that laugh which brought Fern out of her stupor of misery and jarred every nerve in her body. It was such a hateful laugh.

'Married to me! And that pays all the bills, of course. It must be your father's idea of a joke,' he jeered.

She felt the tears dry on her lashes.

'A joke?' she repeated, blinking.

Terence looked away from her big blue eyes. She had an uncomfortable habit of looking at one as though she could see right into one's mind, he reflected irritably.

'My dear Fern, you *know* I haven't got a sou!' he said.

She stared at him.

'But you're expected to support your wife. You've been saying it is your dearest wish. And you've been looking for a job for ages – haven't you?'

Terry poured himself out a drink. Then he turned round and looked back at his wife through half-shut eyes.

'Without much success, I'm afraid, sweetie. Of course I can take to tramping the streets and answering small ads or apply to the Labour Exchange,' he said, with a shrug. 'I'm sure I'd find something like road-mending.'

Fern's heart seemed to wither within her. For a moment she could not speak. Her cigarette burned to a long ash between her fingers. The second blow had fallen and this time it was a death blow to her romance – the old sweet blind belief in Terry. She suddenly saw him for what he was. Mean-spirited, lazy, utterly unreliable. The realisation made her feel sick.

'No,' she whispered the word to herself. 'Oh, *no!*'

It had been bad enough at home with Mummy all today. Poor Mummy, who was a clinging vine and had always let Daddy do everything for her. So pretty still, although in her fifties, so smart. Fond of her bridge, her dinner parties, her holidays in France or Italy or Jamaica. Lapping up flattery.

('You look so young for your age, Mrs Wendell!')

('You're so lucky with your wonderful husband and home, Vivien!')

That was Vivien Wendell. Weeping and terrified, she had clung to her daughter – bemoaning her lot. Fern must take her father's place, she said. She was so like her grandmother – that first Fern who had been a great character – born in Carolina – one of those strong American women who could face any disaster and master it. Young Fern had inherited a lot of that determination and capability despite her 'little-girl loveliness'. Now Fern would have to be all things to her mother.

Bad enough, Fern thought, as she faced her husband, to know that Daddy had vanished overnight as though an earthquake

22

had swallowed him up, and that tomorrow everybody would know the truth. Grim to have to realise that not only was Mummy going to be reduced to a meagre income, but that Fern's own allowance would stop immediately. But at the back of it all, Fern had clung gratefully to the thought of Terry. He was her husband. *He* would comfort and help her mother. He was only a boy and perhaps too fond of the bright lights – but she had always been certain he was fundamentally good and that love could make any trouble, physical or mental, easier to bear. She had longed for his return so that she could find that love and support in his arms.

But there he stood, telling her that he couldn't possibly ever hope to pay the rent of this flat or keep his wife in anything but cheap 'digs'. Then he added sullenly that he had been cheated.

That word was for Fern the *coup de grâce*.

'Cheated!' she echoed in a suffocated voice. 'You've been *cheated?*… But how?…'

He looked ashamed, and made haste to withdraw the abominable word.

'I don't really mean that, darling. I just mean we've *both* been sort of cheated, thinking that your father was a man of his word and that his position and ours were secure.'

Fern went on staring at Terry as though she could not recognise him. Yet there he was, slim, tall, exceedingly good-looking with his thick fair hair and bright hazel eyes and that elegance which was an essential feature of Terry's personality.

'Daddy *is* a man of his word,' said Fern trembling, 'and he is going to prove that he isn't personally responsible for this awful thing. Oh, Terry, how *can* you be so unfeeling ... so ... so...' Her voice broke off. Suddenly she dropped down into a chair and put her face into her hands. She could bear no more.

Terence Barrett tossed down his drink, swore under his breath, then knelt down beside his wife and set about the task of getting himself back into favour. He didn't want Fern to be angry with him and it didn't suit him to be despised, or if it came to a matter of that, found out. He knew that she thought the world of him and had in fact married him against her parents' wishes. For her love and loyalty he was, in his weak fashion, grateful. He was not all bad. As far as he was capable of love – he loved Fern. He admired her character. She was so 'full of guts', as he often expressed it. *And* she was beautiful. He had been physically faithful to her since they married – quite crazy about her in fact – and never wanted anybody else. *But let's face it,* he thought, *I counted on her inheriting a small fortune from the old man. I thought the firm of Boyd-Gillingham, Price & Wendell as safe as the Bank of England. It only goes to show that one can't rely on anything but hard cash in one's own keeping.*

As for old man Wendell being innocent, what did it matter whether he was or he wasn't? ... his firm was implicated, he'd quit, and there wasn't a bean left. Terry had to confess that Fern without a bean behind her was not *quite* so attractive as the other Fern whom he had so gaily led to the altar.

Now he tried to put on some sort of show of love and penitence. He was not unkind at heart and he could see that the poor little thing was badly shocked. He hugged and kissed her. He implored her not to misunderstand him, or anything he had said. It was all because he, too, had had a blow. But *of course* he would get a job now – by hook or by crook. He could drive any car. He might get taken on by some car-firm, as a salesman – or driver.

'We'll battle through, my sweet. Don't despair,' he said, warming up to his part. He remembered with relief that there was at least one more bottle of whisky in the drink cupboard.

Gradually Fern thawed. She had been quite frozen by the way her husband had originally taken her news. But as he talked and talked and made all his new big promises and plans and assured her that he adored her, she tried to believe in him again. But she felt confused and so tired that she couldn't think straight.

God knew, she thought, she didn't want to believe Terry was just a fortune-hunter. She was only too thankful to accept any explanation he gave. She shuddered away from cold, harsh facts. She let him make love to her – gently exploring her body with his caressing fingers until she turned wholly to him – on fire for him again. At last she pulled herself out of his arms and pushed her hair back from her hot, damp face.

'My darling, Terry – what a pair we are,' she said in a shaky voice. 'I must look *grim!*'

He straightened his collar and tie and smoothed back his hair. His handsome face bore the smug self-satisfied look of the male conqueror. He knew Fern could never resist his lovemaking. He had her where he wanted her again. And he was still mad about her. She was devilishly attractive. He eyed her greedily as she put on her cotton frock again. She was a pretty thing – her skin was like peach-velvet, and her waist incredibly small. It wasn't all the money – he *did* love her for herself. He only wished to God old man Wendell hadn't wrecked the boat.

'Your dinner will be ruined, darling. I'd made you something lovely. I expect it's all burnt,' said Fern, smiling at him in her sweet shy way. She had never quite grown used to Terry's crazy outbursts of passion at all hours.

'Never mind, darling, I'll take you out to dinner.'

'What on?' Fern asked with a shaky laugh.

'Oh, I won a tenner at Sandown this afternoon.'

She was too happy again to start wondering why Terry had been to the races instead of keeping business appointments, but she said:

'No, I'll make you one of my mushroom omelettes. Let's keep the money, darling. We'll need it.'

He followed her into the kitchen, wondering gloomily how many of his personal friends *he* would keep when the news broke in the papers tomorrow. But he said nothing. He put on quite a good show for the rest of the evening – even went so far as to telephone his mother-in-law – he knew she was not fond of him – to tell her how sorry he was about everything, and that he would do his best to help.

He insisted on making the coffee while Fern lay on the sofa with her feet up. Then he sat beside her and built up a picture of himself (which he found quite fascinating) as the prop of the whole family. He would do this – he would do that – he would prove at last how much he loved her and how safely she could rely on *him* from now onwards. He admitted that he'd been rather 'naughty' not hurrying into some job he didn't like but he had thought she was secure. Now he knew she wasn't he would take anything that came his way. He would work his fingers to the bone for her.

On and on until Fern was mesmerised. Looking at him with her blue candid gaze, she began to wonder if he had ever said those shocking things when she first told him about poor Daddy. He still seemed to be the husband she adored. She went to bed and slept the night through, exhausted, with

Terry's arms around her; hopeful that all would yet be well.

There was an unpleasant moment, of course, when the morning papers arrived. Headlines were there, horribly to the fore.

LONDON FIRM OF STOCKBROKERS INVOLVED IN FRAUD. SHAREHOLDERS STORM OFFICE ... etc.

And, of course, a photograph of Bernard Wendell. One look at the dear familiar face of her father (handsome and smiling, poor darling), and Fern burst into tears. Her mother then telephoned and went into hysterics. Then Fern had to talk to Aunt Pamela, Mummy's sister. Fern did not much like her, and liked her still less now because Aunt Pam refused to be nice about Daddy and said he must have *known* what was happening and had behaved abominably.

Terence, feeling irritated, had to dry Fern's tears, then he devoured the papers but fortunately found only one little paragraph which stated that his father-in-law had 'got away'; as for the rest – it was plain to Terence that the sooner he and Fern got rid of this flat and did a little vanishing themselves, the better.

It was a chaotic morning. The telephone never stopped ringing. Reporters, and friends who truly wished to sympathise, or those who only wanted morbid details, plus a few of Terence's creditors, trying to make sure that their bills would be paid.

Altogether an unpleasant affair. But Terence did his best to maintain his high level as a heroic comforter. Fern, herself, looked a little older, a little paler and unsmiling, but she behaved, Terry had to admit, magnificently. She called in the family lawyer and, with her mother and Aunt Pam and Terence, they met for a conference. They decided that the old home must at once be put on the market. For a while, Mummy could go and stay with Aunt Pam, who was unmarried and had a small but comfortable home in Highgate. Then Fern suggested she and Terry should dispose of the lease of their own flat and move to cheaper quarters.

'At least I can cook well,' she said. 'I *can* get a job as a cook. I like it and I can make a bit of money that way. Domestic help is more in demand than anything else.'

It was that next morning, looking down the personal column of *The Times*, that Fern saw *the* advertisement, and pointed it out to her husband.

'Look! That's the very thing for us.'

Terence looked.

Wealthy business man with big country house requires married couple, cook-housekeeper and chauffeur, immediately. First-class cooking required. Comfortable modern flat over garage and good salary. Apply: Quentin Dorey, Swanlake Manor, Cuckendean, Sussex.

Terence read this advertisement aloud and then turned his gaze haughtily upon his wife.

'You're not suggesting that you and I should take a job as cook-housekeeper and chauffeur?'

Fern, who had just been going through her jewel case to see what she could sell, and had also taken her sable-tie out of its moth-proof bag, deciding that she might raise a hundred pounds on that, looked at him calmly.

'Why not? Those are the things we two do superlatively well. I cook, you drive.'

Terence flushed. He had one of those fair skins that coloured easily.

'Well, really. To become *menials*...'

'Don't be silly, darling. Thousands of terribly nice men are chauffeurs these days and

31

hundreds of nice women go out cooking. Besides, it means not only a salary, but a home in the country, rent-free.'

'But I say, Fern–'

'And what's more,' she interrupted, 'it'll have its amusing side. We've just got to keep a sense of humour in a crisis like this. I think it'll be rather fun me cooking for my employer's dinner parties and you driving him around in a nice Rolls.'

'If it is a Rolls,' muttered Terry.

'I bet it is,' said Fern. 'Do you realise who Quentin Dorey is?'

Terence gloomily lit a cigarette. It was all very well, he thought, for Fern to talk about a sense of humour – but driving one's own Rolls was one thing, and having to get out and open the door for the chap in the back was another.

'Quentin Dorey,' continued Fern, 'is a financial tycoon. I fancy I've heard Daddy speak of him. You must have seen his name in the papers. Q.D., they always call him. Q.D. down at Monte Carlo, or Q.D. over in Tangiers, or Q.D. flying to New York. And I seem to remember now that I saw photographs of Swanlake Manor when he first bought it. It was featured in one of the magazines. A glorious old place about ten miles out of Brighton and famous because it has one room with a huge cedar-lined cupboard in which Queen Elizabeth was said to have kept some of her hundreds of dresses. I remember, too, seeing a picture of the four-poster which old Liz slept in and which no doubt our tycoon himself now uses.'

Fern had a good memory. She remembered still more about Quentin Dorey. That he was not married. And that he was self-made. When she gave this information to Terry he was even more glum. *Self-made,* fancy having to work for a man of *that* calibre! Whereupon Fern laughingly told him not to be such a snob. Besides, it would be fun joining his staff, she said, warming up to the idea. Why not try? Why not telephone and see if he would interview them? Maybe he had a London flat and he could see them there. Why not strike while the iron was hot? It would at least tide them over this present awful crisis.

'I don't suppose he'd take us if he knew who you were,' muttered Terence, not very tactfully.

Fern coloured and felt that niggling pain in her heart which was still there when she looked at Terry. But she answered quietly:

'He need not know. To him we will just be Mr and Mrs Barrett.'

'Crikey!' exploded Terence in rich Cockney and rolled his eyes heavenwards, but he did not turn the idea down out of hand.

It was he who finally lifted the telephone receiver and dialled the number of Quentin Dorey's Sussex home.

2

A station taxi came to a jolting stop just inside the big wrought-iron gateway of Swanlake Manor. In front of the creeper-covered lodge stood a short, stout man with a weather-beaten face. He held a spade in one hand and a trug in the other and he looked what he was – a gardener.

Fern leaned out of the taxi and spoke to him.

'This right for Mr Dorey?'

'Quite right, miss.'

'We're the new cook and chauffeur,' said Fern brightly, while Terry edged himself further into the corner as though he would rather not be seen. He had to 'hand it' to Fern, he reflected. She was 'game'. He was quite amazed at the way she was taking this unhappy tide in her affairs.

He saw the gardener's expression change from the deferential respect which had first enlightened it to one of surprise. He drew nearer the taxi window.

'Are you, now?' he said. 'Well, I wish you

both good morning. Mr Dorey is in – I saw him just now as I passed the library window. Proper bad sciatica, he's got, and can't hardly move.'

'So we heard from his secretary,' said Fern.

'Mrs Dorey is away,' said the gardener, and added: 'My name's Hatton.'

'We're Mr and Mrs Barrett,' said Fern.

After the taxi had moved off, Jim Hatton went into the lodge and entered the small kitchen where his wife, a buxom woman, younger than himself, with fair bushy hair, sat feeding a nine months old baby.

'New cook and chauffeur have just driven up to the big house,' he said, looking down at his latest offspring. There were two others, a girl of twelve and a boy of eight, whose high, gay voices could be heard in the back garden.

'What are they like?' asked Mrs Hatton.

'Well, I never did have such a surprise as when I saw *her*,' announced the gardener, taking off his leather jerkin, and rolling up his sleeves preparatory to having a wash in the sink. 'Like one of them girls you see on the Telly.'

'What, all made up?' asked Rosemary Hatton (called Rosie by her husband). She raised her eyes from the baby, looking positively excited. There were so few real excitements in her life apart from the cooking and the children. The last cook had certainly been no glamour-girl and had been short of temper, too. Rosie had never enjoyed going up to the Manor when that one was in charge. Rosie 'did' for the Doreys five mornings a week. Jim's mother, who lived with them here, minded the baby. Old Mrs Hatton was at this moment out in the garden taking nappies down from the line.

'I couldn't see proper whether the young woman had stuff on her face or not,' said Jim Hatton, 'but she was proper nice to look at.'

'And what about *him?*'

'Couldn't see.'

'Well, let's hope they settle down. I'm sick of changes up there,' said Rosie Hatton with a sniff.

She could have added that she was sick of Mr Dorey's mother, too; always interfering and nagging. A woman couldn't get on with her work. No wonder they never kept anybody for long. The good ones wouldn't stay and the bad ones got the sack. But Jim had a fine job here with good pay and he doted on the garden and the greenhouses. *He*'d never leave. He'd worked here as an under-gardener when Swanlake belonged to Lord Chavering. Rosie was tired of listening to him talk about the Chaverings and how those were the good old days of the 'real gentry'. Mind you, Jim liked Mr Dorey. He might be a bit sharp-tongued at times and what the books called *'newvoh-rich'*, thought Rosie, but he was an exceedingly nice man. And my goodness what a brain he had. Jim said he'd made a pile of money, and was making more. Had a passion for Swanlake, too, ever since he bought it. Didn't interfere with Jim and the garden and spoke kindly to Rosie whenever she met him. And she wouldn't forget that day when Gary, their boy (they'd called him after Gary Cooper), had broken his arm and she'd dashed up to the big house and Mr Dorey had been right in the middle of important writing but he'd taken out his car and driven her and Gary straight to the doctor and been ever so nice with Gary afterwards.

In the taxi going up to the Manor, Fern was leaning out of the window on this bright May morning, looking ecstatically at the house.

'Oh, isn't it *glorious!*' she exclaimed.

The parkland surrounding Swanlake was so much greener and fresher than the London parks. The sight of a herd of small spotted deer, grazing, brought a little cry of pleasure from her. She was enthralled when they drove into the grounds and she saw the house and gardens for the first time. They were more beautiful, she thought, than in the photographs. The Manor was a magnificent three-storeyed house built partially of Elizabethan brick and partially of stone, with those long, square-paned windows jutting slightly out and framed in beautiful carved stonework, often to be seen in places of this period. It seemed a huge house to Fern, and the gardens, too, looked enormous – formally laid out with clipped yew hedges, some of them shaped like birds. The flowerbeds were already massed with purple parrot tulips, rising from a bank of pale blue forget-me-nots.

There were a variety of trees, a riot of pink, scarlet and golden azaleas. On the left, she could see a corner of the ornamental lake that had given the place its name. And, there *were* swans on it. Fern nodded to herself with satisfaction as she watched the graceful white mother, father, and six pale grey cygnets skimming across the shining water.

'Oh, *do* say you think it's beautiful here, darling!' she appealed to her husband.

'Stately home and all that – yes,' agreed Terry, 'but don't forget, you and I are for the flat over the garage, my pet.'

He was impressed by what he saw, if not as thrilled as Fern. He was still not sure they had done the right thing in taking this job. Not too keen on the idea of being at a jumped-up tycoon's beck and call; having to wash and polish the blooming car as well as drive it at all hours. But Fern had been carrying Terry along on a tide of enthusiasm since Quentin's personal assistant had interviewed and engaged them at the London office.

They had given the rector of the church in Hampstead at which the Wendells worshipped for one reference, and a certain Lady Colway – a friend of Mrs Wendell, whom they had let into the secret of this job – for the other. The rector had promised to say nice things and not mention Fern's maiden name, so they thought they were safe, and Miss Porter, Quentin's assistant, had seemed satisfied. She had done the interviewing because Quentin's mother was away in Sweden for a month, and the couple who used to do the job at Swanlake had gone at a moment's notice. Mr Dorey was in a fix, Miss Porter had admitted, and needed someone down there immediately. It would have been all right if he'd been well and able to stay at his London flat, but a sharp attack of sciatica was keeping him chained to the Manor.

So here they were, and Fern was happy about it if Terry wasn't.

There seemed to be nobody about. Fern and Terry got out of the taxi and pulled their cases after them. Terry paid the taxi-man. Fern lifted the big Queen Anne knocker and banged it vigorously. Now she heard a man's deep voice call from the interior:

'Come in. Come in. I can't get up…'

'It's the sciatica,' Fern whispered to her husband, and the mischievous dimple, which she could never control, appeared at one corner of her mouth. She wished Terry would cheer up, it was all such an adventure. Their little world of luxury and security had vanished but they had youth and strength, and another kind of world was opening up before them.

'Come on, let's pass our test,' she whispered, and walked with him into the house.

'Come in!' repeated the man's voice, this time rather crossly.

The Barretts entered the library. A swift look satisfied Fern that it was one of the most beautiful rooms she had ever seen, full of books. Then she saw the man who half lay, half sat on an olive green velvet Chesterfield, holding a stick across one knee. A big man, his dark upspringing hair peppered with grey. Fern was surprised to note this because she had been told that Mr Dorey was only in his thirties. He must be going grey very young. Everything else about him was young and vital, despite the stick and his present disability. He had a pale, rather arresting face with high forehead and deep-set eyes, grey and penetrating. The nose was too big and the jaw line too strong, yet, as Fern saw immediately, it was a face to be remembered. It fascinated. Quentin Dorey was a man to be reckoned with. A little scaring, in a way, thought Fern. What a critical look he gave both of them as they stood before him. Here was a person to whom no one could lie and get away with it.

'So you're the Barretts.' He snapped the words.

Fern answered.

'Yes.'

'Yes,' repeated Terry, feeling less interested than Fern in Quentin, and much more intrigued by the air of wealth and importance which hung over everything here. Superb period furniture, fine Persian rugs. On a walnut sofa-table by the couch stood a tray with a crystal decanter of sherry and some glasses which Terry eyed enviously.

'Sit down, sit down, and we'll discuss things,' said Quentin Dorey.

Everything about him was rather abrupt, Fern decided ... his voice and his manner. And she did not like his choice of ties or that rather loud check of the coat he wore. He was a self-made man, this magnate, known to the world of finance as 'Q.D.' No breeding – Fern had known that before she came. Yet when suddenly he looked at her and motioned her to a chair, and his lips relaxed into a brief smile, she was conscious of a nameless charm, a warmth that could only spring from some fount of generosity in the man's inner being. It was a complete paradox, Q.D.'s smile, and Fern, who had always been deeply interested in human nature, was amazed by the sweetness of it.

'Sorry not to be able to get up when a lady enters the room and all that, but you see how I'm incapacitated by this damned sciatica.' He tapped his leg with the ebony stick and grimaced. 'Never been so damned angry. Sciatica is something you can't fight. In spite of all the damn-fool injections and pills the doctors are pushing into me, the pain will have its way. Can't get up to town. Live on the telephone.'

Here Terry thought it time to say something, and murmured.

'Jolly bad luck!'

'I think it must be awful. I remember my father having sciatica,' began Fern, then blushed and stopped, recalling that she must not mention that dear beloved parent's name here – or anywhere else for the moment. She added: 'But it'll go as soon as it comes, Mr Dorey. I know you'll suddenly wake up and find it's all better.'

'I hope you're right.'

He pointed to the decanter.

'Pour yourselves out a sherry. I'm going to have one.'

'Oh, I'm sure you oughtn't to with the sciatica,' Fern began again, but once again stopped, this time scarlet with confusion.

Quentin Dorey stared at the young girl, then suddenly bellowed with laughter.

'So that's how you start life as my cook – ticking me off for having my sherry. The bullying kind, are you? Like my damned doctor.'

'Oh, I'm sorry ... please excuse me ... it was most impertinent of me...' stammered Fern.

'Think nothing of it,' said Quentin, 'just give me that sherry and have one yourself. Barrett – pour out.'

Terry rose. He disliked the order but was only too willing to oblige. He was even beginning to be amused himself. But not being as good a psychologist as Fern, he began to hope that if this man was so lacking in education and culture, he, Mr Terence Barrett, who was a public schoolboy and a man of the world (let's forget the play-boy), might use his influence and work on this millionaire. This place *oozed* money. The sherry was the finest. Yes, he might end up as friend instead of chauffeur to the great Q.D.

In an unctuous voice Terry, sipping his drink, said:

'I admire your taste in wine...' and added with a little bow, *'sir.'*

There shot into Quentin Dorey's curiously light grey eyes a speculative and searching look when he turned them upon the young man. As a rule he either 'took to a chap', or didn't take to him. His hunches were generally right. Just as they had been right on the stockmarket for so many years. Handsome fellow, young Barrett, but one of those too-smooth, too self-confident young gentlemen. The kind that Quentin sometimes envied because of their breeding, their *savoir-faire,* but he never quite trusted them. Still, if Barrett could drive the Rolls well and was as careful and experienced as his reference made him out to be … okay. But it was the cook that worried Quentin. He needed someone to take complete control down here. There was chaos out in the kitchen and didn't he know it.

His mother just didn't seem able to cope with, or keep, servants. She wasn't used to a place like Swanlake Manor. She had always lived in smaller houses. Twenty years ago, of course, when Quentin was still a boy, they had been living up in Lancashire, and mother had done some of the housework. But things had changed since then. That was how Quentin wanted it to be. *He* had changed, too. He wasn't quite the brash, awkward Lancashire lad he used to be. He had become a Power … a Name in the world of speculation, among the bankers and brokers. He was rich and successful. Only, deep down in his heart, Quentin knew that he wasn't quite sure how to write his own success story. His mother couldn't help. For instance, if he wanted to be the real lord of the manor and run a big place like this properly, he must rely on his staff … someone to run the place in the way it *should* be run … he must have a housekeeper who *knew* about things. He stared almost incredulously at the young girl whom Miss Porter had engaged, and wondered if that good lady, who had been his secretary for ten years and was one of the best ever, had gone out of her mind. Mrs Barrett looked a mere *child*. How could *she* take charge here? What could *she* cook? Granted, she had 'class', and in a very big way. He did not know much about women's clothes, but she looked elegant to him. But those extraordinarily blue eyes, so appealing under their long black lashes, did nothing to soothe Quentin's worries. They filled him with misgiving.

'You look too darned young for this job,' he barked, setting down his empty glass.

'Oh, *Mr Dorey!*' exclaimed Fern in dismay.

'I relied on Miss Porter choosing the right couple. I've had enough of failures,' he interrupted. 'The last woman couldn't cook and made me blush for shame when I had my friends down to a meal. The one before that went off with some of the silver. There's no one in the village who'll come because we're three miles from the nearest bus stop, and the best ones are in jobs, anyhow. And my mother, who lives with me, makes things more difficult because she can't stand foreigners and won't have a foreign maid in the place. So we're left with this vast establishment and what have we got but Mrs Hatton, the gardener's wife, and an Irish maid who keeps saying that she wants to go back to Connemara. My mother wants me to sell up and go back to London, but I'm not doing it.' Quentin's fist crashed on the table. 'I fell in love with this place when I first saw it two years ago and here I stay. I don't accept defeat.'

Fern and Terry remained silent, slightly overawed. Terry began to wonder if he was going to be such an influence in Mr Dorey's life after all, or, indeed, if anybody could influence Q.D., except his mother, for whose wishes he seemed to have some consideration.

Fern's gaze was travelling around. She noted now that there was a great deal of dust everywhere; that there were half-dead flowers on the stand in the corner of the room; that the beautiful engraved Venetian mirror was blurred with smudgy finger marks. There was even a cobweb on a corner of the oil-painting over the mantelpiece. Her gaze examined this portrait: a woman wearing a ruby velvet habit of eighteenth-century style and with a yellow plume in her hat. She was seated on a grey horse against a background of beeches. It was a painting of tremendous richness and beauty. On one of her impulses, Fern broke out:

'Oh, that is surely a *Winterhalter!*'

Quentin Dorey, who had been just about to say that Mrs Barrett was too young and that he wasn't prepared to have another couple of failures around the place and that they had better go back to London, closed his lips again. He stared at Fern. And now that attractive smile flashed across his strong stubborn-jawed face.

'We-e-ll,' he said on a long drawn-out note, 'so you know who painted my lady on the horse?'

'It is a Winterhalter, isn't it?' she asked shyly.

'It is,' he said, 'and I paid quite a few thousands for it.'

Fern winced. Quentin continued rather loudly:

'And I'm willing to pay more for some of the masterpieces of this world, if and when I can find them. I'm learning about art. And *you* seem well up in it, Mrs Barrett.'

Here Terry put in:

'My wife is a surprisingly cultured young woman.'

Interested suddenly, despite himself, Quentin waved a hand in the direction of another painting at the far end of the room.

'And that?'

'A Van Gogh,' said Fern promptly.

'Like it?'

'Not as much as the other. And they are of such different schools, they oughtn't both to be hung in here together, really. *Oh,* I do apologise...' She bit her lip and put a hand up to one hot cheek, aware that she was once again letting her impulses run away with her.

But the big man on the sofa uttered another of his guffaws.

'We-e-ll, that's rich. So they oughtn't to be hung together. You wouldn't mix your schools, eh?'

'N-no,' she faltered.

'When my leg recovers you must take me round and show me what else I've had hung in the wrong place.'

She stared at him, aghast, afraid that she had offended him. However, he continued quite affably:

'On the other hand you're supposed to be here in order to mix stuff in basins and cook my meals. And serve them up and run my house. Will that include lessons on culture, might I ask?'

Fern gulped but decided not to be afraid of him. She began to extol a few of her own virtues. She assured Mr Dorey that she was a Cordon Bleu cook; that she adored housework, and that she didn't mind about having no help. That she'd work her fingers to the bone to look after such lovely things, and that she wanted to be given a chance. Quentin listened and looked at her with a mixture of doubt and admiration.

'So you're not afraid of work?'

'No – not at all,' she said breathlessly.

'And you can tell me how to seat people at my table, and lay it properly, and do the flowers and help me give good parties, and get rid of all this damned cloud of negligence and disorder that's hanging over my lovely manor house?'

'Oh, yes, *yes*, Mr Dorey!' she said breathlessly, her eyes brilliant.

Terry crossed his arms on his chest. He

51

supposed he would come in for the next onslaught from the great man. He wondered how Fern could stick it.

Then Quentin Dorey said:

'Right, I'll give you a chance – the pair of you. Barrett' – he turned to Terry– 'I don't know the first thing about cars myself, but I understand that you do and that you've driven a Rolls for years. This Lady What-have-you who wrote to Miss Porter seemed to think you were a good man with a car.'

'I think you'll find I can carry out my duties,' said Terry, rather haughtily.

Quentin's gaze swept up and down the young man.

'Well, mind you're punctual, and none of your speeding whether it's on the M.1, or down the Sussex lanes,' he barked.

'I'm going to hate this man,' thought Terry.

'I'm going to like this man,' thought Fern.

'Press that bell,' Quentin told Terry, pointing with his stick at the bell at one side of the big Adam fireplace. 'With any luck it'll be answered by moaning Minnie from Connemara, and she'll show you to your quarters. And by the way...' he added with a sudden twinkling at Fern, 'her name isn't Minnie, it's Maureen. Try and keep her

52

happy if you can, because my mother engaged her and would like her to stay. She's the simple sort of village girl we used to have up in our home in Lancashire. My mother likes that sort.'

'I hope Mrs Dorey won't disapprove of me,' ventured Fern.

Quentin put his tongue in his cheek. He wouldn't like to say how his mother would feel about this young girl taking charge down here. Just as well the old dear was away for the moment, he decided grimly. She had gone over to Sweden. The first trip abroad she had ever taken alone. It so happened that she had been brought up in the Lake District with a cousin younger than herself, who had married a Stockholm business man. The daughter, Greta, was Mrs Dorey's godchild.

Mrs Dorey had at last kept a longstanding promise to go and stay in Stockholm. Quentin had kept it securely from her that (a) he had become incapacitated with this bout of sciatica, and (b) that the last couple (the Howards) had departed. But that was the way he intended to keep it, or she'd come dashing home. She needed her holiday. She was a dear. Loyal and integral as only the Lancashire folk can be, but she just wouldn't accept the fact that 'staff' were no longer what they used to be and that down in the South one had to treat such folk as equals.

Quentin knew where to draw the line. He believed himself capable of extracting good service without allowing too much familiarity from his employees, but mother liked 'em to be humble and grateful and all the things they weren't. He felt a little guilty about the Barretts now that he had engaged them. But he hoped they would get on with the job and prove themselves, so that by the time mother came back they would be nicely settled.

He said aloud:

'I'll tell you two, frankly, I'm not the Lord Chavering type. I'm a north-countryman. I don't deny that I started in my father's cotton mills as a labourer. But I got to a Grammar School, and I won a scholarship. When my father died, I found I had no wish to stay up in the north. I came south to London. I had one ruling passion in life, which has remained with me – high finance. They call me the Great Q.D.' He laughed, showing magnificent teeth... 'The Wizard of Figures. Everything I touch turns to gold. I'm the director of more companies than I have time to control. I've trebled my father's capital and look like doubling that. But there's something more I want...'

'What is that, sir?' asked Terry, fascinated despite himself.

Quentin Dorey, who was only ten years older than this fair-haired young man who was now his chauffeur, half-closed his eyes and looked at the painting over the mantelpiece.

'I want what money has never been able to give anyone, Barrett; what your wife seems to have got; the *know-how*. Like being able to name that painter. And if she proves as good at looking after me and my house as she is with art, I'll double her wages – and yours.'

Terry gave a slightly supercilious smile. But Fern looked at Quentin Dorey's ill-chosen tie and rough upstanding hair, and thought suddenly:

'This man has everything ... and nothing. There's something lost and lonely behind the mask of the big tycoon. But I like him.'

3

A few moments later Fern and Terry, clutching their suitcases, followed Maureen, the Irish maid, through the hall and dining-room to the kitchen quarters. Fern caught a quick glimpse of another glorious room. The linenfold panelling was dark and glossy. A fine portrait, which Fern recognised as a Lely, hung over the Tudor stone fireplace. The curtains were of rich lilac-coloured brocade – the same colour as the velvet on the carved Charles II chairs. A long oak sideboard, shining with the polish of ages, bore massive silver candelabra, and delicate Limoges china dishes that were piled with apples, pears and muscat grapes.

Fern was used to comfort and good taste, but the Dorey home was fabulous. The 'Lancashire lad' must have bought the place with most of this stuff in it, too – direct from Lord Chavering, she imagined. Each new treasure made her feel happy to be here. But Terry saw only the possible value to himself in working for a millionaire. Now he was in a good temper, holding her arm and whispering jokingly into her ear, making her laugh at some of his quips and jests. Terry could be amusing when he wanted to. 'It seems we go slumming where we belong,' was one of his comments.

Maureen proved to be a thin, dark-haired girl with magnificent Irish eyes in an otherwise plain, snub-nosed face. She was untidy and wore a grubby pink overall. She snuffled as though she had perpetual catarrh. When she spoke it was with a rich brogue.

'Sure and I am pleased to see ye both,' she said when they first left Mr Dorey's presence. 'Here is meself all alone for trying to keep things going in this great house, and with only Mrs Hatton to come over and help since the Howards left.'

'Oh, we'll soon put that right,' Fern said consolingly, and when Maureen threw her a mournful glance and said that the sooner that she got back to Connemara the better, Fern added: 'Now don't be downhearted, Maureen. I'll cheer you up and we'll work together.'

'Sure and that will be something new, as I got nothing but hard words from Mrs Howard,' said Maureen.

Fern remembered Mr Dorey's description

of 'moaning Minnie', and concealed a smile. The girl was only about eighteen. Fern, as a married woman, felt superior and decided to look after her and make a few tactful suggestions about that straggling black hair pinned up in an untidy bun, and the dirty pinafore. Goodness! There was a lot to do here. No wonder Mr Dorey was worried about his entertaining; but Fern was not dismayed, she felt that the whole thing was a challenge and she was not going to give the great Q.D. a second chance to tell her that she was too young or incapable of holding the job.

A brief look round the vast kitchen struck a slight chord of dismay in Fern's heart. There was an old-fashioned dresser, a long wooden table, an out-of-date sink. Few of the labour-saving devices to which Fern was used – apart from an Esse stove and the big electric cooker. *And* (cheering sight) a dish-washing machine. The brown paint on the walls was depressing, but everything in here was spotless. Maureen explained that Mrs Hatton washed and polished the kitchen quarters and 'did' the dining-room, the hall and stairs, and the upstairs bathrooms. She, Maureen, had to manage the library and the bedrooms.

'Never mind – I'll be helping you now,' Fern soothed her.

'They don't use the big drawing-room except when they're entertaining, but sure and it's big enough for a dozen pairs of hands,' said Maureen, 'and wait till you see Mrs Dorey.'

'And what is Mrs Dorey like?' asked Terry with curiosity. He was walking up and down the kitchen with quick impatient footsteps, smoking a cigarette. He was thinking that he was going to miss the bright lights of London and get thoroughly depressed in the country.

What the Irish maid had to say about Quentin's mother did not help. In a confidential whisper, sniffling, Maureen described Mrs Thomas Dorey as a great big woman, six foot tall, with a gaunt face and fierce eyes in deep sockets. A bit like Mr Dorey but nothing like so nice as the 'gentleman'. ('God love him,' added Maureen.) He was always kind and doubled her wages last Christmas. Blunt and sharp-tongued, Mrs Dorey was, and expected everybody to wait upon her, and although a person had to grant that Mrs Dorey seldom spared herself, and she was always doing something, she was no real lady in Maureen's estimation.

And no help to Mr Dorey when he had folks staying, as then she'd sit doing her tapestry work and never saying a word but criticising everybody with those fierce eyes of hers.

'Sounds charming,' drawled Terry.

'Oh, never mind,' said Fern, 'we'll soften her up.'

Maureen looked with appreciative eyes at the new cook's pretty blue dress and jacket, with its crisp white piqué collar. She admired the white felt hat pulled low over Fern's glossy brown hair. Pretty as a picture she was, and Maureen was all ready to adore her and be thankful that Mrs Barrett was so young and wouldn't be fussing. As for Mr Barrett, he was as handsome as an angel (God love him).

She took the Barretts over to their flat. The courtyard was as attractive as the old house, thought Fern, with an old well and pump as a centre piece. The buildings were all old and gabled and charmingly covered with wistaria. Terry took a quick look through one of the half-open doors and whistled appreciatively at the pale cream and chocolate Rolls.

'*That's* something,' he drawled. 'Shan't mind being behind *that* wheel.'

Maureen apologised for the flat. She was afraid the Howards had left in a hurry ... a couple of 'no-goods', she said scathingly, and Maureen had only had a few minutes to spare to run over and sweep the place out.

Fern said:

'Don't worry. We'll manage. Now you go back and put on a kettle, Maureen, and I'll come over and we'll make a "cuppa" and talk about lunch.'

'Och,' said Maureen delightedly, 'I could do with a nice cup of tay and I've been worrying about the gentleman's midday meal till you turned up, God love you.'

And she ran off in better spirits than when she had first met the new couple.

When they were at last in the home which had been allotted to them, Terry flung two suitcases on to the floor and broke out into a long list of complaints.

The rooms in this ghastly flat were the size of sixpence. The furniture was ghastly, too. As for those two cheap beds in the bedroom, he was sure that the mattresses would be horrible, if not lousy.

Fern listened patiently. She took off her coat and hat, lit a cigarette and started to unpack.

'It's no good carrying on like this, Terry darling. It may not be as bad as you think.'

Terry snapped open his own suitcase and

flung some of his clothes on to the bed.

'I suppose not.'

'Mr Dorey was *terribly* nice. He treated us in a very friendly way.'

'And what about his mother? From what Maureen says she'll be nothing but a headache when she comes home.'

Fern looked at her husband's handsome, disconsolate face and felt her spirits droop. It was a pity that Terry couldn't take calamity with more courage, she thought, but perhaps this sort of switch-over from being quite well-off and living in your own pleasant home was more crushing to his spirit than to hers. *She* was quite willing to give her new life a trial and not let it get her down.

'Do let's preserve a sense of humour,' she begged.

'I see nothing very funny about it. And the last straw was when Maureen said just now I'd find my *uniform* in the cupboard.'

He marched to the cupboard door, opened it, and took down the chauffeur's uniform; smart enough in its way, dark green with gilt buttons, and a green and black peaked cap.

Fern suddenly burst out laughing.

'Oh, darling, *darling Terry, do* have a giggle with me and not feel so badly. You'll look simply divine in that. You'll soon have

Maureen making you her Pin-up Boy.'

'I shall adore that,' said Terry.

Valiantly she tried to woo him from his black mood. She stuck the cap at a rakish angle on his head and, taking his face between her hands, kissed his sulky mouth.

'You'll always be *my* Pin-up Boy, beloved, and I can't tell you how well that cap suits you.'

Terence gave a quick sidelong glance in the mirror, agreed with Fern, and suddenly hugged her.

'You're adorable and brave,' he said, kissing the tip of her nose.

She was happy again. Her heart was still in his keeping. She didn't like this change of existence much but she saw no object in moaning. Deep down within her she was weeping at the memory of the lovely flat she had had to give up, and more particularly she flinched at the thought of poor Daddy and the disaster that had knocked him out so completely. She had had a most unhappy telephone conversation with her mother just before leaving town. Mrs Wendell seemed to feel, like Terry, that it was a disgrace that her daughter should have to take such a job and live in the chauffeur's quarters.

'None of our friends will ever speak to us

again,' she had wailed.

But Fern knew that wasn't true. People weren't like that nowadays. Lots of their friends would come down here to see them and enjoy a sausage and a cup of coffee in this little place, she was sure. What did it matter to a true friend if you lived in a castle, or a shack? Fern had never been a snob and had no patience with people who tried to keep up the myth of 'class distinction'.

She had no real time now to examine her new home from every angle, but it wasn't very attractive – that she had to admit. Just three little square rooms, a tiny kitchen, with bathroom leading out of it; a rather depressing bath which hadn't much enamel left.

The windows were small and the atmosphere close and sticky on this sunny day. There was lino on the floor of a rather sickly green colour. The whole flat was painted yellow – a bilious colour Fern had never favoured. The curtains were of cheap yellow and green cretonne that had shrunk in the wash. The furniture consisted of bits and pieces of ugly varnished wood. Two 'fireside chairs'. No fireplace; only an electric radiator. No comfort. Certainly a painful contrast both to Fern's own home and Swanlake Manor itself. And it was not particularly clean.

Fern buttoned up one of the white overalls that she had worn when she took her Cordon Bleu course, and looked at an old-fashioned oak-framed print on the sitting-room wall, 'The Soul's Awakening'. She burst out laughing. Terence heard her and came in from the bedroom. He had put on his uniform. Howard must have been a shorter man, because the trousers were not quite long enough for Terence, although the coat fitted well enough. Fern's laughter increased as she looked at her husband's ankles which were just visible.

'Oh, d-darling, it's all so f-f-funny,' she gasped, wiping the tears from her eyes.

Terence gave her a little hug and said:

'Well, I can't see it, but you're damned plucky, darling.'

'I'll get lots of our own things down here and soon make this place look different, providing we do our stuff and keep the job,' she said, hugging him back.

'Well, I suppose as we're paupers now it's something to earn fifteen pounds a week between us and have a rent-free place,' he sighed.

'Come on, darling,' she said, linking hands with him, 'we'll get over to the house and report for duty.'

'With moaning Minnie.'

Fern giggled.

'Well, I'm sure you'll make her eyelashes flutter, darling.'

Back in the big kitchen at the Manor, Fern soon found herself exceedingly busy. It all seemed so gigantic after her tiny kitchen in London, but nothing would have induced her to say so. She asked Maureen as few questions as possible, used her common sense, and speedily opened drawers and cupboards to see where things were kept. She soon decided that she must make considerable changes. The last cook must have had a muddled mind. There was a complete lack of order. Fern had always been tidy. She couldn't bear all this mix-up of pots, pans and dishes. She would spend an hour or two tomorrow reorganising.

One good thing – there was no lack of utensils or china. The cupboards were crammed from top to bottom.

Fern only had time now to throw a quick admiring look at the grey and gold Royal Davenport dinner service on show behind the glass doors of the old-fashioned dresser.

A beauty, she thought. And that beautiful tea-service in the pantry – Limoges. Quite heavenly! But the dinner service that was used daily, Fern could hardly bear. The green and rose service happened to be exactly the same pattern as the one Mummy had in the old home. It carried Fern back nostalgically to memories of the past, to the merry, carefree days with her parents ... before Terry had come into her life. But quickly Fern jerked herself back into the present and carried on with her work.

Quentin Dorey was on the verge of pressing his bell and demanding his lunch when somebody knocked on the library door. He looked astonished at the sight of the young brown-haired girl in a white overall, carrying a tray. His new cook! As she laid the tray down, he noted the spotless cloth, a bowl of steaming *consommé*, cold ham cut thin as pink paper with its fringe of creamy white fat, and *duchesse* potatoes in tempting toasted spirals. From a bowl of French salad there arose the appetising odour of garlic. If there was one thing Quentin liked, it was a touch of garlic with his salad.

'My goodness me!' he ejaculated in a delighted voice.

'I'll come back in a moment for the soup bowl,' said Fern, 'and bring you either cheese or some fruit. I'm sorry I haven't had time to make a sweet.'

'I don't eat sweets. We only have them when there's a party.'

'And I'm sorry there's only Cheddar,' she added, 'but tomorrow I'll see you have a piece of Brie. Or do you prefer Camembert?'

Quentin's satisfaction increased as he answered this. Here was a girl who knew her stuff. A very different show from the one Mrs Howard used to put up. Oh, those awful 'boarding-house meals' as he had called them, with badly chosen, badly cooked meat, and watery vegetables. And Mrs Howard's one idea of a party sweet used to be a trifle or tinned fruit. She had no imagination. Quentin Dorey enjoyed his food without being greedy. He was happy with a good old Lancashire hot-pot well done, as it used to be made up north in his youth. He had also learnt to enjoy French cooking down south. But to 'net' a real Cordon Bleu cook down here in Swanlake – that was going to make his future entertaining very much easier. Quentin leaned back on his cushions. He nodded once or twice.

'Well done,' he said in his brusque way.

He had not yet learnt to pay compliments easily – it was foreign to his blunt northern nature. But he felt that little Mrs Barrett deserved some praise.

Fern felt pleased and her cheeks grew pink, but she shook her head.

'I haven't *done* any cooking, yet.'

He tasted the soup.

'You've put sherry in this. Oh, yes, you've got the *know-how*. And you've made the whole thing out of nothing – out of what you found in the kitchen, *and* presented it well. That's what I call *something*. You should have seen what young Maureen brought me yesterday.'

'Well, if you don't want my husband this afternoon I'll get him to drive me in the staff car to the nearest good shops and I'll give you a better dinner,' said Fern.

'Splendid,' said Quentin.

'Coffee, sir?'

'Cut out the "sir"!' he said with a scowl, 'I'm not one for all that palaver. Plain Mr Dorey suits me.'

'Then I'll only say "sir" in front of guests.'

Drinking his soup, he eyed the girl over the spoon, one eyebrow raised in slightly ironic amusement.

'I can see you're going to make quite a list

of things that should or shouldn't be done here.'

Fern's colour heightened. She fumbled nervously in the pocket of her overall for a handkerchief.

'I ... I...' she began to stammer and stopped. This man was a little formidable and yet not disagreeable. She believed that she would learn to respect what Terry had called 'the jumped-up tycoon'.

Now Quentin said:

'No need for apologies. I want you to do what you think the right thing. You've been used to good service, haven't you?'

Fern, feeling a trifle guilty, avoided this question. She wondered what Quentin Dorey would say if he knew exactly who she was, and that she had never before been anybody's cook.

He went on:

'Well educated, too, that's obvious.'

'Yes,' she said.

He drank the soup to the last drop, appreciatively.

'Fine. This ought to cure my sciatica.'

'I hope so, sir ... I mean, *Mr Dorey.*'

'Everything all right in your domain?'

'I'll soon get things in order, Mr Dorey.'

'Well, I've got company tomorrow – short

notice, but when you're shopping, get something extra for lunch. I've asked a couple of American business friends down to lunch. Meant to try and struggle into a car and take them to a hotel. But now you've come perhaps you'll manage. I'd prefer to eat at home.'

'But of course, Mr Dorey. What would you like?'

'That's your job,' he snapped. '*You* do the housekeeping and catering. And look here – money's no object. Buy the most expensive food you can find, and make the meal tasty.'

Fern looked at her feet reflectively. This man had had a rough beginning and at times a rough way of putting things. Yet there was a kind of blazing strength and honesty about him which she liked. And when he turned those extraordinarily fine and intelligent eyes of his upon her, she suddenly felt the need, herself, to be honest with him. She wished that she hadn't come here under false pretences, as it were, and that she could tell him the whole sordid unhappy story about Daddy and why she had to go out to work. But she dared not. Terry would never forgive her. She turned to go. Quentin called after her:

'Buy anything you need.'

71

She looked over her shoulder.

'Are you sure it wouldn't be best for me to wait until Mrs Dorey comes back? Wouldn't she rather be the one to tell me…'

'*I'm* telling you,' interrupted Quentin in his fiercest voice.

She closed the door quietly after her. She giggled a little on the other side of it. The great Q.D. could not actually scare her but she felt a trifle nervy in her new position as a 'domestic employee'. He would have to be tactfully handled.

Q.D. ate the rest of his lunch and regretted that he had snarled at his new cook. On second thoughts, it had been rather tactful of her to suggest waiting for his mother to come home. At any rate, he hoped to goodness that she'd stick it here. Unlike all the others, who left because they either disliked his mother or hated being so isolated. And what a change, to be looked after by someone who was clean and pleasant to look at after the amiable but untidy Maureen. His mother had engaged Maureen in the first place because she had been hoping to employ a local woman, who did not come in the end on account of the long distance to the Manor. But the local woman was Irish and had this niece in

Connemara and had sent over for Maureen. While Mrs Dorey was away, Maureen lived out with her aunt, and Hatton, who could drive, fetched her and took her back again before dark.

It certainly would be pleasant to be served by someone like Mrs Barrett who, youthful though she was, seemed well able to take control.

Q.D. moved his leg gingerly and found that there was less pain, which put him in an even better mood than the good lunch. But he had nothing to say to Fern when she came in with his cheese and his coffee. He was immersed in *The Financial Times,* and hardly aware that she had come in and gone again, until he saw that his used plate had gone and in its place a well-arranged basket with cheese and bread and biscuits for his choice, and coffee that tasted strong and delicious.

'We-e-ll!' Quentin said aloud, 'I think my Miss Porter has done the right thing after all.'

In the kitchen, Fern sat with her husband and Maureen eating a cold lunch with them. Maureen was being friendly and voluble but Terry ate in silence. He marvelled because Fern seemed so much at home at the head of the kitchen table. She maintained an attitude of supreme indifference to 'having come down in the world'.

Once they were in their flat alone together she even refused to admit that she had 'come down'.

'You're out of date, ducky,' she laughed at him as she unpacked. 'A good cook-housekeeper's job is better paid and just as enviable as any other sort of work, these days.'

Terry lifted a case that she had just emptied and put it outside the door. His handsome face was a trifle sulky. The memory of all that had happened to her father – the débâcle that was responsible for his, Terry's, change of fortune – was beginning to act on his spirit like a slow corrosive acid. On the other hand, he knew they had come here on an agreed salary of fifteen pounds a week between them. That meant fifteen pounds in their pocket.

Already Fern was beginning to put her own attractive touches to this awful flat, he thought. And now as she got out of her overall and stood in front of the dressing chest, brushing her hair, he looked at her with softened gaze. She was wearing only a pale blue nylon slip. She was a sweet thing, he thought ruefully, and wished he could feel the same excitement of love that Fern used to arouse in him. He *wanted* to be nice to her – to help her through this difficult time – but his own discomfort, his overwhelming conceit nagged at him too bitterly. When Fern turned and held out both arms in her loving and appealing way, he drew her close. But his caresses were automatic, and he thought apprehensively of the future.

After a moment he released her and said: 'The Rolls is a peach, I must admit.'

A bell rang in the tiny hall. Terry answered it and at first thought it was the front door. Then he realised that it was the house-telephone from the Manor. The master's voice, Terry thought, with a little grimace. Quentin calling his chauffeur.

'I shall want you to go up to town in the Rolls, leaving here at ten o'clock tomorrow, Barrett. You will call at the Westbury Hotel off Bond Street for a Mr Vandamm and a Mr Wilmot, and bring them down here. Understand?'

'Yes, quite,' answered Terry, and drooping one eyelid sardonically at Fern, who stood behind him, added, 'sir.'

'My first assignment,' he said, following

her back into the bedroom.

'Your second, my pet. You're going to drive me into Brighton. Right now, in the staff car. Maureen says we're only ten miles away and I've got a lot of shopping to do.'

Terry would rather have stretched himself out on the bed and had a 'siesta'. He was more exhausted than Fern, he announced, after today's events. But perforce he took out the Morris traveller and drove down the Brighton road from Cuckendean.

On the way he said:

'We ought to be in the Rolls.'

'You do make me laugh,' said Fern. 'I'm quite enjoying it all. This is rather a wonderful dual carriage-way and *look* at those Downs ... superb! And it's as warm as a summer's day. Hope it lasts.'

'My little philosopher,' said Terry with a sidelong glance at her.

She turned her thoughts to her employer.

'I was told not to count the cost but just to go ahead and give his pals a smashing lunch, so I shall try to buy lobsters if I can get them. I'll make that special *Homard Xavier* which you think so marvellous.'

'H'm, I hope there'll be some left over for me, since I now find myself in the position of having to *wait* for left-overs.'

'You are an old grump,' she laughed.

He looked at her out of the corners of his eyes and put his foot down on the accelerator.

'But you still love me, eh?'

'Yes,' she said and she looked at the handsome head with the jaunty chauffeur's cap on one side. She felt a sudden tightness in her throat. She had been so *very* much in love with Terry when they first married. She wanted passionately to keep things that way. He was still very charming, and when he had taken her in his arms in the flat just now, the old wild thrill had still been there warming her like a flame. Why, then, did she feel so sad and lonely behind the façade of resignation? Why did she feel in desperate need of fresh security – of a reassurance that her husband didn't *quite* give?

As if afraid of what lay before her, she snuggled closer to Terry's side. The car climbed up the road that crossed over the Downs past the windmill and on to the heights from which suddenly they could see the sunlit sea and the great Regency town of Brighton stretched far below them.

Terry was not aware of her emotion. He said:

'Light me a cigarette, honey-bunch.'

She lit it and put it between his lips. He said:

'I was rather tickled by all that Irish stuff that rolled out of young Maureen's lips at lunch. She makes Mrs Dorey sound a bit formidable. I shouldn't think your path will be as easy once *she's* home.'

'No, I don't suppose it will. That's why I want us to get well dug in and for Mr Dorey to find us indispensable before she returns.'

'Did you hear what Maureen had to say about this trip to Sweden?'

'Yes, I heard,' said Fern.

Maureen in her rich rolling voice had acquainted them with the fact that Mrs Dorey had a goddaughter in Stockholm, whom she was probably bringing back with her to stay here. She had stayed before – the first weekend Maureen came over from Ireland.

'Surely to goodness and she's like one of they model girls or a film star,' Maureen had said, 'and looks like making this her home for good and all one day.'

Fern was not particularly interested in gossip, but Terry, out of sheer boredom, had fastened on it and extracted from Maureen the further information that Greta appeared to be in love with Mr Dorey. Mad about him, she was, said Maureen, and Mrs Dorey made no bones that she liked the idea of the match – the way she pushed the two into each other's company.

When Terry had asked whether Mr Dorey looked like responding to such overtures, Maureen had giggled and said she had always heard Mr Dorey was more interested in his business than in marrying, but of course, who was to know? And she had repeated that the half-Swedish girl was very glamorous and that she sang, too – and Maureen had listened behind the door and marvelled at the high notes. Like a nightingale, Miss Greta was, worth listening to.

As Terry drove the car down the broad hill leading to the Western Road of Hove where Fern had been advised to do her shopping, she had a sudden vision of Quentin Dorey installing 'the Swedish nightingale' at the Manor as his wife.

Terry seemed to divine her thoughts, for he said:

'Well, if milord takes to himself a bride – that will be the end of you as housekeeper. I can't see you taking orders from a young girl who probably won't know as much about housekeeping as you, and won't want you here anyhow.'

Then Fern laughed and said:

'Aren't we being a little previous? They aren't even engaged yet. I like this job and I'm going to hang on to it as long as I can.'

The shopping expedition was a success. She found the lobsters and some excellent veal and with all the other groceries that she needed to stock up her larder, she laughingly threw one parcel after another into the staff car.

'I'm taking Mr Dorey at his word and buying what I need for my Cordon Bleu lunch.'

Terry yawned. He could not share his wife's enthusiasm. Fern bought food for her employer's dinner tonight, as well. Terry only half listened as, driving home, she told him what she had planned. Fillet of sole *bonne femme*, followed by a cheese soufflé. Q.D. had said that while he was incapacitated, unable to take exercise, he did not want to eat heavy meals.

Terry glanced at his wife's charming profile as they neared the gates of Swanlake Manor. Her expression of concentration rather annoyed him.

'You seem to take this job so seriously, I don't understand you, Fern,' he grumbled.

She hesitated before she answered. She did not know whether she quite understood herself. The shadow of her father's calamity (hers, too) and her plunge into domestic service hung over her. Yet she was happy ... curiously elated by the challenge of it all.

She looked forward to making a success even of tonight's little dinner which she would cook for Q.D ... and serve to him, herself.

4

There was little doubt in Fern's mind that the lunch party that Sunday was a tremendous success, but it was not without considerable effort on her part. To begin with she had slept badly the previous night. The bed was certainly not comfortable and the little chauffeur's flat was strange and stuffy, despite the fact that they opened all the windows and doors. She woke up with a bad headache – something from which she rarely suffered. Then at half past eight when she was over at the big house preparing breakfast – Q.D. liked a hearty one – a small boy came on a bicycle with a note from the village. It was sent by Maureen's aunt, to say that poor Maureen had a bilious attack and couldn't come to work. Her aunt apologised and said *she* couldn't help because her husband was always home on a Sunday and needed her. So on the one day when Fern most wanted assistance, she didn't get it.

Terry sympathised and said that he would help her once he got back, but he left soon after ten o'clock to fetch the American guests. Fern armed herself with duster and mop and rushed around the rooms that were going to be used. There was so much to prepare for that lunch, too. One of the Americans had now decided to bring his wife, which meant four of them in the dining-room, and it was not simple cooking. Fern had fashioned the rod for her own chastisement by choosing a complicated meal which needed every inch of her attention.

She had little time to remember her headache, although it was so bad by eleven o'clock that she had to take aspirins with her 'elevenses'. In the middle of preparing the lobsters, the great Q.D. rang for her and handed her a pair of shoes:

'Get Hatton or Maureen to polish these.'

Fern kept her thoughts to herself, but she knew that Hatton didn't come on Sundays (which Quentin – vague about domestic affairs like all busy big business men – had forgotten), and she decided not to worry him by telling him about Maureen. As she turned to leave Q.D., shoes in hand, he added that his leg was a good deal better and he could limp around the house today. He also repeated his praise of last night's dinner.

'Keep up the good work,' he said.

So she endeavoured to keep it up – single-handed.

In between preparation, she had to race upstairs to make Quentin's bed and tidy his room. She had little time in which to appreciate the beauty of the wide gracious gallery with its carved rosewood rails overlooking the front hall. But she took a quick admiring look at the dark green, velvety paper on the walls, and the fine row of oil paintings.

Quentin's bedroom seemed to her to express the man's own personality. It was handsome yet austere, with simple mahogany furniture, grey walls and carpet, and rose and brown chintz curtains. Looking at the tallboy, which bore an array of brushes and lotions of a masculine calibre, she saw one expensive-looking but ugly statuette, in appalling taste. The picture over the bed was modern and ill-chosen, too. She thought:

'He goes quite wrong from time to time. Something in him *wants* the best but he needs guiding.'

The various objects that were 'wrong' – obviously bought by him and not the late Lord Chavering – did not make her shudder. On the contrary, she felt that the great Q.D. had a human side ... and that apart from high finance, this 'man of property' was a simple soul, unsure of himself – which, in its funny fashion, was quite endearing.

He drove her almost crazy by ringing for her repeatedly, wanting something or other. Drinks and cocktail nuts in the library. Two bottles of white wine to be brought out of the cellar (he tossed her the keys), and to be put on ice, for lunch. Would she also see that there were cigarettes in the boxes and get a new box of cigars from the cabinet. Always he punctuated his orders with ... 'tell Maureen to do it' or 'if you're busy in the kitchen, why don't you let Maureen answer the bell', but once he grunted, 'I assure you I prefer the sight of *you* – you *do* wear clean overalls!'

That had made her smile. She smoothed him down and kept the secret about Maureen's absence. But her headache was at its worst by the time Terry came back with the guests. Terry was full of the drive, and the magnificence of the Rolls. She was thankful that he didn't add to her load by complaining; but he was no help. Terry had never been a domesticated person and Fern found it best in the end to banish him from the kitchen while she 'got on'.

She was thankful that lunch was ordered

for one-thirty, not before. Then at last, in a fresh white overall, she walked into the library and announced that all was ready.

She caught a brief glimpse of two tall, burly Americans, both broad-shouldered, with crew-cut hair; and of a slim, typically well turned out American woman who gave Fern a pleasant smile and said in a patronising voice, '*Good* morning!'

Fern's cheeks were flushed from the exertion of cooking, and the nut-brown hair was not quite as neat as usual, which made her look charming but not quite the sedate housekeeper she would have wished. Or, if it came to that, not quite what Quentin would have wished, for he frowned at his pretty housekeeper, ever mindful of the fact that there was going to be the devil to pay when his mother came back and saw her. However, his American guests said how 'cute' Fern looked, and how lucky he was. It was difficult to get any sort of domestic help in America.

Quentin certainly felt lucky once the meal was served.

Everything was perfect. The table was laid as he had seldom seen it, with the right silver in the right place; sparkling crystal glass, and a silver bowl of tastefully arranged freesias as a centre piece. The embroidered mats had been well-pressed and were speckless.

Fern then served her *Bortsch* ... a soup which enchanted Mrs Vandamm in particular. It looked so attractive, she declared. Beetroot-red, with the sour cream on top.

There followed the lobster *Xavier* which had always been Fern's speciality. She had boiled the lobsters and cut the flesh into dice, and put them with mushrooms into the shells, adding a perfect sauce and glazing each portion under the grill. With it, she served a French salad. Afterwards, veal cutlets with tomatoes. And she finished the lunch with a pudding such as Quentin had never tasted before. He, who did not like sweets, ate up every piece that Fern served to him.

Mrs Vandamm broke into genuine applause and asked Fern for the recipe.

'*Say!* This soufflé is not in this world – that flavour of toasted almonds and coffee – *my!* What *is* it called?'

Fern politely told her that it was called *Soufflé Brazilian* and was a recipe from the famous Mary Gallati's cookery book.

Fern was certainly rewarded for her efforts by the general praise, but by the time she had cleared away the coffee and cooked some dinner for herself and Terry, she was quite exhausted.

'Poor darling, you must go and lie down as soon as you are through,' said Terry, yawning.

But his mind was not altogether on his wife. He was wondering how he could fix things so that, when he drove the Americans back to town, he could spend a few hours up there with some of his own pals. He wanted to get away from this atmosphere of servility. He was bored, *bored,* playing the game that Fern took so much to heart.

Later that afternoon after Terry set out with the Americans for London once more, the bell summoned Fern to the library.

She found Quentin seated at his big walnut desk. There was a mass of papers before him. He looked over his shoulder at Fern.

'Mrs Barrett,' he said, laying down his pen, 'I want to thank you again. You put up a superb show and I seem to have got me a real chef. You must love cooking or you couldn't do it so well.'

'I do love it,' she nodded, 'and I'm glad you're pleased, Mr Dorey.'

Quentin's mind was much taken up with business and one particularly important letter which he had to write, but he found time to note that the young girl looked pale and that there were lilac smudges of fatigue under her eyes. With genuine solicitude, he said:

'Hope it hasn't been too much for you. You've been on the go all the time. Maureen has been a help, I hope?'

Now Fern confessed.

'As a matter of fact she didn't turn up today, Mr Dorey. She isn't well.'

Quentin's eyes opened wide.

'Do you mean *you've* been doing the whole show single-handed?'

'Yes, but I managed.'

'I'll say you did! Well, upon my word, you're a trump, Mrs Barrett. My guests said they were going back to America to tell everyone that they've seen the most handsome country house in England and eaten the finest meal *in it.*'

'I'm glad you were all pleased,' said Fern, half dropping with weariness.

'Go home and take it easy. Take the rest of the day off,' he said abruptly.

'But what about your supper...'

'Shan't want much after that banquet.'

'But your leg...'

'You leave me a tray with something cold

on it and I'll manage. Now buzz off and do what you're told,' he said with a sudden roughness which belied the kindliness in his eyes. She found those light grey eyes strangely fascinating. Her lips trembled into a smile. Q.D. made her feel like a schoolgirl receiving orders. She said 'thank you' under her breath and turned to go.

Quentin added:

'I expect your husband told you ... he won't be back till later; he asked me if I minded him hanging on in town for a bit. Some parcel or other that you wished him to take to your mother. He said he'd probably have a bite tonight with her. I didn't object.'

Fern stared at Quentin. She saw only the back of his head now because he was bending over his desk again. For a moment she was dumbfounded. Terry had not said a word to her about staying on in London, and as for taking Mummy a parcel ... and dining with her ... nothing could be further from the truth. First of all there was no parcel, and secondly the last person Terry would go and see was Mummy, who wasn't even in London at the moment.

Fern crossed over to her flat, feeling more than ever exhausted and suddenly deeply depressed. She did not know what Terry meant to do in London. Of course, she trusted him. And she was not one to tie her husband to her apron strings. But she wished he hadn't lied to Mr Dorey. She wished, too, that he had told *her* what he had actually intended to do.

Her headache worsened. Her feet hurt after all the unaccustomed standing and running about. The exultation which had been hers because of her culinary triumph was completely spoilt by what her employer had just told her.

She took off her clothes and lay down on the hard mattress, longing for her own comfortable bed in town.

She tried to rest but sleep eluded her. After an hour she got up again, put on her slacks and a shirt, and began to work round the flat.

No good worrying about Terry. He'd explain why he had done this when he saw her, but he *did* know that she was *off*-duty after lunch – it had been arranged that she should have a half day in the week and Sunday afternoon – and she was deeply disappointed because he had not elected to come home and spend the off-time with *her*.

She found she had run out of cigarettes.

She needed a smoke to soothe her nerves. She decided to take the staff car, which she knew how to drive, and go down to the village where there was sure to be some place open where she could buy a packet of cigarettes.

She looked in her bag for change and found only a shilling and a copper or two. She then searched her wallet. There should be a five-pound note in there. She had brought it down from town. But there wasn't a note to be seen. A hasty search through the whole bag and through her coat pockets proved that the five pounds were missing.

Fern's cheeks went slowly red. An unhappy look dawned in her eyes. It was quite obvious that Terry had taken the money. She didn't really *mind* that. It was a standing joke between them that when they were short of cash they rifled each other's pockets, but paid it all back in time. And if Terry hadn't settled his debts in the past, it didn't much matter because Fern used always to have plenty of pocket money, out of that fat allowance she received from home.

But things were different now, Fern thought.

She walked on to her little balcony and stared down at the courtyard where a ginger cat, followed by two fat, playful kittens, stalked over the cobbles in graceful feline fashion. She watched them for a moment, trying to be cheerful again.

The sky was so blue. It was a heavenly day. There was a sound of cawing from the rooks in the high elms at the back of the garage. A lump rose in Fern's throat. No, it didn't matter that Terry had taken that five-pound note. What mattered was that he had been so secretive about staying up in London. And what on earth was he going to spend the money on? Perhaps have a drink with a few friends. She guessed as much. But didn't *he* realise how things had changed? Why, they had hardly been able to settle all their bills before they left London. And Mummy's lawyers had told Terry that things would be very tight financially with the Wendell family; that Mummy would only just have enough to live on until the position was resolved and they all knew where they were.

'Well,' said Fern to herself, tight-lipped, 'no more smoking for me. I'd better learn to give it up altogether.'

It seemed suddenly very lonely. She even felt homesick – a new misery that not even the beauty of Swanlake on this golden afternoon in May could cure.

5

Quentin worked most of the afternoon – writing the kind of letters he preferred to answer personally, rather than dictate to Miss Porter.

The first was to his mother, who had written from Stockholm to tell him that she was thoroughly enjoying the beautiful city and the reunion with her old friends, but that she would be glad to get back to Swanlake.

I don't like leaving you by yourself, too long, she wrote, as there will be nobody to look after you properly…

Quentin smiled at this but decided to maintain a discreet silence about the Barretts. Knowing his mother's fiery nature he preferred to face her with the *fait accompli* regarding the departure of the Howards and the arrival of the new couple when she returned.

The first half of Mrs Dorey's letter was

mainly concerned with descriptions of Swedish scenery and customs, and censoring the latter. Dear mother, thought Quentin ruefully, she was a deal too critical and hidebound. The second half of the letter was connected with Greta. How beautiful the girl was looking; how magnificently she rode and swam and played tennis, and did everything else.

I'm going to bring her back with me when I come, my dear boy and really you must turn your thoughts seriously to the idea of marrying Greta. You need the perfect wife. I won't be with you for ever and she is the ideal one to look after you. Mind you spare some time for her when we get back. Get a few days off – it'll be the first week of June and surely you could let work drop a bit and pay some attention to your private life.

Quentin read that part of the letter with impatience and answered it impatiently:

Don't keep trying to lead me to the altar, Mother. I'm not ready for it. I value my freedom. Greta's a grand girl but...

But what? he wondered, halting and scowling at the Winterhalter over the mantelpiece.

Greta Paulson looked a bit like that creature on the horse, with her golden braids of hair and tall slim figure. A typical Scandinavian beauty. Plenty of attraction, yes. Why, then, didn't he please his mother and propose to Greta? He wanted a wife and children – one day. He knew that it wasn't a good thing for a man to devote his whole time to business and acquiring possessions. Besides, there was a side of him which had for a long time been lonely, despite his mother's companionship. One or two of his friends had made disastrous marriages, but Quentin was not cynical about marriage. He believed in it and in family life. Nevertheless, he had never yet been in love – in love as he believed a man should be – feeling a deep passion, even adoration, for the right woman.

There was a cold side to Greta. He had learned something about it in his association with her. (Not that he had ever tried to kiss her.) But he *felt* a lack of warmth, of real generosity in her nature. He liked generosity in people; that, candour, and courage were the qualities he admired most of all.

Now, he thought, that ladylike little thing who had come down in the world and was his cook-housekeeper – *she* had courage! No doubt about that, though he wasn't so sure about the husband.

But his thoughts were digressing from Greta. He finished his letter to his mother rather abruptly, and began to write the more difficult one, connected solely with business.

The letter which he had to answer was headed: BOYD-GILLINGHAM, PRICE & WENDELL.

It was connected with a very large sum of money which he had (so he imagined) invested through the junior partner, Bernard Wendell.

Q.D.'s square hard face was harsher than usual in this moment. He had been 'taken for a ride' for the first time in his life (so he imagined) through Wendell, and he didn't like it.

For years he used to buy shares on the market through his father's old broker, then the two partners of that firm, well-known to the old Q.D., had died, being both advanced in years. One of Quentin's business associates had warmly recommended Boyd-Gillingham. There was no longer a 'Price' in the firm. Lately Boyd-Gillingham had been a sick man and away continually and many of Quentin's deals had been made through Wendell.

Quentin had found Wendell a charming

man of the old school. He had felt entirely safe with him. It had been a considerable shock when he had phoned the firm one morning recently, found all the lines jammed and later read in the morning papers that Wendell had disappeared from the country. Gillingham was now lying seriously ill at his home in Epsom, and admitted to a deficit in the firm of hundreds of thousands of pounds. It was obvious to Quentin that the brokers had been playing around with their clients' money, at a tempting time, when the boom was on – and with disastrous results.

Until the case was heard, details were not available, but Quentin gathered that the partners had, some months ago, financed one particular deal in City property, backed by the funds which they had misappropriated.

There had been an unexpected demand for withdrawal of clients' money – much buying on margin – and in the end an inability on the part of the brokers to meet their debt for the property deal.

Quentin was involved up to the tune of twenty thousand pounds. Not much, perhaps, for a 'tycoon' of wealth, but too much so far as he was concerned. He wanted that money back. He didn't care which of the partners was most seriously indicted, he held them both culpable. He tried to excuse Gillingham on the grounds that he was sick, and maybe the sickness had spread to his mind, but for Wendell – barely fifty and a fit man – such an action was unpardonable. In Quentin's mind Wendell was 'the rat' who had deserted the sinking ship.

Yet he had to wonder what lay at the back of the affair. What twist of brain or sudden temptation could have led a decent fellow like Wendell to sink in such murky waters?

What kind of private life had he once had? Quentin knew vaguely that Wendell was married, but that was all. Now, undoubtedly, the firm would be hammered. Boyd-Gillingham would take the rap over here and the search for Wendell would go on.

Quentin worked at his desk until a sudden hunger reminded him that it was past time for the evening meal and that he had had no tea. The house seemed very silent. He supposed the little cook was over in her flat having a well-earned rest. He still savoured the memory of that lunch.

He decided to ask his old friends, the Pascalls, down next weekend. Lord Pascall and her ladyship liked good food and now that Mrs Barrett was here, Quentin could risk the invitation. And there was that nice elderly woman, Mrs Grey-Everton – a wealthy widow whose estate adjoined Swanlake – she could come in and make up the fourth for dinner on the Saturday night.

Quentin walked through the deserted house into the staff quarters. A sudden homely longing for a good strong cup of tea took him into the kitchen. He switched on the electric kettle. As he looked around he was struck by the order and spotlessness of the place. He rarely came out here, but whenever he had done so in the past, it had always seemed in a vast muddle.

On his return to the library, a fresh twinge of pain made him grimace and clap a hand against the side of his thigh. Devil take it, the sciatica was coming back, and just as he had made up his mind to get up to town tomorrow in the Rolls. Now all he wanted was his couch again.

That reminded him. Young Barrett was bringing the Rolls down after dark. He'd better be careful – with all that Brighton traffic and the lights against him. Woe betide him if he got so much as a scratch on the Silver Wraith!

Vandamm had mentioned that young

Barrett was a first-class driver. *'He'd better be,'* Quentin thought grimly.

In her flat, across the way, Fern sat alone reading a book – or trying to – feeling not in the least happy about things and with her mind, also, on the Rolls, and Terry driving back tonight.

She loved him, but she could not be entirely blind to his weaknesses. One of them was that when he got into a jocular 'party mood' in that Chelsea set in which he sometimes moved, he *did* sometimes drink a little too much.

It seemed the longest evening Fern had ever spent. She wrote to her mother, giving her an ecstatic description of Swanlake; assuring her that she was going to be very happy here and promising to go and see her soon. She ended with mention of the name which she dared not speak aloud any more but which was ever in her thoughts.

I pray every night that darling Daddy is safe and well, and will soon be cleared of all this terrible suspicion…

Fern stayed up listening to her little radio until about ten o'clock, quite expecting Terry to be home by then. But he didn't come and she felt so tired and miserable that she finally filled a hot-water bottle and went to bed. The May night had suddenly turned chilly.

She was half asleep when she heard the purring engine of the Rolls and the scrunch of wheels in the courtyard. Wide awake then, she sat up and switched on the table lamp. Terry had never changed the flex and it was too short in here. The lamp sat in a comic position on the floor.

Fern waited for Terry, expecting at any moment that he would come in. But he didn't. After a moment, Fern felt uneasy, slipped out of bed, and in dressing-gown and slippers walked out of the flat and down the little staircase to the garage below.

The lights of the car were full on. Terry was standing by the bonnet, smoking a cigarette, his peaked chauffeur's cap on the back of his head.

In the glaring light of the headlamps, the sight of that face made her heart sink. It was so sickly white – and so miserable. And when her darling, handsome, arrogant Terry looked *miserable*, she knew that it was because *he* knew that he had done wrong. Just like a child.

'Terry! What on earth is it?' she exclaimed.

'Why are you so late home?'

He looked at her a bit stupidly.

'Hullo, darling.' Then, as he noted her thin silk dressing-gown, 'Go on up. You'll catch cold down here like that.'

'Never mind,' she said impatiently. 'What's the matter? Why are *you* standing down here?'

'I'm afraid you'll be furious with me when I tell you.'

'Come on, tell me.'

'Well, you know what I am. Q.D. asked me to pick up an important parcel from his flat in town. I remembered the damn thing only when I was three-quarters of the way down here. Always have been vague, haven't I, poppet?'

'Oh dear, what will he say when he asks you for the parcel?' asked Fern in dismay. 'Right at the beginning of your job. You really ought to have turned back.'

Now Terry looked sheepish and pulled at his ear.

'I wasn't all that sure about myself driving all that way again. I felt so sleepy,' he mumbled.

'Oh, *Terry!*'

Now he noticed her shivering and put an arm around her with a contrite expression which she could rarely resist. Terry's nose was just slightly tip-tilted. It gave him a boyish, appealing expression. But she felt really cross with him tonight.

Her mind worked busily as they walked up to the flat after Terry had shut and locked the garage. Terry threw himself on the bed and was about to sink into an exhausted sleep but Fern's brain was wide awake.

'Where does the boss stay in town?' she demanded.

'He has a flat in that big block on the Embankment – Whitehall Court.'

'In Whitehall,' said Fern and looked thoughtfully at her bedside clock.

He caught at her hand and eyed her sleepily.

'What are you planning?'

'Where is the parcel?'

'He arranged for me to pick it up at the porter's office.'

'There'll be a night porter, of course.'

'Yes, but–'

'You go to sleep,' said Fern in a firm voice. 'Come on, sweetie, get your clothes off and go to sleep, or you'll look a wreck when you report for duty in the morning.'

He struggled out of his suit, fighting against the exhaustion and the too-much-drink which were rapidly defeating him. His mind was really too muzzy for the moment to argue or ask Fern further questions. He only said:

'Well, I can't possibly drive back to London tonight. I'll just have to take the rap.'

And after that he passed into oblivion.

He did not hear the sound of a car being started up nor miss Fern's presence in the bedroom. He opened his eyes to find that it was morning and Fern was standing beside him with a large flat parcel in her hands. He blinked at it stupidly and saw the name written across it. She was holding it up in front of his eyes: QUENTIN DOREY, Esq.

Now, fully awake, Terry stared at his wife. She was already up and dressed.

'Here you are,' she said, holding the parcel close. 'Up you get, Lazybones, and tell me you're pleased with me and sorry about last night.'

He stuttered.

'What's this? How on *earth*...?'

'You can deliver it to the boss with his morning mail,' said Fern.

'But where ... how ... did you *get* it?'

A dimple showed at the corner of her mouth.

'While you were sleeping off "the fumes", you monster, I drove the staff car up to Whitehall Court. Incidentally, I found the card which I was sure Q.D. had given you authorising you to take the parcel, still in your pocket, and I presented it to a very surprised night porter.'

In all the months that Terry had been this girl's husband, he had never felt a warmer admiration or affection for her than now. He jumped out of bed and caught her close, hiding his face against her warm neck.

'You went all that way in the early hours of the morning – in that awful staff car – oh, you *angel!* You absolute *honey.*'

'Well, I admit I didn't enjoy the drive.'

'And you must be so tired this morning.'

'I am.'

'But you've saved my bacon in no small way, darling.'

He covered her face with kisses.

'I'll never forget this,' he added. 'You make me feel a cad. But I'll try and show my gratitude.'

She was tired but she felt that it had been worth it – not only what she had done for him but because now Q.D. need never know. (She had fixed that with the night porter.) And it had worried her so badly to think that almost as soon as Terry got here, he should fail to carry out a commission that his employer had given him.

How could she be cross with Terry when he showed her such gratitude and seemed so close to her? She kissed him tenderly.

'Hurry up and get dressed, Chauffeur Barrett. I'm going over to prepare breakfast.'

'I'll be with you in one jiffy, and I repeat – I'll never forget what you've done for me, sweetie.'

'"Never's" a long time,' she called out gaily as she left the flat.

She spoke without real cynicism but there was to come a sad day when she was forced to remember her own words.

6

It was a real 'Monday-morning' for Fern.

Maureen turned up to work but looked miserable and sickly and said she felt it. Before she had been in the house an hour, Fern sent her home.

'You need another day in bed,' she said firmly.

'Glory be, and it's an angel you are,' said Maureen, 'It's the gastric trouble I have.' And, with a sniff, she departed, driven by the handsome Mr Barrett back to her aunt's cottage.

Fern had to face another day with a depleted staff. Mrs Hatton never stayed longer than her three hours but she was a splendid cheerful worker and, over 'elevenses', Fern heard the whole story of her meeting with Jim, the gardener, and their marriage, plus details of the births of each child (which Mrs Hatton gave with gusto). She'd had all the children in a hospital where she'd been treated like a princess, she said.

'You take my advice and have yours that way instead of at home, duckie,' she finished.

Fern, having cooked and washed up breakfast and done all Maureen's rooms as well, was relaxing for a few moments with her 'cuppa' and cigarette. She grinned at the girl they called 'Rosie'.

'I didn't know I *was* having one!'

'Oh, but you will,' said Mrs Hatton cheerfully.

'I'd like one,' said Fern wistfully.

She meant it. She had never had much to do with small children but she had always planned to have a family. She used to tell Mummy that she wanted at least two boys and two girls, because she thought family life the finest thing in the world for a woman. Thinking back she remembered discussing the question with Terry when they first became engaged. In his vague way he had agreed that he would like children, but the trouble with Terry was that he was always so vague; apt to skim over things, never to probe very deep. She had only found that out later, after they were married. Then, when she repeated that she would adore to have a baby, he said:

'Oh, sure, one day, by all means, but let's

have a good time first of all while we're still so young, poppet.'

Perhaps now, as things had turned out, it was as well she wasn't hampered by a child, thought Fern. This job would have been impossible if she had had an infant to look after. At the same time she felt a curious ache in her heart when she considered that now it might not be easy to have that longed-for baby for *years*. It wasn't how she had wanted her marriage to be; but when would her handsome and rather irresponsible husband ever find and hold down a really first-class job and so enable them to lead a different sort of life in which a family could be included?

No good, either, looking back – or even too far forward, Fern told herself. While things were as they were now, better to live only for the moment.

Thank goodness she had thought of driving up to London to get that parcel. It was the first thing the great Q.D. asked for when she sent Maureen in with his early tea.

Once Quentin was dressed and down in the dining-room where he breakfasted – he was the type of man who could not bear trays in bed – Fern went in to see him and discuss the day's menu.

When he remarked that he was glad to see that Maureen had come back to help her, she did not mention the fact that she had sent Maureen home again. Why worry him, since he was kind enough to *feel* worried because he thought she had too much to do.

'My secretary will be coming down for lunch,' he said, 'so serve up a meal for two. We shall be working most of the afternoon.'

'Yes, Mr Dorey.'

'I've told Barrett I hope my leg will be okay enough for me to get up to a meeting in London tomorrow. It's an important one I don't want to miss.'

'Is the sciatica better, Mr Dorey?'

He moved his leg gingerly under the table.

'Still giving me "gyp", but I've got to get up to town tomorrow even if I'm carried there. By the way, Dr Philmore is coming in from Brighton to see me later on this morning.'

'Yes, Mr Dorey.'

Eating his well-grilled kidney and bacon – a dish he particularly liked – Quentin glanced at the slim girl in her neat white overall and thought yet again that he was a lucky chap to have found anybody so efficient. He said:

'I'll be entertaining this weekend. I'll let

111

you know after Miss Porter has done some phoning and arranging for me how many we'll be. If you need extra help on the Sunday why not ask Hatton's wife to come in for an hour or so?'

'I'll ask her if I need the help,' said Fern.

The rest of the day was a rush and she was pretty tired after her nocturnal drive on Terry's behalf. But she felt well rewarded when he came back to lunch looking more cheerful than usual and said that he had been congratulated by Q.D. for remembering all the things that he had been asked to do.

'Said he was glad I had a better memory than Howard,' grinned Terry.'

'Humph,' said Fern looking at him through her lashes.

He touched her cheek with a forefinger.

'*I know.* Don't tell me. It's all due to the little woman.'

Fern laughed but she looked pale and heavy-eyed, and after she had washed up it was Terry who told her she must rest this afternoon.

'You don't need to go shopping. Just give me the list of things and I'll get them in Brighton for you. I'll go on there after I've taken the secretary back to Haywards Heath Station.'

'Miss Porter's rather nice,' said Fern.

'I suppose we owe her this job,' said Terry, yawning.

Fern came up to him and leaned her head against his shoulder.

'Are you beginning to like it better, and not feel so *menial*, darling?'

'Oh, it's okay,' he said.

After what she had done for him last night he hadn't the heart to grouse as bitterly as usual, but he knew in his heart he would never like this sort of work. He considered himself far too good to be anybody's *servant*. He had dreamed far too often of holding down a big important job in a firm of which Terence Barrett was one of the directors.

When he was out driving the Rolls, it didn't seem too bad, but when he had to clean the damned car (as he had done this morning) the unaccustomed physical labour made his muscles ache – and when he was hanging around waiting for 'the boss' to ring for him, he was bored, bored, *bored*. A pity, he thought, as he looked at Fern, that the 'roses and raptures' of passionate love faded after marriage. Fern was always emphasising the fact that they didn't, if you were truly in love, and that she was still mad about him.

But was he mad about her? He didn't quite understand himself, nor did he, at times, think too well of his own nature, but with him there had to be the right atmosphere for 'roses and rapture'. He could be Fern's impassioned lover more easily when they were in town, as in the old days, with a glamorous background. But down here in a position like this … no.

He almost wished that he had Fern's happy nature. For her, adversity did not lessen love but strengthened it. On him it had the reverse effect. It cooled his ardour.

When Fern went into the library to collect the coffee cups, Q.D. and his secretary were already at work again. Miss Porter looked up from her pad and smiled at the young cook-housekeeper. She had heard such good reports from her chief that she was relieved, since she was responsible for engaging the Barretts.

Fern smiled back at Miss Porter. She was a nice brown-haired, brown-eyed woman on the wrong side of forty. She had, perhaps, thought Fern, once hoped for marriage, a husband and children, but had never been given the chance. She was not a glamorous figure. She was short, square and wore glasses. But she was a tireless worker with a fabulous memory. She had become Quentin's right hand once she entered his service. She had in the past run a typing bureau, but it had not been a great success. That was why she had taken the job with Mr Dorey. That he was a 'rough diamond' at times, Miss Porter knew, but she admired him more than any man she had ever worked for. Perhaps in the shy recess of her deepest heart she was even a little in love with him. But he would never know it.

Today, as Nancy Porter looked at Mrs Barrett, she felt the faintest tinge of envy. It must be rather nice to have charge of Q.D.'s gorgeous home, and be always here to serve him.

Nancy Porter was able to give Fern a little respite by telling her that Mr Dorey's friends, Lord and Lady Pascall could not come this weekend, so the houseparty was put forward to the first weekend in June – another fortnight ahead. After Fern had left the room with the tray, Miss Porter said:

'Mrs Barrett does seem the answer to all your problems down here, doesn't she, Mr Dorey? That was a superb lunch.'

These words penetrated Quentin's thoughts, much engaged as they were on the business report he was examining.

'Ah, h'm, yes, that young thing cooks like a French chef. You've done me a service in finding her, Nancy.'

'I hope Mrs Dorey will like her, too,' said Miss Porter a trifle anxiously.

'I hope so too,' said Quentin with a slight grimace which the privileged secretary well understood.

He secretly felt a bit guilty about 'Mum', as the big man affectionately called his mother (nobody else dared to detract from that formidable lady's dignity). He had begun to think that he had been foolish not to tell her about the Barretts. But, of course, he kept reminding himself, it was silly to worry so much about his mother. She could not help but appreciate the new cook.

Dr Philmore had told Quentin this morning that he could drive up to town to his meeting. The leg had definitely improved. He was just not to do too much on it for the moment.

It would have been sensible, Quentin supposed, to stay in London at his flat while he had this leg trouble, but when the attack had first seized him, he had been down in Sussex, so he had remained here. Besides – when he was in London he always dined out and spent the evening with friends. He had no wish to be a prisoner in the flat during such a spell of fine weather. It was better in the country.

The longer Q.D. lived at Swanlake, the more attached he grew to the place. At one time he hadn't bothered about flowers or shrubs, nor known the name of any of them. Nowadays he could talk to Jim Hatton about the greenhouses and what could be grown, and at times even took off his coat and worked a little out in the sun with spade or fork or at the weeding. Exercise was good for a man; kept him fit and young. Quentin had no intention of allowing himself to become one of these fat City gentlemen with a middle-aged 'spread'.

The drive to London was successful. On the way up he talked to his new chauffeur – in his friendly way. He found Barrett quite an intelligent conversationalist. They launched into a debate on private incomes and tax returns.

Quentin extracted Terry's opinion that he did not believe in the levelling up of incomes; the socialistic policy of 'the same for all'. Terry disapproved of everything being taken from the rich to give to the poor.

'I like social services for the nation,' added

117

Terry as he drove the Rolls smoothly down the Brighton road toward Redhill. 'But there must always be those who have the brains and ability to make good – like you, sir,' he added glibly, 'so I think after years of hard work and using that brain, your kind should be allowed to enjoy their earnings.'

'Yes, agreed,' nodded Quentin. 'But I wish I had had your chances, Barrett, when I was a youngster – had gone to first-class school. You and your wife have had real education, I can see that.'

'Thank you, sir,' said Terry with a little smile.

'You've got a wonderful wife,' added Quentin.

'Thank you, sir,' repeated Terry.

'What brought you both down to this sort of work?'

Terry did not answer that question for a moment. His eyes narrowed. Then he said:

'Just bad luck, sir. We had money once, and we lost it through no fault of our own.'

Quentin felt slightly nettled. Neither of these young people seemed inclined to give any real facts about themselves. Mrs Barrett was always as non-committal. What were they hiding (if anything)? How had they lost their money? How had they got it in the first place? Oh, well, it wasn't his business and if they served him well, why worry? he reflected.

'Ambition is what counts in this world, Barrett,' he went on after a pause, and lit one of his favourite cigars. 'When I was a lad I used to dream of this sort of thing...' He waved the cigar in the air, and indicated the car.

Terry gave a short laugh.

'If that's ambition – I've got plenty, too, sir, but I don't look like realising mine.'

'One of the first things you've got to do, is to *like* work,' said Quentin drily.

'Oh, yes,' said Terry, but he spoke without conviction, and added: 'Winning a football pool – twenty thousand or thirty thousand pounds, just for filling in a form, that's my idea of good luck.'

Here, Quentin Dorey snapped at him:

'Not mine. All against my principles. I've no use for that sort of capital gain. Easy come – easy go. I say a chap's got to work hard day and night. Men who inherit wealth or win it overnight – no. They get flabby and live in a sort of mental cocoon wrapped up in egotism. Bone-lazy, they get. You've got to *work*, Barrett.'

'I don't see that my work will get me anywhere, if I might say so,' said Terry bitterly.

That was where he made a mistake. The man at his side turned and looked with narrowed gaze at the young chauffeur. He could see the discontent written on that good-looking face. He sensed the weakness that went with it, too. He thought suddenly:

'This chap hasn't got his wife's character. *She's* worth ten of *him!*'

Frowning, Quentin turned his gaze to the road ahead of him.

He had little more to say to Terry, but no criticism to make of the way in which he was driving. Barrett handled the Rolls perfectly.

When they got back to Swanlake that evening, he found the house full of welcome. Mrs Barrett had arranged flowers in the hall and library, and in the dining-room there was a nice tea waiting for him with thinly cut brown bread and butter. He thanked her as she brought him the tray:

'I'll put on weight if you give me too much. Watch your step and my diet – at least one day of starvation,' he added, grinning at her.

Fern's very blue eyes smiled back.

'I'll watch, Mr Dorey.'

'Didn't you say,' he added suddenly, 'that first day you came, some of the paintings in this house were hung in the wrong place?'

She flushed.

'Please forget that—'

'Rubbish. I like to remember it. Now where would you make the changes?'

A little nervously Fern told him that she had learned a great deal from her father. Bernard Wendell's hobby had been collecting pictures. From childhood Fern had become familiar with London's best art galleries and exhibitions.

But she was a little perturbed when the great Q.D. told her to send for her husband and get him to rehang some of the paintings where they ought to be.

Quentin Dorey was a man of many facets, she thought. The important, sometimes pompous tycoon could become a strangely humble, simple man, passionately anxious to learn.

'And I want to do the right thing when Lord and Lady Pascall come down on Saturday week,' he told her. '*You* decide where to seat the people at meals. You do whatever you think her ladyship would like. I mean about arranging their rooms ... putting flowers around and the proper sheets and towels and soap in the bathroom and so on. *You* know ... attend to the details.'

121

'You can leave it all to me, Mr Dorey,' said Fern, who never liked her employer more than when he groped like this, so endearingly, for information and help. Since his return from London he had given her so many orders, she had not had much time in which to tell him anything that had happened to her during the day. Now she handed him a piece of paper.

'They telephoned this telegram from Haywards Heath Post Office, Mr Dorey. I think I've got it down right. It's from Stockholm.'

'Ah! My mother.'

Q.D. took the piece of paper and read what Fern had written in her neat hand.

Plans changed. Coming home June 1 with Greta.

'Yes, that's it,' said Fern nodding.

Q.D. turned and laid the paper down on his desk. He wondered why his mother had cut her visit short by a week. Of course he would be pleased to see her, but he wished that she had waited a little longer. Now she would be here with Greta on the very weekend on which he had fixed his houseparty. However, there were plenty of rooms in this house.

He flung another order at Fern.

'The party is growing. Arrange whichever suite you like for Miss Paulson and see that my mother's own bedroom is ready and aired for Friday week.'

'Yes, Mr Dorey.'

After Fern had gone, Quentin read the telephoned message again. He grimaced.

He had a shrewd idea of what this meant. Quite possibly someone from the district had written out to his mother and told her about the Howards, and the Barretts being here. That well-known gossip and Mum's best friend, Mrs Grey-Everton, for instance.

Well, he was sure Fern would put on a good show, and he could only hope that Mum would like her.

7

It was a busy fortnight for Fern. By the time the Friday of that second week arrived, she felt that she had been at Swanlake all her life instead of two and a half weeks.

She had grown quite accustomed to her position. Not even her mother's sad letters or phone calls which were full of sympathy for her 'poor brave darling', could stop Fern from fundamentally enjoying her work. And she particularly liked working for Quentin Dorey. He gave her *carte blanche* at Swanlake and seemed more than appreciative of her efforts. Whatever changes she made during the short time she had been in charge, he approved.

Maureen was better and back at work and although Mrs Hatton had had to stay away all Thursday, because she, too, had had a touch of gastritis (it seemed to be going round the village), Fern managed to cope.

Now that she knew that Mrs Dorey was coming home she felt that she must have everything perfect. She could not say that she was looking forward to the return of Q.D.'s mother, after all Maureen's muttered hints about Mrs Dorey being such 'a terror'. But as Fern said to Terry:

'She is the mistress here and I'm just the maid. I've got to remember it.'

Terry eyed his wife gloomily. He was not in a good mood. He did not tell her so but she rather guessed that he was not seeing eye to eye with Mr Dorey, although no actual fault had been found with his work. But it appeared from what Terry repeated to her that when the two men discussed things, they seemed unable to find much common ground. Once Fern had advised her husband to keep strict control of what he said, but he only hunched his shoulders.

'I'm prepared to touch my cap and open car doors but I'm not going to swallow all my ideas and principles just to suit Mr Quentin Dorey, even if I do get the sack,' he said.

This made Fern feel a good deal more anxious than she cared to show, but she touched Terry lightly on the cheek.

'Don't be a noodle, darling,' she said. 'We've got a marvellous home here for the moment. Let's keep it.'

'And when the heck do we get any real

time off? You've been hard at it ever since we came. So have I. What's the good of our high wages if we never get the time to spend them?'

Fern agreed with this and she knew her Terry. It wasn't much good suggesting that he should save a penny, even in their present contingency. She tried to soothe him.

'I knew we were supposed to have been off last weekend, but I couldn't leave Q.D. absolutely alone with that bad leg, could I? After we get through this weekend's house-party we'll definitely take our Wednesday off and we'll ask if we can borrow the staff car and go and see poor mother and then have a nice little dinner somewhere together.'

'Sounds too utterly glamorous...' began Terry with a sneer and then relented because Fern's charming face looked so hurt. He kissed her on the nose: 'Okay, sweetie, that's what we'll do,' he drawled.

Mrs Dorey was due at London Airport with her goddaughter on that Friday afternoon. When Terry suggested to Fern that this might be the development in a big way of the so-called romance between Mr Dorey and Miss Paulson, Fern smiled, but she thought a lot more seriously about it. It would be wonderful if Mr Dorey could meet and marry the right girl, she supposed, but was this just a match *arranged* by a designing mother? If so it would be a disaster. There was something so very sweet and generous about the tough business man. She could imagine him being led into the wrong matrimonial channel – just as he could be influenced into making a wrong choice of ties.

'Really!' Fern laughed at herself. 'The way you try and mother this man who is ten years older than yourself and a hundred times more successful – is quite ludicrous!'

Friday morning was a nightmare. The window cleaners didn't come until the last moment, and there had been a sharp storm of driving rain the day before which left marks on all the beautiful windows. Fern had to telephone half a dozen times in order to get the men to keep their promise to come along.

Then a leak started in the cistern of the staff bathroom. Plumbers arrived and trod with dirty boots over the floors that Mrs Hatton had washed and polished so vigorously. The butcher's van broke down and the saddle of mutton which Fern had ordered for tonight's dinner was late in coming, which worried her.

She rushed from room to room to make sure everything looked right. Terry had driven his employer up to London to the office and they were calling at the Airport to collect the arrivals on the way down.

For the first time Fern had a little time to inspect Mrs Dorey's own bedroom – one of the big front rooms overlooking the lake. It could have been wonderful, Fern thought, but she did not care for Mrs Dorey's choice in colour or furnishing. There was too much pink. The wrong kind of pink. Not the 'shocking, sugary' kind that could look so smart, but a sickly pink. Paint-work, the carpets, the satin curtains, even the tiles in the bathroom were pink. Mrs Hatton had told Fern that Mrs Dorey had had this room done up to her own taste when the Doreys first took over Swanlake. In Lady Chavering's time it used to be all in white and gold.

The furniture was good solid mahogany, but the walls were crammed with pictures and photographs – obviously of Quentin at all ages – on the mantelpiece. One, in an old-fashioned silver frame, of a square-faced gentleman with a moustache, who was Quentin's father.

There were no books, and only one small mirror. Mrs Dorey was obviously not vain.

Funny, thought Fern, one can almost tell a person's character from their bedroom. She could imagine exactly what Nell Dorey was like. A real north-country-woman brought up in the old-fashioned way and maintaining old-fashioned customs; witness the conglomeration of ornaments and pictures in here, which had possibly belonged to Mrs Dorey's mother and grandmother before that. Tasteless to a degree that made Fern flinch. And why that pink when everything else was so dull and austere?

A psychologist would say, possibly, that somewhere under Mrs Dorey's harsh exterior there existed a longing for something gay and girlish – the two things Nell Dorey had never been, even when she was young.

Fern knew, of course, what Mrs Dorey looked like, or at least what she had looked like, because there was a framed snapshot of her in Quentin's bedroom. Tall and straight and narrow-lipped (as described by Maureen). *What* would happen now that she was coming back? *'Quite frankly, I dread it,'* thought Fern.

She arranged some flowers tastefully on Mrs Dorey's dressing table, opened another window because the day was quite warm, and then hurried through the house to see to the other bedrooms. A handsome suite including the Queen Anne bedroom for Lord and Lady Pascall (no evidence here of Mrs Dorey's personal taste). They were coming tomorrow, so she would do their flowers in the morning. A charming corner-room with a pale blue, flowered paper for the Swedish goddaughter. A bowl of freesias for her dressing chest. Then Fern darted back to the kitchen to wait for the butcher's van and prepare the special sauce for the fish course which she was giving them.

Afterwards over to her flat to wash and put on a fresh overall. Tired before the evening began and with a heavy weekend ahead of her. They should all be back from the Airport at any moment.

Fern looked around her sitting-room. It always seemed a little ugly and strange and not really like home. In a way it intensified whatever regrets Fern had about her former life. She was happier, really, at work in the Manor.

She had a sudden nostalgic longing for the sort of evening she used to spend with Terry. Tonight it would be all work and waiting on guests – and no Terry.

To have an intimate meal alone with him – to dance somewhere – as they used to do, in town – had that sort of life gone from them for ever? Now, for a moment when Fern had time to think about herself, it struck her that she had seen very little of Terry all this week. Even when he wasn't driving Q.D. around he seemed to be out. He avoided sitting with her in the kitchen whenever he could. She knew, of course, that he had found a country 'pub' called 'The Golden Fawn' and that he went there regularly after he finished washing the car. It wasn't that she minded. Men were different from women... Terry was certainly different from her in his outlook. Unable to conceal his perpetual resentment against the life he was now forced to lead. But her heart ached at the idea that he needed to find his relaxation away from her. She was terrified that he would do something to offend his employer before he finished.

The saddle of mutton was delivered. That was a weight off the young cook's mind. She started to prepare her vegetables. Then she heard the crunch of wheels and the purr of the Rolls. Running into the hall she looked out of a window and saw that the party had arrived from the Airport.

Her heart fluttered. She felt unusually nervous. She put up a hand to tidy her hair and smoothed her overall. She thought it would be a nice thing to open the door and welcome Mrs Dorey home, personally.

The sun was still shining. The garden looked glorious. Fern had arranged beautiful flowers and plants all over the house, and was confident that it was spotless too. She did so hope that Mrs Dorey would be pleased.

She took a quick look at the two women who stepped out of the car while Quentin eased himself from his own seat, with the aid of his stick. Terry was taking suitcases out of the boot. (Poor old Terry, thought Fern; hating his uniform and his job.)

Mrs Dorey was unmistakable. Fern recognised that tall upright figure in green tweeds, with a green beret on an iron grey head. The face she turned to Fern was just like the one in her photograph, only more lined. Not a kindly or amiable face, although the features were handsome and it was obviously from her that Quentin had inherited his strength of jaw and his purposeful expression. But as Mrs Dorey drew nearer Fern, the girl could see that the eyes were not as kindly as her son's.

The girl – Greta Paulson – was certainly glamorous. Slender, perfectly dressed in a grey silky suit with a touch of white at the throat and a white felt hat on a head as fair and shining as corn in the sun. A lovely Swedish blonde, thought Fern, with sincere admiration. Just a tiny pang of envy shot through her as she saw Greta standing there, powdering her nose, adjusting the brim of her hat. A typical smart, modern girl, careful of her looks, wearing white doeskin gloves and carrying a white leather bag under her arm.

'*Once,*' thought Fern, '*I used to drive down with Terry for weekend parties like this and be the fashionable guest.*'

Now she was the cook. Her hands were already reddened after fourteen days of rough work. She stood here not in chic, lovely clothes, but an overall.

Mrs Dorey came toward her. Goodness, how tall the woman was! Quite terrifying, thought Fern, and wondered comically if she ought to drop a curtsey in front of such a personage. She stuttered:

'Oh ... how do you do ... I mean ... good afternoon.'

'Good afternoon,' echoed Mrs Dorey in a voice that was as hard as her mouth. And she looked down at the brown-haired petite girl and into those fantastically beautiful blue eyes with the utmost foreboding.

Enid Grey-Everton had been right to advise her to come home, she thought. She had been very much put out when she received Enid's letter which had told her of the sudden departure of the Howards and of the way Quentin had installed this new couple.

They appear to be well-educated and not at all the class of person you will like. You know what lady-helps are. Always too big for their boots, my dear. I hear this girl cooks divinely, but is much too young for a household like yours, with a bachelor son in it. And I've heard the chauffeur is already a regular visitor at the 'Golden Fawn'...

That and other tit-bits of gossip from Cuckendean.

It had been enough to make Mrs Dorey rush back to Swanlake. She had said nothing to Greta, of course – merely suggested that they ought to go back as 'Q' (so his mother called him) had been alone too long.

But Mrs Dorey was furious with her son for not telling her about the Howards and furious that the new couple had been engaged in her absence before she could 'vet' them.

She could not say she disliked the young chauffeur. As Greta had whispered in her ear, he was 'very good to look at'. Even Mrs Dorey was feminine enough to agree. Besides which, Terry had been deferential and charming to her and she could not complain of the way he drove. But one glance at Mrs Barrett confirmed her worst suspicions about the wife. She was young and pretty and she was *quite* out of place, with her soft educated voice and her *'how do you do's'*. Besides, Quentin had talked far too much about her cooking. Mrs Dorey had never before known him take the slightest interest in any of the staff.

'Time I came back and took control,' thought Mrs Dorey, and marched into the hall.

Her eyes, which missed nothing, noted the well-polished floor and furniture, which was all to the good, *and* the flowers. But a look of horror crossed her face as she stared up at the oil painting over the big stone fireplace.

'Who hung that up there instead of my flower picture?' she demanded.

Quentin limped up behind his mother. Somewhat sheepishly his gaze met Fern's, then turned away again. But it was not his nature to be tactful. The blunt truth was always good enough for Q.D.

'Mrs Barrett's father taught her a lot about painting and she knows what's what, Mum. She suggested the flower picture was more suitable for the drawing-room and the portrait that hung in there should be in the hall. I thoroughly agree. Don't you?'

Nell Dorey turned. The glance she threw the young girl in the white overall was withering. It made Fern's throat feel quite dry.

'No, I do not agree,' Mrs Dorey snapped, 'and as far as *I* am concerned, Quentin, you can change them back again.'

8

For an instant Fern wished that the ground would open and swallow her up. She hardly dared look at Quentin, but when she did so she caught the suspicion of a schoolboy's sheepish smile on that clever face. She guessed that he was remembering, as she did, last night when Terry had come in and changed over the pictures.

Fern had actually said at the time:

'Are you sure Mrs Dorey won't mind?...' but Quentin had shirked the issue and mumbled something about, 'Oh, we must move with the times, and we can all learn something from those who know better.'

He had gone on to tell them that he had bought many of these valuable paintings and ornaments from the Chaverings. He felt pretty sure, he said, that there used to be an oil-painting of the eighteenth-century school over the hall fireplace when they first came here.

But Fern had still felt uneasy about the absent lady of the house. Mr Dorey was a masterful man used to having his own way. But what would *she* say?

Now Fern knew that she had been right. She dared not look at Mrs Dorey. Greta Paulson came forward and gazed up at the portrait with her wide-set eyes, which Fern noticed were peculiarly fine hazel gold – most striking with that amber hair of hers.

'I think this looks rather good here, Aunt Nellie,' she said to her godmother. She spoke perfect English with a faint, attractive accent.

'Aunt Nellie' tossed her head. Quentin looked grateful, and Fern had far too much simplicity and niceness in her nature to know what was actually passing through the other girl's mind.

Greta Paulson had summed up the situation shrewdly. One look at Fern was enough to make her decide that the sooner Aunt Nellie sent Mrs Barrett away from Swanlake the better. But Greta did not want to appear to be altogether on her god-mother's side. First she must endear herself to Quentin. She had never seen as much of him in the past as of her godmother, but when they did meet she knew that she wanted above all else to marry him.

True – he was not as glamorous as some of

her handsome Swedish or English boy-friends. But he took no particular interest in her except in a friendly amiable way, which infuriated her. She liked men to fall madly in love with her and the very fact that Quentin had not done so long ago had become an irresistible challenge. The brash north-countryman was not altogether her ideal, but there was, all the same, something strong and invigorating about him which her femininity found provocative. Besides, he was very rich. That counted a lot with Greta.

Looking exquisite, she slipped an arm through Quentin's and smiled up at him.

'Mrs Barrett seems to be very perceptive. And how clever of you, Quentin, to find an artistic cook. I really do like this painting out here better than the old flower-piece.'

Quentin was delighted. He patted the elegant hand, then moved away from the girl.

'Thanks. Let's all have a cup of tea,' he said.

'I've laid tea in the drawing-room, and I won't be a moment making it,' said Fern.

She wasn't altogether sure she had liked the way Miss Paulson had used those words 'artistic cook', but she felt that the immediate tension was over. It was not, however, over for Mrs Dorey. She found fault again.

'We always have tea in the *library.*'

Fern coloured.

'I'm so sorry, Mrs Dorey. I thought that when you were entertaining you would like me to open up the drawing-room.'

'Now that's right, come along, Mum, come along!' said Quentin loudly, and with the aid of his stick limped across the hall. He shot a glance at Fern as he passed. She could have sworn that he gave her another schoolboy grin indicating that there was a bond of guilt between them because of the alterations they had made while 'Mum' was abroad.

'Oh, dear,' thought Fern as she hurried off to the kitchen, 'everything's going wrong now, I know.'

In the kitchen Terry sat in a wheel-back chair, legs outstretched, running his fingers through his thick fair hair.

'*Crikey!* What a woman! She nattered all the way from the Airport. She likes this. She doesn't like that. Her darling son was looking ill. She was extremely cross that the Howards had gone. Natter-natter. I heard the whole thing, anti-us, even though she said nothing actually *against* us. She couldn't, with me driving, but I bet she's starting now.'

'Oh, never mind, darling,' said Fern, feeling rather cross, herself, but refusing to show it. 'I must admit it *was* tactless making so many changes in her absence. Mr Dorey would have it.'

'You can see the sort of taste she's got,' grunted Terry.

'Well, taste has to be cultivated. One isn't necessarily born with it,' said Fern cheerfully. 'That isn't against her.'

'As for that blonde bombshell,' went on Terry, 'I wish I'd met *her* when I was just plain Terence Barrett up in town. I had *her* taped. All this: "Good afternoon, Barrett," and telling me where to put her cases, and how not to turn the suéde bag upside down because it contained her perfume bottles. A thorough madam!'

Fern, busily making tea in the big Georgian silver teapot which she always admired and had not yet used, chuckled.

'Poor lamb, you *are* in a bad way. You shouldn't let these little things get you down.'

Terry muttered something she could not hear and busied himself lighting a cigarette. Fern now carried a large silver tray with the tea and hot-water jug into the drawing-room.

It was one of the rooms she liked least in

the house, as it was such a 'hotch-potch' …
obviously Lady Chavering's and Mrs
Dorey's tastes combined. The proportions
were good and there were six beautiful
Regency windows with fanlights looking out
over an emerald lawn to the lake on which
the graceful swans were moving slowly
around the verge.

The rugs on the parquet floor were to
Fern's mind badly chosen – expensive, but
too modern. They clashed with the curtains
which Fern was sure had been chosen by
Lady Chavering. Lovely, in white and gold,
of a Georgian design with shaped pelmet.
Some of the Queen Anne walnut furniture
was good, but there was a horrible new
'suite' – sofa and two chairs covered in a
chintz which did not marry with the
curtains. The paper, in Fern's opinion, had
probably been there in the old days, a
handsome white embossed paper over white
panelling. But most of the paintings were a
complete mix-up of good and bad, like the
ornaments. Fern would love to have been let
loose and allowed to sort everything all out
and start again.

She especially admired the walnut and
glass French cabinet full of lovely Meissen
china birds of all colours and designs on

yellow velvet-covered shelves.

Quentin said:

'Thank you, Mrs Barrett,' when Fern put the tea tray down on a low round table over which she had spread a lace-edged cloth. Greta put in:

'Glorious sight! I'm dying for a good cup of English tea, Aunt Nellie.'

'Well, let's hope it's *good*,' said Mrs Dorey in a meaning voice.

Now Quentin's face wreathed into a smile and his bright eyes twinkled at his mother.

'Eh, Mother,' he imitated the Lancashire accent with which he had been so familiar in his childhood, 'Mrs Barrett knows how to make a good strong cup of tea, and wait till tha' sees what she gives you for dinner tonight. That'll open your eyes, lass.'

Mrs Dorey remained silent, twisting her lips. Her eyes were wide open now – but not with appreciation. The silver was shining. The bread and butter looked well-cut, but it seemed to her that this young woman, Mrs Barrett, was taking far too much upon herself. Where did she find those spoons? Had Quentin been mad enough to give her the key to the silver chest? *Those* spoons were only used when they had titled guests. And all those flowers everywhere. Far too

143

many. Mrs Dorey had also had time to run up to her bedroom to wash her hands and been staggered to see the floral arrangement on her own dressing-table. She *never* put flowers in her bedroom. She considered it a shocking waste, and didn't hold with such theatrical tastes. Oh, *she* knew these modern domestics. A bunch of flowers to cover the dust (although her gloomy and critical gaze had found no dust so far).

She refrained, however, from snubbing Mrs Barrett in front of Quentin. She sipped her tea in silence, satisfied to listen while the young couple chattered. All that really mattered was that Q. should be sensible and propose to Greta before she went back to Stockholm. *'But it is certainly time I came home,'* Nell Dorey reflected. Fancy Quentin entertaining while she was away! She had been warned about Lord and Lady Pascall coming tomorrow, and Enid Grey-Everton, too, for dinner. That young Barrett woman was to have arranged everything on her own. But she would soon be made to realise where the orders would come from in future.

'Of course,' thought Nell Dorey, *'I must go carefully. I know my son. He's like his father. Doesn't like being frustrated when he's keen*

about anything. Likes to be master of his own house. Just like his father over again.'

And Mrs Dorey had learned not to cross old Q.D. too often. It wouldn't do for her to be disparaging too soon about Mrs Barrett; Q. seemed so pleased with her. But later on, Mrs Dorey would take the reins back into her own hands.

Tea over, Mrs Dorey suggested that Quentin and Greta should go and have a chat in the library.

Quentin looked at the lovely Swedish girl with a man's natural appreciation of beauty, but nothing more. It was actually always a surprise to him that young Greta never caused his heart to beat one bit faster. He said:

'Nothing I'd like better, but Greta must excuse me till later on. I've got an hour's writing and some phoning to do.'

'How's that Boyd-Gillingham, Price and Wendell affair going?' asked Mrs Dorey. 'Now *that* was a scandalous thing. Are you going to get your money back, Q.?'

'Have you lost some money, Q.?' Greta put in with a sympathetic smile.

'For the moment,' he said and frowned. 'Mother will tell you about it, no doubt. It's one of my few mistakes. I trusted that firm.'

'Well, I shall always blame Bernard Wendell – the one who took himself off in that guilty way,' announced Mrs Dorey. '*He's* the rogue, I'll wager.'

'Who's to know the true facts until they're published?' said Quentin curtly.

'Well, it makes me furious,' said Mrs Dorey. 'The good Dorey money being misappropriated that way and *no* doubt Mr Bernard Wendell's family have spent it. It makes me sick to think of the lot dripping in mink and diamonds, paid for by *you*, Q.'

'My dear mother – to hear you talk anybody would think Wendell was a gangster with a diamond-decked moll,' said Quentin with a laugh. 'I don't imagine it's at all like that. Believe me, *I'm* not pleased about the way things have turned out, but one can't pass final judgment on Bernard Wendell until one knows more about it.'

'Sometime you must tell me about this Mr Wendell, whoever he is. It sounds an interesting case,' said Greta languidly, her golden gaze seeking Quentin's.

Outside the drawing-room door, a young girl in a white overall stood like a statue of snow – white to the lips. She had opened that door very slightly, meaning to go in and collect the tea tray. She had heard just enough to make her shut the door again swiftly in horror. Turning, she ran back to the kitchen, the tips of her fingers against her quivering lips. Terry, who was stirring a cup of tea and reading the racing news in an evening paper which he had picked up at the Airport, looked up and saw his wife's face. Her expression was enough to bring him to his feet.

'Good lord, what's the matter, Fern? You look as though you'd seen a ghost.'

She was shaking so violently that she had to sit down. She leaned her forehead on her folded arms for a moment, struggling to control herself.

'What's the matter – for heaven's sake?' Terry questioned her again.

She raised her head, her eyes were large and wild... 'They know. *They know,*' she said.

'Know what?'

'The Doreys ... they know about Daddy.'

It was Terry's turn to look concerned.

'I say! You don't mean to tell me that they realise you're one of the Wendells?'

'No, they don't seem to know *that.*'

Terry's face cleared. He wasn't all that keen about his job as Q.D.'s chauffeur, but he didn't particularly want to be given the

147

sack because of his father-in-law's shameful conduct. And it was a question of *faute de mieux*. He had reached the conclusion that this was as good a job as any, with a home thrown in until something more suitable for Terence turned up.

'Then what are you worrying about, ducky, and what did you hear?' he asked.

'I was just about to go in and take the tray.' Fern whispered the words. She was still suffering from shock. 'I just heard Mr Dorey say: *"One can't pass final judgment on Bernard Wendell until one knows more about it."* That, of course, was very decent of him and I entirely agree. Then Miss Paulson said that she wanted him to tell her about Mr Wendell "as it sounded an interesting case..." That was all.' Her voice broke, and tears gushed into her eyes, 'But oh, Terry, it was awful. I couldn't *bear* it!'

Terry put an arm around his wife and patted her shoulder.

'My poor sweet. I expect it did upset you. I'm sorry. But you've got to get used to it. The thing's happened, and if you hear the name of Wendell being spoken of disparagingly in future, you must blame your papa, mustn't you?'

Those last words jarred on Fern. She

moved away from him, her eyes flashing through her tears.

'You never lose an opportunity of being horrid about Daddy. You seem to be less charitable in your judgment than Mr Dorey.'

'That's right, pick on me,' said Terry in a surly voice. 'And, please remember, it's only a newspaper case to Mr Dorey. It's hit *me* – *us* – personally.'

Fern swallowed hard. She was beginning to be mistress of herself again. The old spirit flashed out.

'Well, Mr Dorey's right. Let's wait and hear the facts before we condemn Daddy out of hand. I'm sure – and so is Mummy – that he had a good reason for disappearing.'

Terry shrugged his shoulders, sat down and picked up his paper again.

Now, biting her lips, Fern said:

'I wonder what on earth brought up the subject of Daddy in that room just now.'

She was not to discover that reason just yet. For Terry, without knowing that he was doing so, misled her. He opened his paper and pointed to a small paragraph.

'There's your answer. They saw this. They were reading bits from *The Standard* as we drove home. I saw it, too, but I wasn't going

149

to show it to you and upset you.'

'Thank you,' said Fern under her breath, but there was an aching pain in her heart as she read the paragraph he pointed out. It stated in a few cold, merciless words that the stockbroking firm of Boyd-Gillingham, Price & Wendell had been hammered on the Stock Exchange that morning.

She made an enormous effort not to lose her self-control again. She handed the paper back to her husband.

'I'll go and clear away the tea tray,' she said in a choked voice.

'Well, don't take it too badly, sweetie. At least let's be thankful they don't realise that we are connected with it,' said Terry. 'Now I've got to go and clean the ruddy Rolls. See you later.'

Maureen came into the kitchen. She was gay and friendly as usual, but hopelessly untidy. Despite all Fern's efforts to smarten the Irish girl up, Maureen remained – just Maureen. A gold-hearted, excellent worker, but she would never make a smart waitress; she did not like going into the drawing-room and had begged Mrs Barrett to take in the tea and serve all the meals in the dining-room. Maureen loathed appearing.

Fern was so upset for the moment that she

could not bear Maureen's chatter. She left her to peel some potatoes. Mrs Dorey met Fern in the hall.

'Ah! I'd like a few words with you, Mrs Barrett.'

Mrs Dorey spoke quite pleasantly but there was a threat behind her smile. Fern was not in the mood to take criticism but saw that there was no help for it. And she told herself not to be too silly about the incident. It was just unlucky that she had heard her father's name bandied about in this house. But, as Terry said, she had got to get used to it and continue to hide her own identity, which, in itself, caused her distress.

9

Mrs Dorey led the way into the dining-room where she said they could have 'a little chat'. Nell Dorey had already discussed the new cook with her goddaughter. Greta was upstairs, unpacking. She had agreed that Mrs Barrett looked out of place here, but that it was best not to annoy Quentin, and suggested Aunt Nellie should go easy about getting rid of Mrs Barrett. She explained that she had taken Quentin's part about the picture in the hall for that very reason – 'to keep him sweet'.

Mrs Dorey agreed. She saw the wisdom in this. She was most anxious to keep Quentin in a good mood this weekend – and, indeed, for the whole fortnight that Greta would be staying here.

The 'little chat' fulfilled Fern's worst forebodings.

Mrs Dorey sat eyeing her with obvious animosity, although her thin lips smiled and she was polite enough. But she left no room for doubt as to her intentions for the future.

Swanlake was to be run *her* way or Fern would not run it at all. She did not say it in so many words but, as Fern afterwards told Terry, the implication was there.

'I've looked after my son most of his life. He isn't easy. He overworks and he's so vague that he *needs* my organisation,' said Mrs Dorey. 'One of his nicest qualities is his great kindness of heart. People imagine he is as bluff as he sounds, but I know what a soft heart he has. He can be taken advantage of, you see, Mrs Barrett.'

This particular sentence brought a rather sharp reply from Fern, who had decided not to allow herself to be frightened off by this stern, elderly female. She was certainly a character. Fern liked characters, and once again she was conscious that life was throwing a challenge at her feet – like the old-fashioned glove. So she picked it up and silently prepared for the fight. She was not going to be easily scared away from Swanlake. She adored the place. She also knew that she had so far pleased the great Q.D. and as long as he wanted her here, why shouldn't she stay? She fenced with Mrs Dorey.

'I quite understand what you say, Mrs Dorey, but I assure you that I'm not one to take advantage of other people's kindness.'

'No, no, I'm sure you are not, Mrs Barrett.'

'As far as the alteration of the pictures and the ornaments is concerned, it was Mr Dorey's wish and I carried it out. He and I discussed art and he paid me the compliment of thinking that I had learned quite a lot from my father.'

'Might I ask if your father was an art collector?' asked Mrs Dorey with a freezing smile.

'No, he was a business man.'

Through her glasses Mrs Dorey's sharp eyes noted the burning colour that spread over the young cook-housekeeper's face. Why such a flush? she asked herself, always quick to suspect and assume the worst. She asked:

'What kind business?'

Fern gulped. Coming so soon after what she had heard behind the drawing-room door, she was a little unnerved. And she did not intend to be cross-questioned like this by Mrs Dorey.

'Oh, just in the City,' she said.

'Are your parents both alive?'

'Yes, both, Mrs Dorey.'

'How long have you been doing this kind

of work?'

Again Fern had to swallow. She looked away from those merciless probing eyes. Grey, like Quentin Dorey's, but oh, so different – so much less friendly and less full of warmth. Grey pebbles. Stony.

'I've been cooking for the last couple of years,' she said, thankful that the answer, although non-committal, was at least the truth.

'I hear from my son that Miss Porter took up your references. No doubt she'll show them to me in time.'

Fern made no answer. Her heart was starting to beat with resentment. Worry furrowed lines along her young clear forehead. The Vicar would always help as he had promised, and Violet Colway, who had written that other reference (which had been so cleverly worded) recommending her and Terry, would always stand by her letter. But for the first time since she came to Swanlake, Fern felt miserable and uneasy. On one of her impulses, she broke out:

'If you don't think I am what you want here, maybe you'd like me to leave at once, Mrs Dorey?'

Nell Dorey at once altered her tone. She was much too afraid of what Quentin would do or say if she achieved any such victory on her first day back. Perhaps, she thought in a gloomy fashion, she was being a little too hasty in condemning Mrs Barrett out of hand. Young and pretty she might be, but she was certainly efficient. And it *was* so difficult to get good servants down here. Until something better turned up, thought Mrs Dorey, she had better pipe down and keep the young woman.

'Don't misunderstand me – I was merely asking you a few questions, my dear Mrs Barrett, and I'm *sure* you'll do very well here,' she said grandly, rising to her feet. 'My son seems delighted with what you have done so far.'

'Thank you,' said Fern, unsmiling.

'There are just a few things that you are not doing altogether as *I* like, but we'll discuss these gradually.'

'I've had sole charge of the menus so far. Do you wish to alter that, and choose the food yourself, Mrs Dorey?'

Mrs Dorey would dearly have liked to answer 'yes' but dared not. She was a plain cook herself but only as far as good old north-country cooking went. She did not know the first thing about these French dishes that Quentin seemed to like and wanted to serve to his business friends, or when they gave parties. Hurriedly she said:

'Oh, no, *you* continue to make out the menus. That is what I hear you have been trained to do. I must, however, rely on you not to be too extravagant.'

Fern bit her lip.

'Mr Dorey asked me not to spare cream or wine for sauces, etc. It is difficult not to be extravagant if you want really fine French cuisine. Am I to continue as Mr Dorey wished or am I to cut down?'

Nell Dorey hesitated. This young girl was a cool one, she thought. All this dignity; up on her high horse! Mrs Dorey liked humble service. She liked maids like Maureen who were so scared of her that they stammered when she spoke. There was something about young Mrs Barrett that made Quentin's mother feel uncomfortable. Anybody would think she was *'someone'*. Of course, she was obviously well-educated and had come down in the world, but *who was she* really? Mrs Dorey's long thin nose scented something *not quite right*. As she dismissed Fern she made up her mind to find out more about her – if only out of sheer curiosity.

Later that evening, when they were all in the drawing-room drinking coffee, Quentin asked his mother if she had not found the dinner delicious. She gave him the fond smile reserved for him alone, and answered:

'Excellent, excellent.'

'That saddle of mutton was quite wonderful. We have nothing so good at home,' put in Greta. 'But what a pity in this lovely home you cannot have an old-fashioned English butler to wait at table. Mrs Barrett doesn't *look* very smart. Still, I suppose she has to do the cooking as well – one can't expect it.'

Quentin frowned. He was standing with his back to the fireplace smoking a cigar. His mind had been on some interesting point of business. Now his attention was drawn to the lovely girl on the sofa who sat lazily stirring her coffee, smiling up at him. She had put on a charming yellow dress with a short full skirt. He had to admit that she wore lovely shoes and had delightful ankles. The lamplight turned her hair to pure gold. Why, he wondered curiously, did her beauty seem to him as cold and remote as the snows on her Swedish mountain tops? Yet there was an invitation in the way she looked at him – a promise in those curved red lips that had been there for him ever since Greta was of an age to assert her femininity – ever since he, himself, became a man. He knew well what his mother wished for him. Almost he wished that he could grant her her heart's desire, and marry Greta. But marriage in Quentin's mind meant something much deeper than a passing sensual fantasy. He wanted, when he married, to love his wife with all the strength and depth of his being, and, as far as he knew, the woman to inspire such a love had not yet come along.

He turned his thoughts to the young 'domestic' under discussion. In a vague way he resented his nice hardworking Mrs Barrett being adversely criticised even in a small degree.

'I never think Mrs Barrett looks untidy or like that Irish child, Maureen. She always wears a nice clean white overall. Personally I don't know how she does the double job so well – both cooking *and* serving.'

'Why don't we look for a butler?' asked Mrs Dorey, turning over in her mind the fact that if they got one Mrs Barrett would not be so much seen or heard about the house. She would be more in the kitchen.

'My dear mother,' said Quentin impatiently, 'we've discussed this business of a butler before. I don't particularly want one.

I can't be bothered with some fussy, elderly gentleman's-gentleman helping me to drinks and cigars – helping himself to them as well! I'd rather look after myself and pour out my own drinks. If you want another maid in the place – get one.'

Mrs Dorey looked nettled. For the last year she had been trying to get maids here and had failed, and she did *not* like foreigners. Enid had had trouble with a German girl, and those Italians at 'The Golden Fawn' – so rumour had it – were not at all satisfactory. And the only Swedish girl whom Greta's mother had sent over had found Swanlake too isolated and rushed back to Stockholm. The girls from abroad (even if one could put up with them) wanted to come to England and see life – not be buried on the outskirts of a Sussex village.

Greta, sensitive to what Quentin was thinking and feeling, hastily praised the cheese soufflé which Fern had sent in as a savoury. The subject of Mrs Barrett was then dropped. Quentin went off to the library to put a business call through to London. He seldom stopped working, even at night.

'I shall go to bed early and you can stay

down here with Quentin and get him to play you some records,' said Mrs Dorey, smiling at her lovely goddaughter.

'That will be nice,' said Greta softly.

Mrs Dorey leaned closer to her.

'I think we may be worrying ourselves unnecessarily. All Quentin is interested in is the food, certainly not in the girl.'

'Besides, she's got a very good-looking husband living with her,' said Greta. 'I'd let things stay as they are at the moment if I may venture to say so, Aunt Nellie.'

Then the two women hastily stopped talking as Fern came in to collect the coffee cups. Mrs Dorey brought herself to thank Fern graciously for the dinner. Gravely Fern accepted the compliment, gave both the 'ladies' one of her swift sweet smiles, and bade them goodnight.

'She isn't a bad little thing,' drawled Greta.

Mrs Dorey half closed her eyes and leaned her head back on a cushion.

'All the same, I wonder … I wonder where that girl and her husband really came from. I think there's something *queer* about such a couple taking this kind of job.'

10

One night towards the end of June, Quentin Dorey left the offices of a big Swedish timber firm in London – in which he had a financial interest – and stepped into the Rolls. Terence was outside, waiting for him.

'Home, Barrett,' he said briefly.

Terence touched his cap in that slightly ironic way which did not pass unnoticed by his employer, but he drove the car skilfully through the traffic in Lombard Street.

One thing Quentin had to grant this young man, who had now been his chauffeur for a month, was that he drove well. But it was the only thing he did do well in Quentin Dorey's estimation. It hadn't taken the latter long to sum up his chauffeur as being lazy, unpunctual at times, and often much too big for his boots.

As a rule Quentin Dorey was too busy to think about Barrett, but when he did so, it was to realise that he did not really care for the boy, as for instance he had done for dear old Milligan, the chauffeur who had once driven his father, and who had had to retire through ill-health and old age.

Milligan had been a really good man and a devoted servant. Never, Quentin told himself wryly, could one call young Barrett either of these things. Yet there was nothing bad he could definitely pin on Barrett, and the reason why he kept him was always written quite glaringly across Q.D.'s consciousness. It was because he liked and respected Barrett's young wife.

Thinking about Mrs Barrett, Quentin frowned at the recollection of an unhappy incident yesterday. There had been an open clash between the little cook and his mother.

It had been over the choice of wines at a dinner party which the Doreys had given the previous night. As a rule Quentin, himself, saw to the drinks, but he had been so busy last night that he had only had time to rush down from town, change into his dinner jacket and take his place at the head of the table.

The guests, Admiral Sir John Shawney and his wife, were important to both Quentin and his mother. They had just bought a Georgian house near Horsham and could be counted as near neighbours;

more especially as the Admiral was on the board of directors of a company in which Quentin had an interest. Rather cunningly, Mrs Dorey had used this forthcoming dinner as an excuse to keep Greta longer at Swanlake. She would make such an ideal 'fourth' when the Shawneys came, as their son, Oliver, would be with them.

Quentin was not blind to his mother's matchmaking. Greta had lately been thrown across his path at every available instance. Mrs Dorey had been unusually coy when she said to him before the Shawneys came: 'Perhaps Greta will take a fancy to young Oliver. You'd better look out, dear!'

Quentin had laughed tolerantly, anxious not to upset his mother. As a rule, with his mind fixed on business, he did not have time to worry about her little 'schemes' for him. But when he thought more about them, he was annoyed. Greta was never anything but attractive. When she played and sang her Swedish folk songs, he felt almost sentimental about her. She had a charming voice. But, funnily enough, nothing that she did or said found lasting response deep down in Quentin. At times he had begun to wonder if he had a heart to give to any woman. However, it was evident that he had *feelings,* he told himself. One of the strongest traits in his character was his passion for justice. Concerning last night's clash between his mother and Mrs Barrett, he felt that a wrong had been done to that little cook and he wasn't going to stand for that even if it meant his taking her part against his own mother. By God, he thought, as Barrett drove him home this evening, it was lucky his chauffeur hadn't announced already that his wife had decided to go. But, of course, Mrs Barrett had said she would forget the episode and Quentin was sure she was not the type to break her word.

How difficult it all was! How impossible women were to handle, the great Q.D. reflected dismally, especially 'Mum' when she got her hackles up. Right from the start she had objected to Mrs Barrett, and without good cause. The girl worked like a slave and never complained, and the only time that Quentin could say that his dinner was not up to standard was when she had made a soufflé and they had kept her waiting until the damned thing was spoilt. That wasn't *her* fault. She had been told to serve dinner at eight and they hadn't gone in until nine, because Quentin had got talking to a guest about gold-mining in South Africa – a subject on which he was always verbose.

Quentin had known nothing about the row last night until the party was over and Greta had gone to bed. Then his mother broke out in denunciation of Fern.

'I can see she doesn't like taking my orders and wants to run the house herself, but tonight she deliberately flouted my orders, and I won't stand for that!'

When Quentin had asked what had happened, he was told that Mrs Dorey had ordered the best claret to be served and Fern had brought an iced hock. It was a deliberate going against her wishes, Mrs Dorey declared indignantly.

At this Quentin had rubbed the back of his head and tried to remember exactly what they had had for dinner. Of course – salmon.

'But you can't drink claret with salmon, can you?' he had begun.

'Nonsense,' broke in Mrs Dorey. 'You can drink claret with anything. Anyhow, it was not *her* place to make the alteration.'

'Now look,' Quentin had said. 'Mrs Barrett is in charge of the food, you know.'

'*And* of the drink?'

'That's my job as a rule but...'

'Tomorrow I shall give her notice,' broke in Mrs Dorey.

It was at that point that Quentin lost patience with his mother.

'You'll do nothing of the sort. She's a first-class person and we've had peace in this house and wonderful food ever since she came. It would be sheer madness to let your personal dislike of the girl drive her out.'

'So you think it's just personal dislike?' his mother breathed, red and furious.

'You know that it is, Mother,' he said with a tight smile.

At that pitch, a knock came on the door and the subject of the discussion herself walked in. A rather pale, harassed-looking Fern without her overall and wearing a cotton frock.

'Excuse me,' she said, 'but I had to come and see you once I heard the guests drive away. I did not feel I could go to bed until I had sorted things out.'

Mrs Dorey looked speechlessly at the girl. But Quentin gave her a kind smile and said:

'Come in, come in, my dear.'

'*My dear*, indeed!' thought Mrs Dorey. 'Q.'s off his head, being so familiar.'

And she forgot all her goddaughter's

admonitions to her not to have a row over Fern because Q. would be upset. Mrs Dorey was frustrated and disgruntled. Greta had been here three weeks now and Q. had not made a move towards her. He had just been as he always was, friendly and non-committal.

Of course, Mrs Dorey knew perfectly well that she had no real justification for thinking that Q.'s attitude towards Mrs Barrett held even the slightest touch of familiarity. He had called her 'my dear' just now as he might have done with a child. Funny that she disliked that young girl so much. Or was it because she knew that Fern Barrett was an educated girl, and that she knew so much more about high-class entertaining than Nell Dorey had ever done?

'Now let's get this clear,' said Quentin. 'There's been an upset about the orders for the drink, hasn't there, Mrs Barrett?'

'Yes, I've come to apologise,' said Fern. Her eyes were very bright and rather defiant in her small pale face, although neither of the Doreys saw how her fingers shook. She had clasped them behind her back. She stood there like a schoolgirl in disgrace.

The Doreys chorused:

'Apologise?'

'Yes,' said Fern. 'I fully realise that I went over your head, Mrs Dorey, which was very cheeky of me. But you just *can't* drink claret with salmon! It *must* be white wine and I thought perhaps you'd forgotten that it was the salmon when you ordered the claret, so that's why I changed over. I know you were angry but I do feel … I do feel...' Her voice trailed off.

Quentin stared at her, a half-smoked cigar between his fingers. He ran a hand over his thick grey-flecked hair. 'Heavens!' he thought in dismay, 'Mrs Barrett looks as though she's going to burst into tears. Why, the *poor little thing...!*'

Fern went on in rather a choked voice:

'Mr Dorey said that it was an important party and he wanted to make a good impression on Admiral and Lady Shawney. I *knew* that red wine with the salmon would be dreadful, but of course I realised,' she added in an agonised voice, 'that Mrs Dorey must have *forgotten* we were having fish.'

Mrs Dorey was about to state vehemently that she never forgot anything, but decided to hold her tongue. She was aware that the girl *knew* she had not forgotten, because she had said: 'Bring in the claret with the salmon,' when she gave her orders. And the wretched

169

girl was probably right about the hock. That was what annoyed Nell Dorey. She was generally right. Because Fern was now being generous and trying to save Mrs Dorey's face, in front of her son, Mrs Dorey felt an even greater dislike of her. But she preserved a complete silence.

Quentin said:

'Now come, come, don't let's all get heated about this. *Of course* my mother didn't realise about the salmon, Mrs Barrett, and I think it was very astute of you to have changed the drink. The Admiral said he had never tasted a better hock and it was perfectly cooled, and of *course* you've got to drink white wine with fish. I think my mother was a little upset, but she isn't now that she understands your motive, are you, Mother?'

This question, Nell Dorey thought, held quite a menace. Oh, how like his father he was! She could see old Q. standing there. He would never let anyone get away with a mistake – not if it was royalty. Q. would have fair play; well – Mrs Dorey decided to cool down. She wouldn't like it if young Q. suggested she should move into a home of her own. She wanted to go on living with him here.

Somehow or other, she brought herself to

170

tell Mrs Barrett that everything was 'quite all right'.

'I'm sure you did it for the best reasons, and let us forget about it,' she said stiffly, 'and of course you were correct – I would never have ordered the claret if I'd remembered about the fish.'

The two women's gaze met. Fern's eyes were hurt rather than victorious. Mrs Dorey's gaze was the first to waver. Q. looked from one to the other. Poor old Mum, he thought, always getting on her high horse, but such a good soul deep down. He both honoured and respected her. He was grateful for the deep devotion she had always given him. Nevertheless his heart in this moment went out to the 'little cook', as he had come to think of Fern. She looked so small and tired and worried.

'Have a glass of something to buck you up,' he said, and turned towards the drink cupboard. But Fern stopped him.

'No, please, I wouldn't dream of it, Mr Dorey.'

'I should say not!' thought Mrs Dorey.

Fern added:

'I'm glad everything's all right now. I'm sorry about it all.'

'Forget it, forget it,' said Quentin, 'and we

mustn't have too many parties in succession.
I don't like overworking you. You looked
fagged out.'

'I don't mind how hard I work,' Fern said,
'as long as I needn't feel I'm doing the
wrong thing.'

'The trouble is that you generally do the
right thing and that's more than we can
always say for the Doreys when they're at
home,' exclaimed Quentin, with a cheerful
laugh.

'Q!' exclaimed Mrs Dorey, appalled. And
after Fern had gone she accused him of
overstepping the mark. Mrs Barrett gave
herself airs enough, she said, without his
admitting that the Doreys made *mistakes*.

But now her son's handsome grey eyes lit
up with the purest humour. He patted her
back, and laughed.

'Mother, you're impossible. We Doreys
have our good points and plenty of them but
don't let's lose sight of the fact that we also
have our deficiencies. We haven't always
lived amongst, or entertained, people like
the Admiral, or many such other folk who
come to Swanlake. And we want to do the
thing properly. So why be ashamed to learn,
even from our little cook? She's no ordinary
cook, now, is she?'

'I'm sick of hearing you praise her,' Mrs Dorey flashed, but there the conversation had ended because Quentin had said he was fed up with the whole petty affair and was going to bed.

This evening, on the way home, Quentin remembered the whole episode and regretted the fact that his mother wasn't more broadminded. Enid Grey-Everton's friendship did her no good, he thought, frowning. Enid was one of the sort to insist on calling the domestics 'inferiors'. Time such an attitude was eradicated. That little girl had been the superior one last night. It would have been absolutely wrong of her to have served up Mum's choice of wine with the fish. What *would* the Admiral have thought?

Mum could be very awkward and there was going to be more awkwardness tonight, Q. thought gloomily. Deliberately (Q. was aware of it) his mother had arranged to go into Brighton to the theatre and have supper with Enid, which meant that he would be left to dine alone with Greta. He did not want to be alone with her.

'Greta is beautifully brought up and knows everything, and that's the sort of help you need, since you keep on saying that you want things done properly at Swanlake,' Mrs Dorey had told him, when he went into her bedroom to say goodbye this morning. 'Why don't you make up your mind to marry her?'

'Because I don't want to get married,' he had snapped back.

But here he was, the big business man unable to get out of the net his mother was spreading for him – without being deliberately rude. He just couldn't leave Greta to dine alone.

'Barrett,' he addressed his chauffeur, 'what's on at the local cinema – Haywards Heath?'

Terence said that he didn't know.

'Well, whatever it is, I want to see it,' said Quentin darkly. 'I shall need you with the car immediately after dinner to drive Miss Paulson and myself.'

'Very well, sir,' said Terry.

But his eyes were dark with anger. He had expected to put the car away and be off this evening. He knew that, as a rule, his employer drove himself on short journeys, but until that leg was absolutely well the doctor had forbidden Q.D. to use it. Pressure was bad for it.

11

Once back at Swanlake, Terry marched into the kitchen. Maureen was off tonight. Fern was alone, preparing a small dinner for Q.D. and Miss Paulson. Terry tossed his cap on to a chair and unbuttoned his coat.

'Out with Q.D. again after supper. I couldn't be more livid,' he said angrily.

Fern looked up from the sauce she was mixing.

'What's happened now?' She spoke rather wearily. Her voice had lost some of the bright gaiety which it had held in the old days.

When Terry looked away from her and muttered that he was just 'tired', that was all, she made no answer. Usually she would have sympathised. But she was sick of Terry's grumbling and the petty annoyances which he continually brought to her notice. He had no time or patience for *her* upsets, and they had been many and varied since Mrs Dorey's return from Stockholm.

Fern had, oh, so nearly decided to leave

Swanlake last night, after the wine incident. But she had always had a strangely logical mind. Though she resented Mrs Dorey's disagreeable attitude towards her, Fern had to agree that this was an occasion when Mrs Dorey had some cause for complaint. Fern *had* deliberately flouted her orders. That was why she had decided to make the apology. Otherwise, after the sharp reprimand which Mrs Dorey had given her, Fern would have 'handed in her notice'.

She was glad that it had all turned out well. Glad that she had decided to go and see the Doreys before they went to bed. But it had taken some courage on her part and she could see that there would be more trouble in the future. Why did she want to stay? Was it *only* because she and Terry had their little flat and a good salary? Or was it because serving the great Q.D., personally, was a real pleasure to her?

Self-educated, often mistaken, sometimes even embarrassing, he was such a *darling*. Such a warm-hearted, human person. She had grown attached to Q.D. in what she supposed was quite a silly way. She was passionately anxious to do the right thing for him and to keep him satisfied. It was quite unbearable, the way his mother made trouble for him; hard sometimes for Fern, even with her logic and tolerance, to excuse the older woman just because she adored her son. Nothing could be worse than a jealous, possessive mother. And as for this business of Greta Paulson, Fern had found herself worrying about that, too, absurdly. It was not her business who Q.D. married. But with a sure feminine instinct Fern felt that Greta was not the right girl for him.

One learnt all kinds of things about a person when they lived under a roof with you for any length of time, Fern thought, and she did not always see the charming, honey-voiced Greta as the world saw her. She knew another one – a lazy, hideously untidy Greta, who left her bedroom in indescribable confusion and expected Maureen and Mrs Barrett to clear up everything for her; and who also had a nasty vicious little temper. Fern had been witness to that, too.

One afternoon as Fern was walking past the lodge, Greta drove up to the gates in the staff car which she had borrowed to take herself into Brighton for a 'hair-do'. She had almost run down one of Mrs Hatton's children. Certainly it had been the little boy's fault, but Greta had sprung out of the car and screamed at him. She had scared the child abominably.

It had been Fern who picked the boy up and kissed and comforted him while Greta drove on.

'Well,' Fern had thought, 'I wonder what sort of a mother *she'll* make one day!'

No – somehow Fern didn't want Q.D. to marry Greta Paulson.

This evening before Mrs Dorey went to Brighton she had come into the kitchen and said:

'After you've taken away the coffee cups, you needn't hang around or wait up for me, Mrs Barrett. Just leave a Thermos with some hot milk by my bed.'

Then with that coy smile that Fern felt to be almost worse that Mrs Dorey's scowl, the older woman had added:

'I expect you know what we're all hoping for, with my son and Miss Paulson. It's so thrilling.'

'Yes, of course, Mrs Dorey,' Fern had answered.

Fern finished her cooking tonight but felt none of the usual pleasure in what she was making. She was strangely depressed. Terry's attitude towards her didn't help. He hadn't even kissed her when he first came into the kitchen. And she was quite sure that his annoyance at having to drive Q.D. to the cinema wasn't so much because he was tired, as because he couldn't get down to 'The Golden Fawn' as usual.

While they were making beds together this morning, Maureen had said something to Fern that was not meant to be unkind, because Maureen was just a gay, tactless gossip. But it had struck home.

'Sure and there's a gorgeous Italian girl at "The Golden Fawn" helping in the hotel and newly come from Rome, they say. A real glamour girl, Mrs Barrett. If I were you I'd keep an eye on that handsome angel of a husband of yours...' and Maureen had laughed. She was always laughing. She meant no harm to anybody and she adored Terry because he teased her. But all day Fern had remembered her remark about the lovely Italian girl and Terry.

A few days ago Terry had come to the flat with an Italian record. One of those sentimental love-songs that the latins do so well. Terry sat listening to it, playing it several times over, and when she asked him where he had got it, he said up in town. Later she had idly picked up the record and examined the label. She discovered that it was not an English record. It had been made and issued in Rome.

At the time she had realised that Terry had lied to her, but had taken little notice of it. But after all that Maureen had said, a faint suspicion entered Fern's mind that the glamour girl from 'The Golden Fawn' had given the record to him.

She had never wanted to be a jealous wife, but if Terry was forming a friendship with the newcomer to 'The Golden Fawn', she wished he would tell *her*, his wife, about it. The fact that he never mentioned the girl was wrong and made her feel worried and miserable. Nevertheless, pride forbade her asking him about it.

Fern said now:

'I had a letter from Mummy by the second post. She's upset because she hasn't heard from Daddy lately and doesn't know how things are going.'

'Oh, bad luck,' muttered Terry. But Fern could see that his attention was not on what she said. She stopped talking to him.

Quentin had sent a message by Terry to Fern to say that he wanted early dinner. But now, at seven o'clock, the library bell rang for Fern. She found her employer lying on his sofa, nursing his bad leg, which was still troubling him.

Greta stood with her back to the fireplace, sipping a glass of sherry. Fern suddenly envied the girl who looked so cool and elegant. Greta wore a pale grey, flowered silk suit, and real pearls around her throat and in her ears. She gave Fern a charming smile.

'Good evening, Mrs Barrett.' She spoke with great friendliness, but somehow Fern remembered the Hatton child and Greta's impatience and loss of temper. True, it must have frightened her to think that she so nearly ran the little boy down, but it had been a deal more frightening for the boy.

'Our plans have changed, Mrs Barrett,' said Quentin. 'You can tell Barrett I shan't be wanting the Rolls tonight. Just ask him to bring the Morris round to the front door. Miss Paulson is taking me for a drive.'

'Will you be wanting dinner later, then, Mr Dorey?'

'What's in the pot?' he asked, smiling at her in his genial way, 'because if it's anything that'll spoil, we'll have it early just the same.'

'I think I can delay it half an hour,' said Fern.

After she had gone, Greta was clever enough to praise her.

'I always tell Aunt Nellie that you've got a

treasure in Mrs Barrett.'

'Eh, tha's right, lass,' said Q. adopting his Lancashire accent, and warmed towards Greta because she sided with him.

He'd been rather annoyed when she refused to accompany him to a cinema this evening. It was far too lovely, she said. *She* would drive the staff car and take him out on this beautiful summer evening to hear the nightingales down by Cuckendean Forest, which was famous for its bird-song at night. All very romantic and not at all what Q.D. favoured, but it would have been churlish of him to insist on the cinema.

Fern delivered Q.D.'s message to her husband. She could not help but see the pleasure this gave him. Then when she added that Miss Paulson wanted the staff car as she was going to take Mr Dorey for a drive, it being such a gorgeous June night, Terry's face fell again.

That meant a three-mile walk for him to the 'local' if he wanted to see Tosca. Tosca of the smooth olive skin, big black eyes and huge provocative mouth. A real beauty was Tosca, and as gay as anybody could expect to find a girl in a hole like Cuckendean.

She had come over to England to work with another Italian who was in a job five miles away. Of course she was a *good* girl – so Tosca told Terry – religious like so many of her race. But Terry wondered how long she would remain impervious to his blond English good looks and charm. It was a lot more amusing being with her than with poor old Fern, these days. If she wasn't worrying about her father, she was worrying about her mother, or too tired to speak – this wasn't strictly true, but these were the excuses Terry weaved for himself when his conscience told him that he was not being very loyal to his hard-worked wife.

Dinner over, Terry actually helped Fern to wash up, which was unusual for him. The pleasure was a little dimmed by the fact that Terry kept whistling the catchy melody from that Italian record, and it was altogether spoiled when he announced that he was going out instead of returning to the flat with her.

'Where to, darling?' she asked.

Now he lied – as much because he didn't want to upset Fern as to cover his own tracks.

'Got a date with a fellow in the village. I met him when I took the Rolls in for service the other day. He's driving over to see me in Cuckendean. He's in rather a big job with

Rolls Royce and might do something for me – something that would help us get away from this slavery.'

'Darling, one can't call it *slavery*–' she began.

'Well, you know what I feel about all the cap-touching, and you being bullied by that old so-and-so of a Mrs Dorey.'

'I understand her,' said Fern quietly.

'Well, you've got a big heart but I reckon our time here will be short, anyhow. Possibly a proposal from Milord will take place to the tune of the nightingales,' said Terry with a laugh. 'Didn't you say that the beautiful Swede was driving him to the Forest?'

Fern made no answer. Everything seemed to crush her spirits tonight. She was conscious of a sudden dread of ever having to leave Swanlake Manor, and Q.D.'s service. She had begun to make her life here. It had begun to *mean* something real and more than ordinarily interesting in her shattered world.

After Terry had left her, Fern wandered about the little flat smoking a much-needed cigarette and trying not to wonder if Terry had told the truth about this Rolls Royce man from Brighton. She wouldn't dream of spying on him but she wondered if she went

184

down to 'The Golden Fawn' at this very moment she would not find Terry passing the time with his Italian girl instead of a man from Brighton.

She felt lonely, upset and quite different from her usual cheerful, optimistic self. This morning's mail, bringing an unhappy letter from her disconsolate mother, and another from her best girl-friend, had not helped. The girl-friend was flying out to Nairobi to be married and expressed the hope that Fern would go out and stay. As if she could, now! That happy carefree life of the past was over. Everything seemed to crowd down upon her tonight. And suddenly Fern flung herself on her bed and burst into tears.

In the middle of this fit of sobbing – rare for Fern – she heard the staff car being driven into the courtyard and a voice calling – the voice of Q.D.

'Are you there, Barrett? Will you put the car in for me, please?'

Fern got on to her feet, blew her nose and hurriedly wiped her eyes. Glancing through her window, she saw Quentin standing down below, alone. It was only half past nine. He hadn't been out with Greta long, she thought. He had probably dropped his guest at the front door and brought the car round here himself. She could not help wondering what had happened between those two. She could also see that Quentin took it for granted his chauffeur was at home. He must have seen lights on in the flat. She had no option but to answer Mr Dorey. But the last thing she wanted was to face him, and let him see that she had been crying.

12

Keeping herself hidden behind the curtains she called out of the window:

'My husband isn't in at the moment but I'll tell him as soon as he comes. Just leave the car there, Mr Dorey.'

He sounded surprised when he answered:

'What's Barrett doing – taking a walk?'

'I … yes … exactly.' Fern's reply was somewhat disjointed.

Quentin frowned. He stood still a moment, lit a match, cupped it with his hands and held it up to the cigar he had been smoking and which had gone out.

The little cook didn't sound very cheerful, he thought. He slammed the car door behind him and took a step forward. He stubbed his toe on a loose cobble and muttered a round oath which brought Fern back to the window. Now she leaned out.

'Oh, have you hurt yourself, Mr Dorey? Is it your leg?' she claimed.

'Yes, I've jarred the confounded thing,' he said and rubbed the back of his thigh ruefully. 'I didn't look where I was going.'

Fern, concerned about him, ran down the stairs. Darkness had fallen. The night was warm. The sky was studded with stars. There was no moon but the light from the open window of the flat shone down on Quentin, then lit up Fern's face when he turned to look at her.

'You shouldn't have bothered to come down,' he said and stopped. At close quarters he could see that little Mrs Barrett had been crying. Her eyelids were swollen and her lashes still wet with tears.

'*You* don't look too happy!' he added in his blunt way.

'What about your leg?' she asked, feeling her cheeks go hot but ignoring this comment. 'Can I help you back to the house?'

'No, thanks,' he said. 'Like a fool I didn't put my stick in the car and I suppose I shouldn't have driven even these few yards, but I can walk. What a lousy thing sciatica can be! Starts up at a second's notice if one isn't careful. I'm thoroughly fed up with it.'

'Take my arm,' she said.

'I don't need to. The pain's passing. It was just a spasm, stubbing that infernal toe. It jarred the whole leg.'

Now they looked at each other in the soft

glow of Fern's lamplight. And suddenly the big business man, who had little time in his life for sentiment, felt an amazing pang of pity for Mrs Barrett because she looked so unhappy. Childishly, pathetically so, even though she was trying to smile at him, and offer her support. His mind leapt to conclusions. Perhaps something was wrong between her and that husband of hers. Why should Barrett be out 'walking' at ten o'clock at night – and without her? *Why* had she been crying? Quentin was not one to mince words but he knew no subtleties. He frowned down at her.

'Something's wrong. What is it?'

'What could be?' she asked, dismayed, and wishing she had never come down and let him see her like this.

'You've been crying.'

'Oh,' she thought, 'how awful, how tactless of him to say so even if he has noticed!' Yet how kind, how sweet this big bluff man could be. He should be much too busy to concern himself with the personal troubles of his housekeeper. And surely he wanted to get back into the house to his golden-haired Swedish siren? Hadn't they fixed things up in Nightingale Wood? Wouldn't there be an engagement announced tomorrow?

But Quentin was persistent, and not without curiosity.

'Had a tiff with that husband of yours?'

Now her face flamed.

'Certainly not,' she said indignantly.

Quentin put his tongue in his cheek.

'No business of mine, of course.'

'No, it isn't!' she said in a muffled voice.

An awkward silence. Quentin rubbed the back of his leg where that stinging nerve persisted. He was still not happy about the little cook. He forgot that his guest was over there in the Manor House waiting for him. He was, in fact, reluctant to rejoin Greta. She was upset. She hadn't said so but he knew that she was. He had been pretty cool and obviously she was resentful because he wouldn't make love to her while they sat listening to the thrilling sweetness of the nightingale (who was a better lover Quentin Dorey had told himself wryly, than *he* would ever be!). But then he didn't feel he wanted to sing love songs to Greta. Her beauty had been unearthly down there under the stars on this sweet summer's night. Why was it, then, that he felt so much more tenderly towards this girl Fern – she looked such a child – in her crumpled cotton frock with her tear-stained face and untidy hair? A very human Fern, not at all like the efficient, neat Mrs Barrett on duty. Quentin was still convinced that she had had a tiff with her husband. He felt a blundering fool yet blundered on.

'You can always come and tell me if there is anything wrong, you know. I'd try to help.'

Any resentment she had felt, because he was probing into her personal life vanished. He was the limit ... he had no graces ... but he was a *poppet*. Oh, the strength, the solidity of the man, with his rugged, square face. Oh, how wonderful it must be to be in the care of such a one as Quentin Dorey! She had the most ridiculous longing to blurt out her difficulties: her fears concerning Terry and that Italian wench at 'The Golden Fawn'. But nothing would have induced her to betray Terry or so easily admit that she wasn't happy. She said:

'It's awfully kind of you, Mr Dorey – awfully nice indeed of you to be concerned about me, but I assure you I'm all right. I ... I've just got a migraine.'

'Nonsense,' he thought, 'you don't suffer from migraine, my girl, but I'm not going to press you. It isn't my affair.'

He turned to limp away. It was at that moment that Terry appeared on the scene.

He came through the gate into the court-yard. His heels clanked uncertainly on the cobbles. He was singing. An Italian song. The song on the record that he kept playing and which Fern had grown to detest.

'"Io t'amo mia bella ... bella ... bella ... amorata."'

He wasn't singing very well, and with a gaiety that had its roots in the bottle, Quentin Dorey at once decided. As Terry drew near they could see his flushed face and glassy stare. Fern tried not to notice, although she felt agonisingly sure that he had taken one 'over the odd' tonight. Terry grinned foolishly at his employer and then at his wife.

'Oh, hullo,' he said, and added with a glance at Mr Dorey: 'Evening, sir.'

'Evening,' returned Quentin curtly. 'Put the Morris away, will you, Barrett?'

'Of course, sir, and jolly good luck to the old Morris. I miss her when I'm away from her,' said Terry and laughed loudly.

Now Fern's heart sank to the very depths. Cheeks scorching with colour, she stood there in a deathly silence, praying that Quentin would not notice Terry's condition.

Terry began to hum the Italian song again and climbed into the driver's seat of the staff car. He switched on the engine and the lights. Leaning his head out of the window, he called out:

'See if the garage doors are wide open – I'm going to back Miss Morris in, Fern duckie.'

It was on the tip of Quentin's tongue to tell the boy to leave the damned car alone and go straight into the bathroom and put his head under the cold tap. The young fool had been down at 'The Golden Fawn', of course. Well, he wouldn't say anything in front of the little cook and upset her. Quentin had enough delicacy not to wish Fern to be made to feel ashamed. But he knew now, all right, what had been distressing her. Abruptly he said:

'Goodnight both of you,' turned, and limped off.

As he neared the Manor House, he heard the Morris engine starting and stopping, starting and stopping. Grimly he thought:

'I shall have a few words to say to you, Master Barrett, tomorrow. No chauffeur of mine is going to take a glass too many, whether he's on duty or not. There's human life to consider when a chap's driving.'

Fern meanwhile had lost her temper. She pulled Terry by the arm out of the Morris.

'You get upstairs, my boy. I'll garage the car.'

'What's the matter with you?' began Terry in an aggrieved voice. 'Don't you think I'm capable of driving?'

She made no answer, but took his place and slammed the door. Later when she faced him in the bedroom, she blazed at him.

'You idiot! You absolute *idiot*, Terry!'

Once more he tried to bluff things out, but Fern, her blood up, went for him in a way she had not thought herself capable of. She told him that he was 'round the bend'; that he was endangering their job, that it had been obvious that he was 'lit up' and that Mr Dorey must have seen it. Then when Terry started to excuse himself on the grounds that his 'friend from Brighton' had persuaded him to drink too much, Fern interrupted:

'I don't believe you've ever met a man from Brighton. No doubt you were drinking toasts to the big black eyes of your Italian *amorata!*'

The words were out before she could restrain them.

Now Terry looked thoroughly surprised and uncomfortable. He unbuttoned his coat and flung it on the chair. He muttered:

'Nothing like a chap having a jolly reception from the wife when he gets home.'

Fern flung herself on her bed and put both hands over her ears as though to shut out the sound of his voice. All the loneliness and frustration she had felt while she was waiting for him to come home welled up into a suffocating misery. She could forgive him having had the odd drink too many, or the flirtation over the bar with the Italian girl (if that was all), but what she couldn't forgive was the fact that Mr Dorey had *seen* that he was drunk. That Mr Dorey *knew* tore the flag of her pride to tatters.

Terry stood there, the fumes of alcohol clearing from his brain while he stared aghast at his weeping wife. He had only seen Fern cry like this once before – when she had learned about her father's ruin. He had not meant to hurt her. He had not, of course, intended to be found out. How the devil, he wondered, had Fern heard about Tosca? And, of course, it was a disaster that the big man himself should have been down here to see when he came home.

Quite sober now, Terry sat on the bed and

pulled Fern into his arms.

'I'm sorry, darling. Honestly I am.'

'Leave me alone,' she sobbed.

'Fern, darling, I'm *honestly* sorry. I got talking and laughing with the chaps and you know what I am…'

'I know that you're quite irresponsible and that was something I never imagined when I first married you.'

'Fern, don't you love me any more?'

He asked the question in such a lugubrious tone that she had to look up at him. Oh, what a hopeless person Terry was, she thought; yet the old charm was there to draw her back to him. He looked so boyishly contrite and those very handsome eyes of his were so full of tenderness, she had to climb down and forgive him.

'You know I still love you, Terry … that's the trouble.'

'I believe you do,' he said in a humble voice, and pulled her closer and kissed the top of her head with real satisfaction.

She flung her arms around his neck.

'Terry, surely you and I mean more to each other than this? Surely you're not so bored with me that you have to go to "The Golden Fawn" for your fun?'

He chewed his lips and did not answer for

196

a moment. Uneasily he remembered Tosca's fascinating mouth and the way she had looked at him through her long silky lashes and called him her *'bambino'*. She had slipped out of the hotel to see him off. For a moment he had lost his head and kissed her goodnight, passionately. Of course it *was* sheer passion. It was Fern he really loved. He was just weak – bored with his job rather than with Fern – that was the trouble.

'I won't leave you alone again, sweetie, and I'll go on the wagon,' he said and meant it, as he lay there across the bed holding her against him, kissing her wet, sad little face.

In the end he made her laugh and dispelled her fears. Before they slept that night they were lovers again. But it wasn't so good after breakfast when he stormed into the kitchen, his face like a thundercloud, waited for Maureen to leave him alone with Fern, then started to utter imprecations against his employer.

The great Mr Dorey had ticked him off, he said furiously. Accused him openly of being 'bottled' last night, and told him to lay off the liquor and going down to 'The Golden Fawn', or lose his job.

'What business is it of his *what* I do when I am off duty?' began Terry.

Here Fern interrupted. She was in the midst of washing up the breakfast things. She had been quite happy because she had felt close to Terry again and generously wiped out the memory of his stupid behaviour. Now her fears and worries came back. It was always a worry when Terry was in one of his moods and she hated to feel that Mr Dorey had had to administer that 'ticking off'.

'Well, you did ask for it, darling,' she said.

'So long as I don't crash one of his cars, what's my private life got to do with him?' Terry demanded loudly.

Fern put away a saucepan she had just dried. She began to swill out the sink, then with troubled gaze looked out of the window at the grey haze of a misty summer's morning. The weather was not as fine as it had been yesterday. A white vapour lay over the lake which was usually so bright and shining. It wasn't going to be a good day in any way, she thought.

'So you take *his* part—' began Terry sulkily.

Then Fern swung round.

'Darling, I can understand that he doesn't want his chauffeur to be the sort of man who *does* get bottled. I know you don't drink too much, but you can't carry your drink, and you've got big responsibilities as a driver.'

'I'm fed up! Why don't we pack it in?'

Fern felt tired and depressed again.

'Oh, Terry, do be your age!' she said wearily. 'You always want to pack it in and give up, every time something happens to annoy you. *I'm* not quitting, anyhow. I like my job here.'

'I believe you've got a schoolgirl crush on the big clever business man,' sneered Terry.

'That's the silliest thing I've ever heard you say!' she exclaimed. 'Do get out of my kitchen and leave me alone. I've got work to do, if you haven't.'

'Sorry,' he muttered, always as quick to regret his worst side as he was to show it.

After he had left her to get the Rolls out of the garage – he was driving Mr Dorey up to London – Fern tried to forget what he had said. She had Mrs Dorey to see ... the day's menu to discuss ... Maureen and Mrs Hatton to organise, and lunch to prepare.

But the thing Terry had said kept coming back into her mind. A schoolgirl crush on the big business man! How utterly absurd! She admired Q.D. enormously. But a *crush* – fantastic! She was a married woman and Terry was her other half ... the man she loved and belonged to … she wasn't the type to have 'crushes' on other men.

When she saw Quentin before he left the house that morning she was terrified that he would mention last night but he did not refer to it. She had run into him in the main hall just as he was going off to town. She asked politely how his leg was and he answered, equally politely, that it was better. Then with a quick embarrassed glance at her, added:

'Now don't work yourself to death today, young woman. Take it easy. Give us a simple dinner. I'm putting on weight with all your delectable dishes and sauces.'

She made a laughing reply. He shut the front door behind him. Certainly he was walking more easily she thought. And now she had to go and see Mrs Dorey, which would be less agreeable.

That good lady was in the library examining household bills. She had little to say to the young housekeeper about the food. She had reluctantly learned to leave the menus to Fern. But she was shorter and sharper than usual when she informed Fern that Miss Paulson would be leaving the Manor at the end of the week and flying back to Stockholm.

It would have given Nell Dorey such inestimable pleasure to be able to announce an engagement; and let Mrs Barrett see the writing on the wall; Greta would certainly not keep her on if she was coming to live at the Manor as Quentin's wife. But that wretched Quentin hadn't come up to scratch last night. Greta was upset and said she had had 'a horrid disappointing evening'.

Although Mrs Dorey knew nothing about last night's incident with Barrett, because her son had not discussed it, she had sensed that Q. wasn't too pleased with his chauffeur. She could only hope that he would eventually become more displeasing and that Q. would give him notice and thus have to get rid of this girl, too. Fern's cool dignity never failed to annoy Mrs Dorey.

It was a bad day at Swanlake – for everybody.

13

By the time another month had gone by, Fern realised that she and Terry had been in their jobs at Swanlake for nearly nine weeks, and that she had completely settled down, but that Terry hadn't. And Terry never would.

She couldn't say he hadn't tried. With his lazy, pleasure-loving nature it was, she supposed, more difficult for him than for many men. July was a particularly hot month. Terry had a great deal of hard driving to do on congested roads in the heat and dust. The Rolls had to be kept spick and span, as well as the staff car, and the chauffeur had to be at the beck and call of both Quentin and his mother. On the other hand, Quentin was considerate and never asked Barrett to work on his off-days, even if he was wanted. Terry had to grant him that.

Since that evening after which Quentin had called his chauffeur to task, Terry had not drunk so much. In fact he spent most of his evenings with Fern. But it had been a trying month for her. She had continually to be at Terry's back, rousing him in the morning, having to call him again and again before he would wake up and get out of his bed; nag and nag (which she hated) until he went down to the garage to wash the car; write down his orders on little bits of paper which she kept giving him to remind him of the jobs he had been wanted to do. Terry had such an atrocious memory. It was always Fern who had to soothe him when he came home in a dark mood and coax him out of it. Fern who had to try and maintain a happy and cheerful attitude at the flat. And Terry seemed at times to her to resent being forced to stay in with her.

Things were not easy. And Fern was no saint, as she told herself frequently and with bitterness. When there was entertaining at the big house she was often exhausted. She herself needed a little comfort and support instead of having to tackle her husband's problems. Sometimes she felt that she was getting into such a nervy state that it made her snap, where ordinarily she was easy-going and good-tempered.

The same applied to her attitude towards Mrs Dorey, who never lost the opportunity to be disagreeable and ungrateful. It wasn't always easy for Fern to remain aloof from these petty annoyances or to be her bright smiling self in front of Mrs Dorey. Then there was Maureen to tackle, and soon a fresh help would have to be found in Mrs Hatton's place. At any moment now the gardener's wife would have to go into hospital for an operation and she was Fern's stand-by – always cheerful, and so much more reliable than Maureen. Life was full of minor domestic complications for the cook-housekeeper.

Quentin Dorey's sciatica had completely gone. He was back in London full steam ahead with his work. Once or twice a week he stayed up in his flat. Then he used the train, leaving his chauffeur in the country. On such evenings Mrs Dorey entertained her own cronies in the district and took great pleasure in being especially pernickety about the menus and altering Mrs Barrett's whole routine. It was as though she wanted to try and excite Fern to anger and rebellion and so seize the chance to get rid of her. But somehow Fern kept her temper, no matter what she felt.

August was the warmest and most golden month of this year – shedding a new and languorous loveliness over the grounds of Swanlake. And it was during the first week of this month that Quentin allowed himself a holiday.

It was always one of Mrs Dorey's most difficult tasks, persuading him to leave his work even for seven short days. But he had the sense to take that much breathing space, and had made up his mind to join a friend on board a yacht and take that brief holiday at sea.

But forty-eight hours before he was due to go his mother fell ill for the first time in the life of that strong healthy north-country-woman. It was a sudden affair and, for a brief time, a serious one.

Fern, when she took up Mrs Dorey's early morning cup of tea, found her in consider-able pain and looking ghastly. She immedi-ately called Mr Dorey, who rang for the doctor. Within an hour, Mrs Dorey was in an ambulance being conveyed to a Brighton hospital to be operated on for appendicitis. Furious, but battling against her pain, Nell Dorey managed to snap out a few words to Fern before the ambulance men carried her down the stairs.

'It is all most inconvenient and I am sure it's unnecessary them wanting to take me away,' she grumbled. 'What will happen here?'

Fern, forgetting their usual antagonism, sympathised, but gently told Mrs Dorey not to worry.

'I'll look after everything – just as you would like it,' she said.

'Well, I hope to find things have been done as I *do* like them when I get back, Mrs Barrett,' said the sick woman angrily.

Fern looked down at the feverish, drawn face and thought:

'One can't help admiring the old thing … she's as tough as you make them and in her way so full of pluck. If only she was a little nicer about me!'

But Mrs Dorey wasn't nice and had a last sharp word for her young housekeeper before they finally took her away.

Quentin followed the ambulance in his own car. On his return home, he went into the kitchen and spoke gloomily to his housekeeper.

'I've never seen my mother so ill. I don't like it.'

'Of course you don't, Mr Dorey,' said Fern in her most gentle voice. 'But I'm sure she'll pull through. Dr Philmore said that surgeon in Brighton is first-class.'

'Well, I shan't go up to London today. I'll wait and hear how my mother is, then go to see her.'

'I hope she'll only be away a couple of weeks.'

'Well, I shall cancel my yachting holiday.'

'Oh, must you?' asked Fern and then blushed and added: 'I didn't mean to be impertinent but I feel you need that week. You've been working so hard.'

His thoughts wandered from his mother to the young girl standing there in her white overall, looking, as usual, calm and impeccable, he thought. He hadn't had much time in his busy life to notice *how* she looked until today, but it struck him that she was too pale and – could it be – *older-looking?*... Somehow she had lost that look of radiant youth which he had associated with little Mrs Barrett when she first came.

'Pot calling the kettle black,' he grunted. '*You* work too hard yourself, and *you're* not taking a holiday. But I shan't go away until my mother comes home again.'

She did not say how glad she felt. She hardly even dared admit to herself how much she would have missed him. What a son! How lucky that crotchety old woman was to have him. And how marvellous it must be for any woman to belong to a man on whose fidelity and kindness she could *rely*.

'Tell Barrett I shall want him to drive me into Brighton as soon as we get the okay from the hospital,' said Quentin abruptly and walked out of the kitchen.

She knew that he was worried. She, herself, was quite anxious about Mrs Dorey. Although nobody thought much about an appendix operation these days, Nell Dorey wasn't so young, and any operation had its risks.

As she passed the library door she heard her employer's voice, obviously talking to Miss Porter.

'Come on down by the two-thirty train. Take a taxi to the Manor and bring all the mail with you...'

The atmosphere at Swanlake was tense until a telephone call from the hospital informed Q.D. that his mother had got through her operation successfully. Quentin himself walked out to the kitchen to tell Fern.

'Oh, I'm so glad!' she exclaimed joyfully.

He looked into the blue brilliant eyes and felt an inexplicable closeness to this young girl who worked for him and, indeed, for all of them, so loyally. He could see that she was really glad and he also knew quite well that 'old Mum' was often very unpleasant to her. She didn't hold it against her. Nice of her.

'Thanks,' he said abruptly, 'I must say I feel relieved.'

'Will you be dining alone tonight, Mr Dorey, or having friends in?'

He knew then, absurd though it was, that he wished that there had been no Barrett and he could have asked the little cook to serve up the dinner and eat it with him. There was so much he would like to talk to her about. Not business – as he discussed it with Miss Porter. But the kind of interesting things that Fern knew about. The curtains on the big window at the top of the staircase were badly worn and in need of renewal. He would really have liked to have asked young Fern's advice about the new material. He was terrified that his mother would choose something not quite right. He had a schoolboyish desire to play a little game and get Fern to buy the stuff and then tell Mum that *he'd* chosen it. (Not that she'd believe it and then there'd be trouble, he decided.)

When they had discussed those curtains, Mrs Dorey had said:

'Why don't you get Greta to bring you over some of that gorgeous stuff they make in Sweden. They have wonderful materials and she'd choose it with *such* taste.'

Always pushing Greta into his arms, he had thought grimly at the time; not giving up hope, even though once again he had let Greta go back to Sweden without proposing. But old Mum was indefatigable. She had now arranged for Greta's mother, as well as her daughter, to stay a fortnight down here, which would include the celebrations for Quentin's thirty-fifth birthday.

Greta was obviously as determined as her godmother to make Quentin marry her and, in the end, Quentin sometimes thought with dry humour, they'd achieve it, if he wasn't strong-minded. It was a pity there was always that *something* missing in Greta; a something that not even her classic beauty or the nightingale's song could provide for Quentin. Yes, he wanted ridiculously to invite 'the little cook' to dine with him and have a long talk. He felt that somehow it would be a relaxation – that he could tell her things about himself and his boyhood; discuss his most secret thoughts – in a way he could never have done with Greta. What was there about Fern that so intrigued him?

He wanted to know things about *her*, too. What she was thinking; what lay behind that grave look of attention she always gave to his commands, and that quiet way she had of saying: 'Yes, Mr Dorey,' and, 'No, Mr Dorey.'

He would like to have reached out a hand and said: 'Be my friend and call me Quentin. And "Fern" is such a charming and unusual name. Blow me if I wouldn't rather call you Fern than Mrs Barrett...'

Impossible, of course. Far too familiar.

Fern's quiet voice roused him from his diverging thoughts, repeating her question.

'Will you be dining alone tonight, Mr Dorey?'

He replied briefly:

'Yes, I will,' turned on his heel and walked away.

He did not talk to Fern during dinner but told her when she went into the library that Mrs Dorey was doing well and that when he had seen her at the hospital earlier on, she had just opened one eye, recognised him and fallen asleep again.

'You go on over to your flat after you've cleared away. Don't wait up for anything further,' he said abruptly when she served his coffee. 'I shall probably take a long walk later on.'

'It's going to be a glorious moonlit night,' she said. 'It'll be beautiful down there by the lake, I imagine.'

Now he swung round and looked at her. She was putting the tray down on his desk. She then emptied an ashtray and moved quietly from the room, without looking back at him. He came to the conclusion that he had never known a girl with less coyness about her. It was that cool dignity and reserve of Fern's that somehow appealed to all that was deep and unattainable in the man. He was quite aghast to find that once again he wanted to learn more about her. To discover things that she liked and didn't like, and, above all, he wanted to know whether that good-looking irresponsible husband of hers really made her happy.

After she had left the house, he felt that it became no more than an impersonal museum full of treasures. He wondered why he spent so much time making money and what it was all for. He had never before felt so restless, so dissatisfied.

Fern went across to the flat to find no Terry. Not since they had had their last 'upset' had he let her spend an evening alone. Tonight he had promised to take the staff car and drive her up on the Downs to get a breath of fresh air this gorgeous summer's night. Instead she found a note from him on the bookcase, saying that he had gone down to the pub on business.

'*Real business this time, my pet,*' the letter said.

Somehow it didn't make her laugh; neither did it make her cry. There had been moments lately when she had wondered whether Terry was worth all the heartache and worry that he had caused her since they came to Swanlake. She supposed that she was at fault this evening because she had been so sharp with him during supper. But he had put a very dusty Rolls Royce into the garage and she had kept telling him that he ought to go and wash it, and finally he had jeered at her.

'Doesn't she want her darling Mr Dorey to have a dirty motor car in the morning, the poor man?'

Then she had flashed back:

'If you're in a job, you should do it properly, Terry. But if you want to get another rocket from Q.D. – it's okay by me.'

'Well, I've got my own ideas about that,' he had answered. 'I happen to have a scheme about which you know nothing, my

213

dear; but if it comes off, I might not need to take further rockets from your precious tycoon.'

When she had asked for an explanation of these words, he had given none. Once or twice this evening, busy though she was, she had remembered them and felt strangely uneasy.

Her precious tycoon! He was always so silly about her relationship with Q.D. But she had felt it beneath her dignity to protest that the said tycoon was neither precious to her, nor *hers,* and that Terry was just being childish.

Was he down there in 'The Golden Fawn' fooling around with Tosca tonight?

She shut her mind against the idea and her heart against its hurt – the withering of the warm tender love she had given Terry ever since they got married. But she felt disillusionment, like a blight, creeping across the bloom of that love, threatening to destroy it.

14

Terry came home at half past ten – sober enough, but in a strangely jubilant mood which did nothing to raise Fern's spirits. She hated being suspicious, but the moment he entered the bedroom (she was lying in bed reading), sat down on the edge of the bed and leaned down to kiss her, she thought she detected an unfamiliar perfume. A feminine, rather exotic, sort of scent, which was quite strong, as Fern rested her forehead against his shoulder.

Now, she thought, now is the time for me to keep my head but to be absolutely straightforward – like Q.D. – not to skirt around the things that hurt you but bring them out into the open, face them and deal with them. She pushed Terry away. She closed her book and laid it down. She looked steadily at her husband's fair flushed face. Handsome, marvellous-looking Terence Barrett, whose wife she was! It seemed to her a thousand years since those other days in London when they had been so happy in their little flat – everything to each other. She thought:

'Oh, Daddy, poor Daddy, what a lot you're responsible for. If only you hadn't run away! If only Mummy and I knew more about that whole horrid affair. If only I could wake up and find that all was well and there had never been this miserable change in my life.'

'Sorry I've been so long, sweetie, it was big business and I may say I have great news for you,' said Terry brightly, and lit a cigarette and blew a cloud of smoke up to the ceiling. He made some little smoke rings and puffed them out, a trick at which he was rather good.

She said:

'You smell of scent. Lanvin's *"Scandale"*, I think. Does your business friend use it?'

'Darling, don't be ridiculous.' Terry laughed loudly.

She sat bolt upright, pressing both hands down on the bed. Her cheeks lost their colour.

'I want you to be quite truthful with me, Terry. I'd like it better if you would. I know you go down to "The Golden Fawn" to see that Italian girl who is helping down there. It's her scent I can smell, isn't it?'

His gaze wavered before Fern's and he

hunched his shoulders.

'I never knew you were a jealous cat.'

'I never have been before, but tonight is different. Perfume clings, you know. You didn't realise that, perhaps.'

He thought that there was no further use in lying to her. His smile faded. He scowled.

'Okay. I'll own up. There is a girl down there called Tosca. I find her rather cute and I admit I kissed her goodnight tonight.'

Fern's heart seemed to give one dreadful agonised heave of misery; and of shame. The misery was for herself and the shame for Terry because he had broken the promises which to her were sacred.

Now he began to gabble, which Terry always did when he had something to explain, combined with a guilty conscience.

'I didn't mean anything serious and I give you my word of honour (if you'll accept it) I didn't mean any harm. She's one of these pretty, warm-hearted Italian girls. You know the type, and she's crazy about me. She asked me to kiss her goodnight and I did. But, for heaven's sake, Fern, what's in a kiss? Anybody would think I had broken our marriage vows.'

She felt very cold and desolate but she did not lose her composure. She reached for the packet of cigarettes on her bed, lit one and smoked for a moment in silence. Then she said:

'To you a kiss may not be important. It is to me.'

'You're an idealist, my sweet.'

'I thought you were one, too.'

'Oh, I have my ideals,' he said loftily, 'but you can't be so mid-Victorian as to object to the odd kiss. Anyhow, I'm a man. All chaps are the same. You ought to hear some of the married men down there at the bar – letting it be known how glad they are to get away from their wives and what they do...'

'Don't tell me. I don't want to hear.'

'I'm not glad to get away from you, Fern. You know that.'

'I don't know anything any more,' she said in a strangled voice.

'Oh, don't be so dramatic. I tell you, lots of married men have fun with the odd barmaid or some girl they happen to meet casually. I've admitted that I kissed Tosca. I'm not lying to you any more. I'm still utterly devoted to you.'

'Are you?' Fern spoke bitterly. 'Then we have different ideas of utter devotion. I know that since we took this job you haven't found being with me exciting any more.

Since our last row you've certainly stayed more at home and taken me out on our days off, but you never behave like a man in love. I daresay I get tired after all the work, and don't look nearly as attractive as I used to. Your Italian girl is a new thrill.'

'I tell you all men have their off moments!' he argued angrily.

'Have they?' she wondered. 'If Q.D. were married, would *he* go out and kiss a girl in the local pub? It won't have been the first time with Terry. This thing has been going on for some weeks. Would Q.D., if he were married, behave like that? Terry's like an undergraduate always "wanting fun", and needing fresh excitement. But Q.D. is a serious man. If he had a wife, he would want to stay at home with her.'

She smoked her cigarette furiously, her fingers shaking; hating herself for even making the comparison between Terry and her employer. It was a comparison that had only just leapt to her mind, but she found it a trifle shocking, because Terry came off so badly.

Now she listened to him assuring her that Tosca meant nothing to him, and that anyhow he would not be seeing much more of her because they were leaving Swanlake.

That made Fern sit bolt upright again.

She stared at Terry with startled eyes.

'*Leaving Swanlake* – what do you mean?'

'I mean that I wasn't just making an idle excuse when I told you I had a date with a chap at "The Golden Fawn". He's an American. I'd met him once before – soon after we came here – he's over on business and dropped in for a drink on his way from London to Brighton, where he spends weekends. He has plenty of money and rich relatives in Florida. He took a fancy to me and said he thought it was iniquitous that I should be doing this job when I had the brains and the personality' – here Terry coughed modestly – 'for better things. He said that he'd help me to get away from it. You, too. Of course it includes you.'

'What are you talking about, Terry?' Fern asked in utter bewilderment.

He went on to explain that the American had written to his relatives in Florida. Out there, English cooks were at a premium. Good cooks like Fern. There was no need for her to accept a few pounds and a miserable flat in this country. In fact, this chap's cousin would no doubt offer them a firm job right away. Fern as a lady-cook, and Terry as a sort of secretary. That was what the American suggested. His cousin was a millionaire. The salary, he said, would be astronomical. They always paid colossal money to English employees. Terry ended excitedly:

'All we'll have to do is to get our visas and take ourselves over there.'

Fern listened to this discourse in complete silence. Her heart sank lower and lower. Her pulse jerked; her throat felt quite dry. She knew, then, in a flash – in an undeniable moment of truth – that the whole idea was abhorrent to her. She did not want to go to America and work out there. She had never cared about the idea of America, anyhow. It didn't appeal to her. She had been brought up to appreciate traditions, antiquity, old and beautiful things, and when she travelled she liked it to be in Europe. It horrified her to think of living in a smart apartment, cooking for an American millionaire, thousands of miles from her own country; from Mummy who would be lost without her. From all that she, Fern, had ever known and loved. *And from Swanlake.* No – she didn't want to leave Swanlake, *or Quentin Dorey.*

Terry walked up and down the bedroom, rhapsodising on the prospects of Florida.

'Sure, baby, we'll have a swell time,' he mimicked the American accent. 'Everything will be paid for and we'd be able to save, and we might even settle out there and take American citizenship, as my pal suggested. America is the country where the money lies and the prospects of the future. England's finished.'

Now suddenly Fern sprang out of bed, put on her dressing-gown and tied the girdle with a quick angry movement. Her cheeks had grown hot and she had started to shake from head to foot. Never since she had loved and married this man had she felt so hostile towards him. And it was a hostility that terrified her by its implications.

'Now I've heard everything!' she said. 'And more than enough. How dare you say that England is finished? You, an Englishman.'

'Hundreds emigrate.'

'Not I – and that's definite. Nothing would induce me to forsake my country or adopt a new one and stop calling myself an Englishwoman. I wouldn't, even if our country went broke. But we happen to be in the middle of a boom. Industry has never been more flourishing. You've just been listening to a lot of propaganda and hot air from one of these Americans you meet casually in a bar, and who probably can't even substantiate his offers about work and earning all those dollars abroad.'

'He's waiting now for a letter to confirm the offer from his relatives.'

'You told me you had some big scheme on hand. I suppose this is it. You didn't even consult me, your wife.'

'I thought I'd wait until I had something concrete to offer you. My American says the letter should come before the weekend.'

She trembled.

'I don't want to go to America, Terry.'

'There you are! I knew you'd put up a protest and spoil all my fun.'

'Fun!' She repeated the word. 'Is that all you ever think of, Terry?'

'Oh, don't be so silly!' He almost shouted the words. 'I've said that I've been offered a *job*. My friend said that you probably wouldn't have to work very long as I'd soon make masses of dough and be able to keep you in luxury.'

She felt her teeth chattering although her face burned. She moved to the open window and leaned out to draw in a breath of the cool night air. She heard an owl hoot over in the parkland, and followed came the piercing call of a nightjar flying from tree to tree.

'This is England, and this is an English home, and my work lies here,' she thought. She stood there, her back rigid, refusing to turn around and face Terry while he went on talking, talking, trying to make her change her mind. She could see that he was all set to go to America. She even began to wonder if it was her duty as a wife to say 'yes' ... that she would go with him if the job was offered. But why should she? Why cook for an American family who were all strangers to her just in order to make more money – and be thoroughly miserable, away from her own people?

'You might even meet up with your father,' she heard Terry suggest cunningly.

Still she made no answer, her hands tightly clasped at her side. She couldn't, of course, meet up with Daddy. They didn't know where he was ... he never gave an address for Mummy to write to. Except for the odd notes they received from him telling them that he was alive and well, he might as well be dead to them. Now, suddenly, Fern turned and faced Terry.

'I don't want to go away. I just can't leave Mummy alone.'

'She isn't alone. She's got her sister.'

Fern looked up at the sullen, handsome face, feeling utterly bereft.

'Terry, doesn't it matter to you at all what *I* want? Don't you realise what it would mean to me to have to turn my back on everything and everyone I know and go out to Florida to cook for total strangers?'

'You must be dotty, my child. Think of Florida and the sunshine and the wonderful time we could have.'

'It isn't the sort of time that would be wonderful to me,' she whispered.

'Then I think you're damned selfish. You're stopping *me* from going out to the chance of getting my living properly.'

That made her feel dreadful. She felt absolutely hopeless. She did not know where her duty lay – to her husband, to her mother, or to herself. But apart from anything else she could see that America would be no place for Terry, where everybody tossed down highballs and 'went gay at parties', and nobody thought much was wrong with the odd kiss; there the values were all different, and the life was different from the steady, rather more sober way of the English.

'If only I could go over to the big house and ask Q.D. what he thinks I ought to do,' she thought. 'He's so strong and wise. He'd help me.'

Now there leaped into her mind the impassioned hope that confirmation from Florida would never come and that

American whom Terry had met was 'all hot air'. Breathing hard, she said:

'Well, don't let's get too excited about things. It may come to nothing.'

'But if it does come to something, I want to know that you'll go with me.'

'Please don't try and pin me down tonight. Let me think about it.'

He remembered Tosca, warm and responsive in his arms. She had kisses a fellow would remember and want again. *There* was a girl who would like to go to Florida with him, by golly. *She* wouldn't turn down such an offer. Of course he had guessed that Fern would kick up at the idea of leaving her mother while the crisis about her father was on, and he had always known that she wasn't all that keen on the States. And now that some of the excitement was over, he had the grace to notice how white and tired Fern was looking. He knew how badly he had behaved.

With one of his quick changes of mood, he tried to take Fern into his arms.

'Honey, don't feel so wretched. I've only been working on this Florida idea to try and give *you* a break as well as myself. And I thought if you still loved me, which you always say you do, you'd be glad to go with me anywhere.'

For the first time since she could remember, she felt no warmth and no wish to respond to him. She was quite cold. The joy of loving Terry was wearing very thin. She said:

'I suggest we wait and see if this firm offer ever comes, then we'll discuss it again. But Terry – let me say here and now that I, personally, don't want to go to America and leave my mother. All she has to look forward to is seeing me occasionally and knowing that I'm somewhere around.'

'Oh, all right, we'll leave it until the letter comes from America,' muttered Terry, letting her go.

He went into the bathroom. She heard him turn on the taps. She sat down and hid her face in her hands. She felt as though she had been beaten by a gale; that it was still blowing around her, threatening to sweep her right off firm ground. She felt unsure of herself, and very unsure of Terry. This marriage was beginning to be so different from all she had hoped and believed it would be. To her, fidelity in all respects was supremely important. She could not *bear* the memory of that perfume... Tosca's Italian scent. It nauseated her. And it frightened her to know how little she wanted to leave Swanlake. *Was* it a woman's duty to follow her husband wherever he wanted to go? Or should there be a compromise? Shouldn't they each try to see each other's point of view and stay where they could both be happy? And now the most terrifying question of all shot into her mind.

Wasn't it true that a woman who was really fully, completely in love with her husband would always put him first ... go with him to the ends of the earth?

'Oh God,' she thought, 'God, have I stopped loving Terry that way? Is that the trouble? Has he killed that old complete love that made me marry him? *Oh, God, don't let me lose it. Bring it back!*'

But as she lay beside Terry that night, hour after hour, listening to his deep, calm breathing, she felt as though she could never sleep peacefully again. She knew that part of her prayer, at least, was unanswerable. It was difficult, if not impossible, to recall absolute love when once it had been wrenched out of your heart by pain and disillusionment. All you can do is to remain affectionate and tolerant, and faithful until the end.

15

One sultry afternoon during the third week in August, Fern walked down the lane skirting some fields belonging to Swanlake Farm. She was going back to the Manor.

The men had just finished gathering in the corn. For two days they had been working – women and children, too – anxious to get the beautiful dry golden sheaves under cover before the fine weather broke. Everybody seemed to think there was going to be a thunderstorm tonight.

Fern, wearing a cotton frock and dark glasses, felt hot and tired. It was her day off from cooking. Terry was 'off', too, except when he had to fetch Q.D. from Haywards Heath station. And tomorrow, Saturday, Mrs Dorey was coming home.

It was the end, as Fern realised, to the peace and relaxation she had enjoyed at the Manor running the house alone. At least it had been peaceful so far as the domestic routine went. Even the menace of losing dear cheerful Rosie Hatton had decreased.

She had been so much better in health lately, her doctor had decided that she should postpone her operation. Fern always enjoyed Mrs Hatton's three hours up at the Manor – she was such a delightful, helpful and spotlessly clean worker. Devoted to the Doreys, like Jim, her husband, whose garden was such a picture and who often worked long after hours for sheer joy of his labours – a rare virtue in these days.

But there had been no peace in Fern's youthful heart so far as her own personal life was concerned. Since the night when Terry had threatened to drag her to Florida with him, he had scarcely mentioned the job, but she knew that the possibility of this American friend coming forward with a firm offer was still there – like an ominous cloud across her horizon. She dreaded what such an offer might entail. As the days and weeks went by she grew to love Swanlake more and more. All the time Mrs Dorey was in hospital, she had found Q.D. so kindly, so easy to serve, and often ready to talk to her on some subject of interest to them both. He had actually asked her to suggest a new material for the landing curtains.

'Just between ourselves, Mrs Barrett – what would you hang there?'

She had suggested a pale olive-green brocade with a faint gold thread. It would make a handsome background, she said, for the gilt-framed paintings that hung on the staircase walls and along the gallery, and look charming with the leaf-brown carpets.

Quentin at once approved.

'I reckon you've hit the mark – just right. You have fine taste. I'll ask my mother, later on when she's about again, to get patterns. Of course, I won't say you thought of it – *I'll* take the kudos. Will you allow that?' he had added with the boyish, slightly mischievous grin that occasionally lit up his firm, granite face. Fern adored that smile. Somehow it always made her feel relaxed with him – confident that she never need be afraid of the Big Man who could snap and even snarl when he was annoyed.

They had had an impromptu dinner-party last Saturday. Miss Porter had phoned Fern from the office to warn her that Q.D. would be bringing two business friends down for the night. A scuffle for Fern to get hold of Maureen – prepare guest-rooms, drive into Haywards Heath to shop – fix a good meal – and have everything as Q.D. liked it (which meant it must be perfect). Q.D. was pleased with nothing less, as Fern now knew.

Everything had proceeded according to plan. She gave the three men prawn-cocktails, followed by escallop of veal in mushroom and white wine sauce and a cheese soufflé that had brought frank praise from both guests.

Afterwards she had been tired but pleased because Q.D. had taken the trouble to put his head in at the kitchen door and wave his cigar at her, and say:

'Well done! First class! You're a wonder. Don't know what I'd do without my little cook...'

The words, the pleased smile, had warmed her heart. He was so kind to her – so appreciative. But afterwards she wondered, miserably, what she was going to do if Terry ever came to re-open that Florida idea. It hung over her like the Sword of Damocles. She had told her mother about it when she went to see her last Sunday, and Mummy had practically burst into tears and begged her not to go.

'I couldn't bear to lose you as well as Daddy,' she had said. Just as Fern had known she would do.

To add to Fern's discomfort, Terry had not been very gay or companionable lately. He had seemed depressed ever since their last row, and taken to going down to 'The Golden Fawn' again. Fern let him go. She was beginning to feel too heartsick to try and stop what he called his 'fun'. What was going on between the girl, Tosca, and him, she did not know – did not want to know. It hurt too much. But at these times he was cool and indifferent to his wife and it seemed obvious that he had found another interest. Yet there were intervals when Fern knew that he still cared for her deeply – and said so. Then she longed to be back on the old footing with him again. He could still be so charming when he wanted – so lovable. He was a confusing mixture and he kept her on an invisible string that he had only to pull – and she was back in his arms. An unhappy position for any wife she told herself ruefully.

The longer this state of affairs persisted, the more, somehow, Fern found herself clinging to the security of her job with Quentin Dorey; and the more she appreciated all that he stood for in the shifting sand of her new world. Things like honesty, truth and loyalty.

Sometimes, remembering that conversation she had overheard when Greta Paulson was here, concerning her father's firm, she felt sick at heart because of her own false position. She could well believe that Quentin's mother would soon show her the door if it ever became known that she was Bernard Wendell's daughter.

She walked through the gardens and around the back of the house to the courtyard. There was a fig tree growing against the red brick wall on the left of the garage. It always delighted her, and Q.D. had one day told her to help herself if at any time she saw the figs ripening. Hot and thirsty now, she stopped to pick a couple of figs and split and eat them. They were pink inside and sweet and delicious. It took a summer like this to ripen figs in England, she thought. She had never seen a herbaceous border look more magnificent. Jim Hatton had pointed out some of his prize blooms to her this morning. Mr Dorey liked dahlias. They were magnificent. The big feathery ones – red and yellow and rosy-pink.

Fern reminded herself to ask Hatton for a bunch to arrange in that tall alabaster jar on the marble-topped table in the hall. She must also ask for roses for the drawing-room. No flowers in Mrs Dorey's bedroom this time, Fern thought with a faint smile. Nell Dorey didn't 'hold with such nonsense'.

The old tyranny was bound to begin again after tonight, but she was glad the old lady had recovered and could return to her well-loved son. Glad for *her* sake.

Fern had visited her twice in hospital. Each time Mrs Dorey had been cool and formal – politely thanked her for the visit, the flowers, the laundry that Fern had brought from home, but she had not come an inch nearer to being really friendly.

'The old girl loathes us both and the sooner we quit the better,' Terry had said to Fern only last night.

She had not answered. Better to remain silent rather than start an argument. But Fern knew that she did not want to leave Swanlake even if Mrs Dorey 'loathed her'.

Mr Dorey was dining in town tonight. Terry would not have to go into Haywards Heath to meet his train for another couple of hours. And Terry, so far as Fern knew, was in the flat. He had said he wanted to go to sleep on this hot, thundery afternoon. But Fern had chosen to go out and watch the corn being taken in and have a chat with the farm people. They all knew her now and were her friends.

Mrs Banford, the farmer's wife, told Fern how Mr Dorey had been out in the fields working with them last night. In old grey flannels and a cotton shirt, sleeves rolled up, hair rough – and the inevitable cigar in his mouth – he had sat driving the tractor and trailer for two or three hours. He seemed to enjoy it. He made them laugh, in boisterous spirits, full of jokes. He ordered beer for them all. What a grand man he was, Mrs Banford exclaimed. Didn't Mrs Barrett agree? One of the real gentlemen of this world.

Yes, that was it, Fern had decided. One of the *real* gentlemen was Q.D. Self-educated, standing alone, a law unto himself – as solid and fine as a rough-hewn monument.

She reached her flat and walked up the little iron staircase. She hoped Terry would be in a good humour and that they could spend the rest of the day in peace, and go, as they had planned, into Brighton to have supper and take a stroll along the sea-front.

She found the flat empty. The bedroom was as Terry had left it; the imprint of his head still on the pillow; the ashtray full of cigarette stubs. It didn't look to Fern as though he had slept very much. There was a 'whodunit' on the bed.

She took little notice of this. She was beginning to find it futile to allow herself to

236

be upset by anything her handsome rascal of a husband did or said.

They had a television set in the sitting-room now – it had been sent over to them by the Big Man. He thought it might amuse them, he said. Fern had been touched and delighted. Terry made one of his typical remarks.

'Makes me sick – trying to buy us, and bribe us to stay.'

Queer, Fern thought, how she had immediately felt the impulse to leap to Q.D.'s defence, more especially when Terry added that all newly-made rich people were vulgar.

'That's one thing *he* never is,' she said quietly. 'People with money are justified in spending what they want on reasonable comforts and art, and I don't think Q.D. would ever try to *buy* service.'

She felt damp and hot, had a cool bath and changed into a cotton-frock. Terry used to like this one – white with grey and yellow flowers. She wondered sadly if he would even notice what she had on nowadays.

An hour later, while she was preparing supper, she heard the telephone bell ring and ran to answer it.

It was Terry. His voice sounded strained and anxious.

'I've done it now. I really have bought a packet of trouble.'

Fern's face flushed with anxiety.

'Oh, Terry, *what?*'

'I've crashed the Rolls.'

'Crashed the Rolls!' she repeated, horrified.

'Well, I've been crashed into – let's put it that way,' came Terry's voice with a miserable laugh.

'What happened? Where are you?'

'At Bolney Cross-roads – you know, on the Brighton road not far from that Tudor Tea-House.'

'But what were you doing out in the *Rolls?* When I left you, you said you were going to rest this afternoon.'

A moment's silence.

'You'd better tell me.' Fern spoke again. 'Don't hide anything from me if you want my help, Terry.'

'Well, it isn't that it's such a bad crack, really. It's the other car that's out of action. I'm waiting now for the police, and so on.'

'Terry,' said Fern, paling. 'Oh, *Terry!*'

'I want you to get out the staff car and go and meet Q.D.,' he said. 'You know his train's due in half an hour from now and I shall never make it.'

'Who were you with?' The question leapt

to her mind before she could restrain it.

He answered dolefully:

'You'll hear sooner or later so I'd better tell you. Tosca. She'd always wanted a run in the Rolls and I promised to take her. I was driving perfectly okay when some fool of an old woman tried to pass me and lost control and barged straight into me. There's a nasty dent in my off-side back wing. It's buckled up, in fact. There'll be all hell let loose when Q.D. knows.'

Fern was silent. Her hand holding the receiver trembled. How often these days, she thought, Terry reduced her to a state of nerves. But, ever practical, she remained calm. This was no time for upbraiding Terry because he had taken Tosca out in Q.D.'s car. But she knew exactly what *he* would have to say about it, and if Q.D. knew his chauffeur had been giving the Italian waitress a joy-ride, he'd give Terry the sack. He would *have* to.

'Oh, I don't want to be sent away and I don't want Terry to get into a scrape that will ruin his reputation,' she thought in misery. 'Oh, what can I do?'

Then an idea leaped into Fern's mind.

'Listen! I've thought of something quite crazy but I think it will work. Has anyone come yet to take names and addresses?'

'No.'

'The accident has only just happened?'

'Yes. Nobody's worrying about the Rolls. They're attending to the other driver. She's been cut by flying glass. Nothing serious, thank God.'

Fern looked at her wrist watch.

'I'll be out there in a few minutes. Tell Tosca to go off and wait for a bus in the shelter and stay there and not let it be known that she was ever with you. Make her go, quickly. I'll park the staff car somewhere and be with you by the Rolls when the police start questioning. They must think I, your wife, was with you when the accident happened. Do you see? It'll look so much better, when we eventually tell Q.D. the story.'

'But you've got to go and meet him—' began Terry.

'I'll phone the station. They know Q.D. I'll ask the station master to tell him there's been a little accident and ask him to take a taxi home.'

'Oh, my God, what a girl! What a sport – and what a brilliant idea!' said Terry, but Fern cut him short.

'Don't try and flatter me. Just get your

Italian girl-friend out of the picture. I'll be with you as soon as I can. It's bad, but better that Q.D. should think that *I* made you take *me* out in the Rolls.'

16

'Now,' said Quentin, 'might I ask for an explanation as to why I had to take a taxi from the station, and where my chauffeur is?'

Fern stood in the library in her characteristic schoolgirl attitude, hands behind her back. Quentin was in front of the fireplace. He had just poured himself out a whisky and soda and lit a fresh cigar. She had never seen him look so disgruntled. He eyed her under thick, lowering brows. Oh, those light grey penetrating eyes, she thought, did they see everything that was in one's heart? She felt quite sick with nerves and misery. If there was one thing she hated, it was having to lie. But she had to do so now – for Terry's sake. She said:

'Terry sent his humble apologies. He's had rather a nasty shock, otherwise he would have come to make his apologies in person.'

'Where is he?'

'In bed. I made him take some aspirin and lie down.'

'I presume he's had an accident.'

'Yes,' said Fern, catching her breath.

'In the Rolls?'

She nodded. Q.D. eyed her with merciless scrutiny. She looked as white as her overall, he thought. He continued the cross-questioning.

She answered in a terse, cold, little voice. She didn't feel either terse or cold. She felt hot with shame and anger because she could not tell him the truth. She had to repeat the story that she and Terry had agreed upon before Quentin Dorey got home.

'*I* ... am responsible. It's all my fault. I begged Terry to take me out in the Rolls. He kept on saying he was not allowed to use it for personal pleasure. I'm afraid I ... I nagged until he gave in. The accident was not his fault. You'll see that when the evidence comes out. It was the other car that ran into us...'

She stammered a little, her face very flushed, her lids lowered.

Q.D. listened, continuing to sip his whisky, and draw an occasional breath from his cigar. Somehow, in a moment of lucidity he knew perfectly well that little Mrs Barrett was not telling the truth. She was no 'nagger', he thought. But he let her continue … this stammering confession of her guilt. All her fault, *all*. He mustn't blame his chauffeur, she kept repeating.

Then silence. Fern stood there in an agony.

She could not begin to think what Q.D. would say if he had been told the facts. How Terry had been out with that *other* girl, joy-riding; his arm around her shoulders. Fern could only thank heaven that the whole thing had taken place when there was nobody there to see Tosca, save the woman in the offending car, who didn't have a clear conception of what the passenger looked like. So when Fern took Tosca's place – who was there could testify to the 'switch-over' of passengers? That part of the story was safe. When Fern gave evidence, which she would have to do, she must perjure herself for Terry. It made things look so much better if his own wife was in the car with him at the time of the crash.

Fern had hardly been able to think straight since that horrible episode. She had seen the Italian, who had started to whimper and weep and beg the Signora to forgive her but Fern had cut her short and told her to keep out of sight. Before the breakdown gang or the police arrived on the scene, Fern drove the staff car down a side lane and left it there, hidden. She had gone home with Terry in the Rolls once the wing had been knocked straight enough to free the wheel. Later Terry went back alone, to the Bolney Cross-roads to collect the Morris. He returned home tired and in a rage, but, at least, had expressed his gratitude to Fern for what she had done.

'I don't know why I did it,' she had said. 'I don't know that you are worth any more sacrifices. You and that girl – oh, *God!*'

'I'm sorry,' he muttered.

'I hope you'll be pleased now if we both lose our jobs,' she had added in a strangled voice, then been considerably surprised when he said:

'That *would* be a disaster, I admit. As far as I can see, the Florida job isn't coming off. I haven't seen that American again.'

In the midst of the crisis, she had felt her heart leap with relief. But now in Quentin Dorey's presence she had an unnerving suspicion that the Big Man was not likely to forgive or forget such an episode lightly.

Quentin meanwhile, was struggling with himself in a manner of which she had no idea. It had been on the tip of his tongue to demand that that unreliable, arrogant young bounder of a husband of hers should be got out of bed and brought here. Why the heck wasn't he taking his own medicine? What was he made of, to let his wife take the rap? And Quentin didn't believe a word of Fern's story. *He just did not believe* that a girl of Fern Barrett's calibre was capable of persuading her husband to break the rule about the Rolls and risk dismissal.

Now he met her gaze. He was confounded by the expression of stark misery in those heavenly blue eyes of hers. She no longer seemed to him a hired cook in a white uniform. She was just a young, beautiful, brave girl trying to defend a husband who must have let her down many times before this. She hadn't mentioned the word 'drink' but he'd like to bet the boy had had a couple before ever starting out on the road.

It wasn't such a heinous crime, after all; only a buckled wing, and the boss had been forced to take a taxi home. Nothing. No – it was the principle of the thing. In ordinary circumstances he would have given Barrett notice. Not because of the accident but because he disliked him and knew that he was a rotten husband to this girl. Oh, yes, he knew more than Fern imagined. He'd heard all about the Italian down at 'The Golden Fawn'. There had been far too much gossip about the Dorey chauffeur for it not to have trickled eventually to the ears of his employer.

Now, suddenly, Fern spoke.

'Would you like us to leave, Mr Dorey?'

He rapped out:

'No, I wouldn't. It's the last thing I want.'

Her head sank. The hot colour scorched her neck and throat and she could feel the tears scalding her eyelids. She made a valiant attempt to remain cool and dignified and failed totally. Her voice broke as she said:

'I'm so sorry about it ... but it was ... all my fault. Terry is very ... cross with me...'

Now Quentin Dorey thundered:

'Cross with you! That's rich. Cross with you! Wasn't he in charge of the car? Did he *have* to take you out in it and act the silly fool?'

'I made him,' said Fern desperately.

Quentin had a lot to say but he didn't say it. He held his peace. If ever he was tactful, it was now. The blunt man of vision and dogged purpose had no wish to probe further, because the truth was all too apparent and it was equally obvious that

247

this young girl wanted him to believe what she was saying. She had her own personal reasons. And, by golly, she had pluck, he thought. Well – he wasn't going to spoil her victory. If this was the way she wanted things and it would make her feel better – then let it rest. Let that abominable young scallywag lie in his bed, and hide behind his wife. He, the employer, would accept Mrs Barrett's evidence and excuse Barrett accordingly.

He said:

'I take it you don't want the sack, eh?'

Fern did not mind the lack of delicacy about that particular question. It was spoken with too much kindness. Now she raised her drenched eyes and answered:

'No.'

'And I don't want you to leave,' he said gruffly.

Now he took a step towards her. He looked down into those drowned blue eyes that were so infinitely appealing in their sadness. He looked at the soft quivering mouth. He looked at the brave, straight young back, and for him it was a moment of revelation – a revealing of *himself* – unrecognisable but undeniable. Just for a few seconds, Quentin Dorey's hard granite surface cracked, and all that was tender, emotional, passionate showed through. He was distressed by the intensity of his own feelings. *He knew that he loved this girl.* He was in love with her. It was a feeling that had been developing deep down inside him ever since she came to Swanlake. She had done more for him than she could ever know. Not only in terms of service as a cook-housekeeper, but as a woman. She had shown him what no other woman – Greta included – had ever done. That he was lonely and deeply in need of the love and companionship of the right woman. To him this young girl was the right one. But she was already married. And that knowledge was very embittering.

'*Oh, my God,*'he said under his breath, laid down his cigar and his glass and put the tips of his fingers against his head as though his own thoughts confused him.

'What is it?' asked Fern anxiously. 'Mr Dorey, are you ill?'

His hands dropped from his face. The muscles on both cheeks were working. He said:

'You little ninny ... don't you understand... Don't you know why I want to keep you here with me so much? It isn't just because you cook so damned well, I've fallen in love with you. *Do you hear?*'

She gasped. For a moment she could hardly believe what she had heard. But with the amazement there came a lightning flash of incredible joy. For her, too, the truth was made clear and undeniable. *She loved Q.D.* Not in the gay girlish way she had first loved Terry, but with the deep love of a more mature Fern who had learnt to suffer – who knew that what a woman needed in life was a man she could respect and admire as she did Quentin Dorey. Perhaps he hadn't got Terence Barrett's breeding or education. But he had everything else – all the fine qualities that go to make up a real *man*. The millionaire was of no account to Fern. None whatsoever. It was just Q.D. the man. Dear lovable Q.D.

Their gaze met again. The two in this second were dominated by each other. Then Q.D. spoke:

'I should never have said that, should I?'

'I'm ... glad that you did.'

His eyes lit up.

'Then you aren't angry?'

'No. I just thank you. I think it's so wonderful of you to have said it.'

'I mean it. That's the trouble. My dear, dear little Fern, I mean it.'

He was resisting the strongest impulse to catch hold of her and feel the sweetness of her in his arms.

She said:

'I'm going to tell you something. I love you too ... but I'm married, and I gave Terry a promise. That sort of promise is for ever. It has to be.'

For a few seconds he did not take in the last part of her speech. He only heard her timid admission that *she* loved *him*. He was flummoxed. He, the cool financier, who had all the resources and daring that make it possible for a man to gamble, to strike a hard bargain, to pull off a coup, felt himself shaking. Little Mrs Barrett, his little cook, had been transformed into the woman of his dreams. He had so far achieved every success, every treasure he coveted. This one alone was beyond his reach. For the first time that he could remember, he did not know what to say or to do.

Then Fern spoke:

'I'll *have* to leave your service now, won't I?'

That broke him.

'No,' he said. 'Fern, my dear little love, please don't go. If you do I'll feel that everything will go out of my life.'

Her eyes looked enormous.

'You can't mean that,' she said incredulously. 'I can't mean as much to you as all that.'

'But you do, my dear. You do.'

'But I've got my husband...'

'I know. Good God, don't you think I realise it?' asked Quentin roughly, and turned from her and began to walk up and down the study like a caged creature seeking a way out; knowing himself barred and defeated from the start. He, Q.D., who used to boast that he did not recognise the word 'defeat'.

At last he came to a standstill in front of Fern. He looked pale and stern and strange to her, but she felt that she knew him better tonight than she had ever known him. She understood him perfectly. It was with a kind of muted joy that she looked up at him and considered the fact that he loved her, and had told her so.

'I know you're married,' he went on, 'and that I can't ask you to undo the knot. I wouldn't be able to live with myself if I were the kind of chap that breaks up a marriage and filches another man's wife. Thieving doesn't appeal to me. What I win in this life I like to win by fair square methods, and honest work.'

'I know that,' she said softly, 'I *know*.'

'I don't even feel I've come between you and Barrett. You haven't been happy with him for a long time, have you?'

She bent her head.

'I used to be devoted to Terry. I thought myself in love with him. In the physical sense I suppose I was–' She flushed and looked away from Quentin. 'Lately I must say he has done his best to kill my feelings.'

'I've seen that for myself. He isn't worthy of you.'

'Oh, don't flatter me, please.'

'Good heavens, I'm not trying to flatter you, you silly child. My feeling for you is beyond that. I think you're wonderful in every respect and I can't think of anybody I'd like more to live with. Yes, Fern, if you were free I'd like to marry you tomorrow and bring you back here to run my home, not as an employee but as my adored little wife.'

He said it so proudly that some of her own dogged determination to keep faith with Terry faltered. The tears ran down her cheeks.

'Oh, *Quentin!*...' For the first time she spoke his name.

253

Hearing it brought his last defences down. He caught her and crushed her in a bear-like hug, typical of the man, she thought. Awkward, a little rough, yet so warm, so strong and infinitely satisfying. Her small slim body relaxed against his big one for a few seconds. She pressed her tear-wet face against his shoulder. She thought:

'This is heaven … this would be the kind of heaven on earth that every woman needs. It makes one feel no harm could ever come to one again. That he would look after one for ever, and protect one against life – against death, itself.'

'Fern.' She heard him speak her name very tenderly. 'Little Fern.'

For another memorable moment she felt the warmth of his cheek resting against hers. There clung about him the aroma of his cigar, his clean masculine scent. And that embrace, forbidden, never to be repeated, was something that she would always remember. But she didn't want him to kiss her. With the tears drying on her lashes, she said so.

'Don't, don't kiss me, please.'

'I understand,' he said.

He let her go. He walked across the room and, pulling aside the curtains, let the night air cool his face. He could not recognise himself in this man of turbulent passions that must necessarily be controlled. He had never wanted so much before to kiss any woman's lips.

'I love this girl,' he told himself grimly, 'I love her and I can't have her. Q.D. has found the one treasure his millions can't buy.'

Fern took a handkerchief from her pocket. She held it against her eyes, struggling for control. After a moment she said:

'Don't you think Terry and I *ought* to leave now?'

Quentin swung round.

'In a way, yes. But in another way, no. I couldn't take it. I couldn't bear you to walk out of my life. We're both sensible people, Fern. We don't have to lose our heads. And it's a sign of weakness to run away from danger.'

'You would say that,' she said with a sudden laugh.

'It's true. The way to tackle a menace is to face up to it – overcome it. You're a married woman. I can't do anything about you, but I can become your friend and I will, and I'll stay your friend for as long as you need me.'

For a moment she was too moved to

answer, but all the love and respect she felt for him lay in her eyes as she smiled up at him.

'I think you're too marvellous.'

'Rubbish. I feel as weak as hell about you but I intend to keep my head, because I want to keep *you*. I want you to stay here and go on running my home. It's been the biggest pleasure I've known for years, having you around, Fern. It's going to mean even more now to me, but stay – *please* stay, Fern.'

'But what about Terry?'

'We'd better not discuss him. The mere thought of him disgusts me. To be lucky enough to have a wife like you and do everything to lose you – good heavens – he wants his brains tested!'

'He hasn't got a very strong character,' she whispered.

'You knew about that Italian girl?'

'Yes.'

'You forgave him?'

'Yes, so long as he wants to stay with me and tries to be decent, I mustn't desert him.'

'You're a grand girl,' said Quentin, and turned away from her because it was too great a temptation to pull her back into his arms. 'I won't see so much of you in the future,' he added abruptly. 'I'm going to be pretty busy, and once my mother is settled home again I shall go on that yachting holiday.'

'Yes,' said Fern in a small voice.

'My mother isn't always very nice to you,' he continued, frowning, 'but please try to forgive her. She doesn't mean it.'

'I don't know what she'd say if she *knew*...' said Fern with a deep sigh.

'No, I don't know either,' said Quentin with a sudden boy's smile.

'Won't you ... won't you one day get married, Quentin?'

'No. At the moment I feel that if I can't have you, I don't want anybody.'

'I'd better go back to my flat,' she said, turning towards the door. 'I ... I'll tell Terry that you'll overlook the accident to the Rolls – if I may.'

'Yes,' said Quentin heavily, 'tell him that, and I'll talk to him in the morning. By golly, I wish I could tell him the truth ... tell him how I feel about you and that I'll knock the breath out of his body if he doesn't treat you properly.'

She looked back at Quentin over her shoulder, a faint smile on her face.

'I can take care of myself. Don't worry

about me.'

'I love you,' he said under his breath and gave her a long deep look that made her tremble.

She whispered:

'We must never say that to each other again. It's finished. If I'm to stay here, it must never be said again.'

He bowed his head and picked up his half-smoked cigar.

'Agreed. And if it gets too difficult – then you'll have to go. But we'll give it a trial, eh?'

'Yes, we'll give it a trial.'

It was only when she was outside the library door that she stood a moment against it, her heart palpitating hard, her eyes tight shut. She was trying to tell herself that the whole of that scene was not a dream and that Q.D. really, truly had told her that he loved her.

And while she stood there, she wished, suddenly, she had told Q.D. about her father. She didn't suppose her story would have much personal interest for him ... yet she wished she had told him.

17

That next twenty-four hours were the most difficult in Fern's life. The unexpected admission of love between the big man and herself had come as a considerable shock to her whole nervous system. She felt she would never be the same again. With Terry, her husband, her life could never be the same again, either.

Terry accepted what she had done for him in a sullen fashion. He admitted that he was relieved that he was not going to be fully blamed, but when he saw Fern after his usual morning interview with his employer, he was cross and ungracious about it.

'The boss says that he understands that it was *you* who had forced the issue, but that I ought to have had the strength of mind to resist you,' he told Fern with a short laugh.

A little acidly, Fern reminded him that it might have been very much worse if Q.D. had known *whose charms* Terry had found it difficult to resist.

Terry then became difficult about Tosca. It

was obvious, he said, that he wasn't going to be able to see any more of the Italian girl without causing trouble, so he would have to 'lay off'. But he intimated to his wife that life was going to be pretty deadly down here in future.

Fern said nothing, but Terry's attitude was hardly a help. She went on with the cake she was making for Mrs Dorey's tea. This morning she knew beyond all doubt how much she loved Quentin, and how utterly she had stopped loving Terry. He was revealed to her this morning quite clearly as an egotistical, worthless person. Only the fact that she wore his wedding ring and had vowed to be faithful to him kept her with him. She had a vague idea that if she ran to Q.D. and told him that she couldn't stand the situation, he might even discuss divorce, and offer to take her away. But that was unthinkable. She would never do it. She wasn't even tempted. But when she looked at Terry this morning she knew that she was going to remain faithful to a vow – a principle – rather than to the man himself.

Little did he know, she thought bitterly, the difficulties that now lay ahead of her. The bitter sweetness of having to live here under the same roof as Quentin, now that their feelings for each other had changed. The *anguish* of it.

Things seemed worse once Mrs Dorey returned. As soon as the old lady was installed in her own bedroom, where the doctor wished her to remain for a day or two, she made it plain to her young housekeeper that she was in a bad mood. Glad to be home, yes. But she found constant fault with almost everything that Fern did or ever had done at Swanlake.

Fern listened to all the acrimony in dead silence. She was miserable and her nerves were on edge but she was not going to allow Mrs Dorey to upset her. Q.D. wanted her to stay here, and for his sake as well as her own she must make the best of a bad job.

'As long as he needs me, I'm not going to let Terry or Mrs Dorey drive me away,' she thought stubbornly.

Mrs Dorey also drove home the point that her friend Mrs Paulson and Mrs Dorey's goddaughter, Greta, would be coming down to Swanlake next week.

'And this time,' she said, with a significant look at Fern, 'I think we can safely say there will be great developments. I think you understand.'

Fern dug her hands into her overall

261

pockets and chewed hard at her lower lip. Yes, she understood. It gave her a sick little feeling to think of the beautiful, talented Greta coming back to Swanlake ... and of all Mrs Dorey's efforts to unite Greta with her son.

Maybe in the face of what had happened, Q.D. might think it the best and wisest thing to get married in the end. What was the good of being hopelessly in love with a married woman?

'*Whatever happens, I look like being the loser all the way along,*' Fern thought wretchedly.

Now there followed an unhappy week. Quentin kept away from Swanlake. He spent at least four or five nights up in his London flat on the plea of business. The yachting trip, which was to have come off as soon as his mother returned, was postponed yet again. Urgent affairs were, in truth, cropping up in all kinds of unexpected quarters, and there was one financial problem in which Q.D. was particularly involved and which was causing him a good deal of anxiety.

He, personally, was unhappy and even if less emotionally involved – being a man – he suffered. So he flung himself into business matters more violently than usual, as though trying to shut out the longing that he felt for

Fern Barrett.

He found it difficult to be civil to his chauffeur. He used the Rolls less, and the train more.

Terry did nothing but grumble about him to Fern.

'I can't stand these jumped-up fellows – they all get too big for their boots and Q.D. is thoroughly bad-tempered and boorish these days.'

Fern listened in silence. She wanted to rise up in defence of Quentin but she said nothing. She had not seen Q.D. to talk to alone since that unforgettable night of the accident. He seemed to go out of his way to avoid her. She tried to understand but it hurt badly. The old warm friendly basis of their association had vanished. Like this, working under his roof, her job became a torture rather than a pleasure. Yet she could not bear the idea of going away – of never seeing him again.

On one occasion when she was sitting in her flat with her husband, watching the television, she noticed Terry staring out of the window, looking so bored and cross that she felt a sudden wish to bridge the gulf that had been widening between them lately. She was unhappy and lonely, herself. She got up, walked to her husband, and put an arm around his shoulders.

'Terry darling,' she said, 'let's be friends and go down to the lake. The moon is rising and it's a heavenly night.'

He flung off her arm. It wasn't that he meant to be gratuitously unkind – he just had no sentimental feelings left for Fern. The gentle pressure of her friendly hand left him cold. He had seen Tosca this morning. She had stopped his car in the village and told him that she was going mad because he did not go down to her any more.

'How can I?' he had asked. 'I'm being watched.'

She had begged him to slip away if only for half an hour. He knew that he wanted her. She was brown and velvet-eyed and sensuous, and she flattered his vanity. She paid him compliments and didn't criticise him. Marriage was a trap. He had been cheated by old man Wendell and he resented the fact that Fern knew him for what he was.

'I don't want to go to the lake. I'm not in a romantic mood,' he said roughly.

'Terry,' she said, and her lips quivered, *don't* let's go on like this. It's too miserable. Nothing's worthwhile if we can't get along together.'

'Nobody said we didn't get along.'

'There are times when I think you hate me,' she said in a low voice.

He scowled at her.

She looked very thin; not very well, he thought. She was completely changed from the gay, amusing girl he had married. Amusing – and well-off. He felt half responsible for her misery, yet some devil prompted him to lash out at her; his own frustrated desires made a cad of him.

'I don't hate *you* but I hate your father, and you can blame him for the whole bag of tricks,' he said.

'Terry–' began Fern in a blaze of indignation.

But he had gone. Out of the flat, slamming the door, and she heard the staff car's engine running below and wondered if he was going to break all the promises he had ever made.

But she was still fiercely determined not to break hers. She would *not* run across to the big house for sympathy and see *him* alone. That was not to be.

Her loneliness and grief that night were almost past enduring. But there was worse to come in the morning.

Terry went off early, driving his employer

in the Rolls to Birmingham on the new M.1 road. They were not coming back till tomorrow, either of them.

Fern went to the kitchen, unwilling to listen to Maureen's chatter or talk even to nice Mrs Hatton. She dreaded Mrs Dorey's acid tongue, and felt no interest in her cooking. It was not to be for *him*.

Then Maureen came into the kitchen and said that Mrs Dorey wanted to speak to her. Madam, she said, was sitting out on the terrace in a deck chair in the sun reading her post.

Fern rolled down her cuffs, smoothed her overall, and walked out on to the terrace. The old lady was sitting there with a light cashmere rug over her knees. She was getting stronger every day and almost back to her normal self. She was reading a letter, but at Fern's approach she laid it down. She glanced at the young housekeeper over the rim of her glasses.

'Ah, yes, I want a word with you, Mrs Barrett,' she said. And there was a strange new malevolence in her voice and eyes which made Fern's pulses move uneasily. What had she done now? What was wrong *this* time?

It wasn't long before she knew, because

Nell Dorey came straight to the point.

'I've been making a few enquiries,' she said in a smug voice, 'I've been making them for quite some time, following some information that Mrs Grey-Everton got for me, and now I know. I know that you and your husband have come here under false pretences. You are no cook and chauffeur. *Your* maiden name was Wendell, wasn't it? You are Bernard Wendell's daughter.'

The sun was in Fern's eyes. She blinked and put a hand up to shield them. Her heart beat at an uncontrollable rate. She felt rather sick.

At length she found her voice.

'That's quite right, Mrs Dorey. I am Bernard Wendell's daughter. Does it make my presence at Swanlake particularly undesirable?'

'In more ways that one,' said the older woman in a voice of bitter satisfaction. 'Perhaps *you* don't know it, Mrs Barrett, but your father almost ruined my son. A great portion of the money lost by his firm was our family money – funds which my son had entrusted to *your* father to invest.'

18

Fern stared down at Mrs Dorey, her face ashen. This was a shock which, she felt, robbed her of all her remaining dignity and self-confidence. She could hardly believe what she heard. Of course, she knew – because she had unintentionally listened to that conversation about the firm when Greta was here – that the Doreys were interested in the Wendell case. But it had never entered her head that her own father had had any financial dealings with Q.D. himself.

Her brain felt addled. She put a hand nervously to her forehead. For a moment she really could not think what to say or do. The older woman looked up at her triumphantly.

'Well – what have you got to say, Mrs Barrett?'

'This terrible, cruel woman,' thought Fern. 'It isn't easy to believe that she is Quentin's mother. They have the same dogged determination – but he uses his for good and she for evil.'

Suddenly Fern burst out:

'I haven't anything to say, except that you are right. I *was* Fern Wendell before I married Terence. It's true, too, that I haven't had much experience of domestic service. We came down here as a couple because we needed the job, the home and the money. We felt that we were capable of doing our stuff. I think I've proved that I *am* capable of doing mine – haven't I?'

'Oh, I grant that you are an excellent cook,' said Mrs Dorey icily, 'but, as you can well imagine, if we had *known* who you are, we would never have engaged you. I do not blame my son. I blame Miss Porter for not making sufficient enquiries about you.'

Fern's head shot up again. Breathing fast, she exclaimed:

'Am I to account for what happened in my father's business?'

Mrs Dorey gave a thin-lipped smile.

'Oh, no. Nor for what he did. I can even feel sorry for you. But I still say that you had no right to come down here under false pretences.'

'I didn't mean to do so and I don't want you to be sorry for me either, thank you!' flashed Fern with some of her old spirit. She wasn't quite broken yet, and she intended to stand up to Nell Dorey until the bitter end.

'Well, there's nothing more to be said. You had just better pack up and leave Swanlake immediately.'

'If that's how you feel about things, Mrs Dorey.'

'I certainly do, and my son will share my sentiments once he hears the facts. He has the greatest contempt for Mr Wendell, and though I regret having to remind you of it, my dear Mrs Barrett, my son and I are very much the losers through your father.'

'You have no proof that it was my father's fault and I don't think he is the guilty one, anyway,' said Fern trembling from head to foot.

'He must be the guilty one. *He* ran away.'

'He ran away for his own private reasons which we don't yet know, but which I'm sure he will one day explain to us. Then my mother and I are sure his name will be cleared!'

A glint of admiration entered Mrs Dorey's eyes as she listened and looked at the young girl's white passionate face. Oh, she was a plucky one all right! She had her wits about her. And there was more to her credit than the credit of that sly, bad-lot young husband of hers! Mrs Dorey granted her that.

Fern added:

'I'll go and pack. As soon as Terry gets back we'll leave.'

Suddenly Mrs Dorey felt worried. Having achieved what she had been trying for so long to do and scored a crushing victory over Mrs Barrett, she failed to feel either contented or proud of herself. Her conscience smote her. Her behaviour was scarcely Christian or charitable, and she had been brought up in the north country in a good Christian family. At the same time, why should one harbour the daughter of a *criminal?* she argued with herself. Of course the girl did look ill and unhappy, and she'd certainly done a good job since she came to Swanlake. What a nuisance it all was!

Mrs Dorey cleared her throat and managed a small capitulation.

'I don't want to turn you out at a moment's notice. You've always worked well down here. I have no complaints against *you,* Mrs Barrett. It's just a pity you had such a father.'

'I honour him and believe in him and I refuse to hear one word against him!' flashed Fern.

Again the light of an unwilling admiration in Mrs Dorey's stony eyes. She said:

'We won't go into that. But we must both

271

remember that Mr Dorey and Barrett are in Birmingham, not due back until tomorrow. I suggest you wait down here until they get home.'

'Yes, I suppose I shall have to,' said Fern.

But somehow she had a desperate longing to get away before seeing Q.D. again. Oh, God, what a tangle it all was. It had been bad enough to suffer the pain of knowing that she and Quentin loved each other without hope. But those words 'false pretences' which Mrs Dorey had just used struck to the very core of her being. Would Quentin, himself, feel now that she had had no right to take this job? Would he feel as his mother did, that because she was the daughter of the man he imagined had tried to ruin him, she was no longer welcome at Swanlake, would he feel that his very confession of love had been a mistake?

'I can't bear much more,' Fern thought, and turned and ran rather than walked back into the house. In the hall she collided with Maureen, who dropped the dustpan and brush she was holding. As she bent to pick them up she looked at the young cook's face, and what she saw written on it startled her.

'Holy Mother of God, what's wrong? You're looking as though you'd seen a spook, me darlin'!'

Fern could not face the good-natured Irish girl. She could not even go back into the kitchen and risk being talked to by Rosie or Jim Hatton, when they came in for 'elevenses'.

She forgot her work entirely. Forgot that she had been about to make a specially light soufflé for Mrs Dorey's lunch.

She fled across the courtyard, passed the familiar fig tree, and rushed blindly up into her flat. In a kind of despair she looked around it and at all her little efforts to make a home here. But *home* it had never been, and she knew it now. Home had meant the Manor – the rooms in which *he* moved, and ate and slept. Everything that was his she had grown to love and care for, as she would have done her own or her parents' treasures.

It was all over – this job that had become so dear and exciting – and ended in such a devastating way. When Q.D. got home tomorrow his mother would tell him immediately who *she* was.

'I don't want to see him,' she thought. 'I don't. *I mustn't.* In case he, my dear kindly one, begins to feel less kindly towards me and shows it. If he did that I'd never, never get over it.'

Feverishly she began to pack. When a knock came on the door, she opened it to find Hatton, the gardener, standing outside. He carried in his hand one glorious pinky-golden rose on a long stalk, with glossy, deep green leaves.

'I've picked this for you, Mrs Barrett,' he said, looking awkward. 'I took it into your kitchen but Rosie told me you'd come over here. I cut it for *you* because you always said it was your favourite. My best bloom this summer. *"Peace".*'

For a moment Fern could not speak. The little touch of gallantry, coming at such a time, almost moved her to tears. She had always found Jim Hatton friendly and willing to instruct her about growing plants. Often she had gone down to watch him in her spare time in the greenhouses, potting his begonias, or budding a new rose, marvelling at his deft 'green' fingers.

She took the beautiful rose and bent her head over it to inhale its fragrance.

'*Peace,*' she thought. '*Dear God, where is there any peace for me now?*'

'The missus said she didn't think you were feeling up to much and would you like her to bring you over a cup of tea?' continued Hatton.

That woke Fern up. It brought home the recollection that she was still in a job. It wasn't fair to leave Rose and Maureen to cope alone, especially as Mrs Dorey would be expecting her lunch. She could leave the packing until later tonight. This afternoon she would phone Mummy. Of course she wouldn't tell her the truth – it would upset her too dreadfully, but she'd warn her that she and Terry were leaving Sussex for reasons of their own, and would be looking for another job, immediately.

She said to Hatton:

'Tell Rosie not to bother. I'll be coming over. I'm quite all right, Hatton, and thank you for my rose. I'll put it in water at once.'

'When you've got a minute, Mrs Barrett, I wish you'd take a look at them new Michaelmas daisies that are coming on in the big border. I reckon they'll be a fair treat at the end of this month.'

'I'll take a look,' said Fern.

But she thought: *I won't be here to see the daisies come out, or any other flowers at Swanlake, ever again.*

When she was back in the big kitchen, Mrs Hatton insisted on making the little cook a cup of tea.

'You do look bad, love. Has that old so-

and-so upset you? Maureen said that it was when you came back from seeing her that you turned so queer.'

Fern looked away from the kindly eyes.

'I'm quite all right, Rosie, don't bother.'

'Mrs Dorey can be rude, and don't I know it. She isn't like *Mr* Dorey.'

'No, she isn't like Mr Dorey,' echoed Fern, stonily.

And later when she was mixing her soufflé, unsmiling, Rosie watched for a moment and said:

'Fancy going to all this trouble for the old cat's lunch.'

'A job's a job,' said Fern.

Mrs Hatton felt that there was something here she didn't understand. Mrs Barrett seemed to have lost all her usual charm and good humour this morning. What *had* happened?

Doggedly Fern continued to prepare that lunch and in due course served it.

Mrs Dorey had just started walking about normally and could go into the dining-room for her meals, now. She had to admit that she was surprised and a little embarrassed when the girl to whom she had been so brutal placed a perfect meal in front of her. Now and again Mrs Dorey stole a look at the white young face and felt even more embarrassed. She was beginning to wish she had never come out with the truth. She had had a little chat on the phone with her friend Enid. Enid had said:

'Oh, I wish I'd never *told* you about the Barretts now. I can't *think* what Q. will say if his precious cook leaves.'

And Nell Dorey was thinking very much the same thing, while she ate her lunch. She even toyed with the idea of suggesting that she and Mrs Barrett let bygones be bygones and that they forget all about Bernard Wendell. That Fern should stay on – without mentioning anything to Q.D.

She began to dread her son's return and her own part in this unhappy affair.

'I'm a foolish old woman,' she thought, 'I'm always doing nasty things and then being sorry for them.'

Q.'s father used to reproach her for her bitter tongue and unkind ways.

'You're a good woman and I shouldn't think you've ever done what the world calls "a wrong thing",' he used to say. 'But you can be so wrong with all these little malicious, unpleasant ways of yours. Why not try and drink the cup of kindness more often?'

Nell Dorey remembered those words today and was miserably ashamed of herself.

'I'll ask Mrs Barrett to stay and to forget all I said,' she decided. She rang the bell and summoned the housekeeper just before the evening meal.

With the greatest difficulty she began:

'I've been thinking this over, Mrs Barrett, and I'm sure this is going to be a great shock to my son. He's had a lot of business troubles on his mind and I don't want him to have to be involved in domestic worries as well. I've got the Paulsons coming next week, too. I – ahem–' She broke off, hating herself, hating the quiet dignity of the pale, serious-eyed girl who stared her straight in the face. She said no more.

Then Fern spoke.

'I understand perfectly, Mrs Dorey. It would be very awkward for you all round if I go, but I'm afraid I couldn't possibly stay under the circumstances.'

Mrs Dorey sniffed. She must be mad, she thought, climbing down like this. She had been trying to get rid of the girl for months. Q. would have to put up with it. So she tossed her head and told Fern to do as she pleased and walked out of the room with as much dignity as she could muster.

The girl was proud, she thought. And of course, the Wendells were a good family. They had once been wealthy and must have had a fine home. Just *fancy* Mrs Barrett – a Wendell – cooking for them here. What a story to tell – when she could tell it!

Fern finished the dinner, left her kitchen clean and tidy and walked across to the flat.

She wished that Terry was home so that she could tell him everything, talk to him and hope that he, at least, would stand beside her; see her through this calamity. For calamity it was. They couldn't expect much in the way of references from Mrs Dorey.

It was a long, lonely, bitter night for Fern. She stayed up until long after twelve o'clock, packing all her personal things; Terry's, too. It was only when she lay in bed, too exhausted to sleep, that she began to worry about Q.D. again. She shut her eyes, and saw the wonderful look in his eyes when he had drawn her into his arms. She felt again the glorious blissful security of his embrace. The idea that tomorrow morning she would be leaving Swanlake and Quentin for ever seemed like death to her. 'One can die while one is still alive,' she thought. '*Quentin, Quentin, I love you. I need you.*

Never more than now.'

When she woke after a broken night's sleep, it was to the bitterness of a wretched dawn.

She pictured herself leaving Swanlake later today with a husband she no longer loved, but to whom she must keep her word. It was a grim prospect. It did little to cheer her. She got up early, long before anybody else was awake, and walked around the grounds, looking at everything with the deep, fond, brooding gaze of one who knows she is seeing them for the last time.

She had taken some bread with her and fed the swans – that, too, for the last time. How graceful they were, she thought, curving their slender necks, dipping their beaks into the limpid water that looked so exquisitely opalescent in the early light of the August morning.

She took a look at Jim Hatton's prize Michaelmas daisies, and at the rose borders that were pearled with dew, at the standard roses lining the path that led from the house – each one heavy with clustered blooms – pink, scarlet, golden and white.

The morning was full of bird-song. It was going to be a warm, beautiful weekend. She thought of Quentin being driven back in the

Rolls by Terry, little knowing what was waiting for him.

His mother had said she didn't want him to be upset by domestic worries.

'Heaven knows I don't want him to be upset, but I can't stay now,' she thought. 'He won't want me to when he hears who I am, anyhow.'

If only it were not her father's firm that had been concerned with Quentin's investments. What a painful, *appalling* coincidence. 'Anything but this,' she thought, frantic with the anguish of her thoughts, her shattered life.

But she felt that it was imperative she should pull herself together before Terry got back. He wouldn't be sentimentally disturbed because he was leaving Swanlake – he had never really liked it. But he would be worried about the financial position. They hadn't enough money saved to enable them to stay out of a job for long.

It was while Fern was clearing the kitchen after lunch that she heard the telephone bell ring. She answered it in the library. Mrs Dorey had gone upstairs to rest. She had no telephone in her own bedroom. She disliked it.

The colour rushed to Fern's face as she

heard a deep, familiar voice.

'Is that you speaking, Mrs Barrett?'

'Yes, Mr Dorey,' she said automatically, but her right hand went to her throat as though she felt a lump in it. She didn't want to talk to him. *She didn't want to.*

'Fern,' he said, using her Christian name now, 'I just want to tell you that I'm leaving the Rolls up in London and I'm coming down by train. Could you meet me in the staff car? I propose to get in at three thirty-two.'

Startled, she said:

'Is Terry staying up in London then?'

'Yes.'

Q.D. spoke in such a queer voice that Fern's pulses jerked.

'Oh, what's happened to him *now?*'

'He's quite all right, so far as I know. He just isn't coming down with me and I don't feel like driving, myself. The big car's a big heavy on that leg as yet.'

'Oh, what's happened to him?' she asked again, and she thought, *'There can't be something more ... Terry can't be in trouble ... things can't go on piling up like this!'*

She heard Quentin again.

'I don't want to talk on the phone. I'll tell you all about it later. Just meet me, will you?'

'But there's something you've got to know first–' she began.

But he had rung off.

She went back to the kitchen in a state of nervous agitation. This was a development she hadn't bargained for. Quite obviously, Terry was in trouble again and the Rolls was out of action. Whatever it was, it meant she would have to see Q.D. at the station. 'Well,' she thought, 'at least I'm going to be the one to tell him the truth myself. I shan't let Mrs Dorey do *that* to me. I'd rather he heard from *me*. I just won't tell her that I'm going to fetch him. I'll just vanish with the staff car before she knows I'm missing – and I don't care!'

19

When Quentin saw Fern's slim familiar figure standing in the station yard by the Morris, his heart seemed to turn over. She was wearing that blue linen suit and little white hat which she had worn when she first came down to Sussex. He loved her so much and he felt in a turmoil. Perhaps what he had to tell her would make a difference to her – to them both. He felt his heart knocking like a frightened boy's as he walked towards the Morris, and lifted his hat to Fern.

'Hullo,' he said awkwardly.

'Hullo,' she echoed and got back into the car.

As soon as they were on the road she began to question him.

'Tell me, please, Mr Dorey, what's happened.'

'Not as long as you talk to me in that darned formal fashion.'

For the first time for a very long while Fern smiled. He was such a dear. And whatever he had to tell her, she could not but be thrilled at the sight of that rugged face again. She had caught the warmth in those light handsome eyes of his. Oh, just to have him sitting here beside her and being able to sniff the familiar cigar smoke that clung to him eased a little of the pain and loneliness in her heart.

She said:

'What has happened to Terry this time? Please tell me, Quentin.'

'He's gone.'

Startled, Fern took her eyes off the road for a fraction of a second, then stared in front of her again. She felt her face flame.

'What do you mean – *gone?*'

'That's all I know up to date – he has vanished. Quit my service. When we got back from Birmingham – he knew that I was lunching at my Club and sent a letter to me there – I found this note informing me that he had left my services at a moment's notice, and that he wanted no salary. He asked me to give you this.' Q.D. tossed an envelope on to Fern's lap.

'Oh, Quentin!' she said in dismay, 'what *does* this mean?'

'Better read your letter and find out,' said Quentin bluntly.

She drove the car out of Haywards Heath

and deliberately switched to the left, on to a by-road where they could be quiet for a moment, away from the main traffic.

She tore open her envelope and scanned the letter.

Darling Fern,

I expect you will think I'm right off my rocker and let's leave it that I am and always have been – but I never was as practical or philosophical as you. This business of our having to work as we've been doing lately has got me right down. It's also been obvious that we haven't been getting on as we used to and our marriage is a disappointment to you. On the other hand, I know your views and that there can never be any question of divorce. In fact I know you so well, my dear, I shan't waste time asking for a divorce. I'll just suggest we stay married but separate for a while. I'm going off on my own for a bit. Goodness bores me and you're too nice, Fern, and too good to me. In a funny way, I feel you've made a bad bargain and you might be better without me.

Well – that American chap turned up again the night before I drove Q.D. to Birmingham. I didn't tell you then because I wanted to think things over. Now I've decided. His firm wants an English representative in Spain. They're tied up with some Spanish commercial business. As you know, it's the one language I'm good at, owing to the fact that I took a commercial Spanish course when I was a boy. I've always wanted to go to Spain. This American has got me in with his firm, in Madrid.

They demanded a snap answer and they said they didn't want a married chap on the job. So I am going as a single one. Of course, I'll send you some of my salary, and write regularly, and if I do well maybe you'd like to come over and join me.

I expect you'll stay on at Swanlake now, where you're such a success. No doubt Q.D. can soon find a new chauffeur and put him up somewhere and let you keep the flat. But I'm off. I've got my night bag with me. You'll find me at the Hotel Molinos, Madrid, and maybe you'll put a big case with my suits and other things in it and have it sent over by air-freight.

Forgive me if I've caused you a lot of pain. I might even make up for it in the future if I'm a success in my Spanish enterprise.
God bless.
Ever yours,
Terry

Fern finished reading this and looked up at her companion. Quentin was watching her gravely. He thought she looked shockingly ill and he felt worried. She said:

'I'm absolutely staggered. I never thought Terry would do a thing like this to me.'

'You'd better tell me what's going on.'

'You might as well read what he says,' she said in a low voice.

Quentin took off his hat, threw it on to the back seat, leaned a little out of the car window to get some fresh air and read that letter. It sickened him, as had most of the things that young Barrett had said and done.

'Well, of all the cool customers!' he said. 'Commend me to Mr Terence Barrett. Typical, I'd say. A total lack of consideration for you, for his employer, or for anyone but himself.'

'He seems to have walked out on me,' said Fern with a wry smile.

'Adding the suggestion that you should join him if he makes good. Very generous,' said Quentin, with a short laugh. 'By golly, Fern, for a chap to leave *you,* asking for a separation, knowing full well, as Barrett says in this letter, that you don't believe in divorce – it's iniquitous. Does he think you are going to go on working and waiting until he chooses to send you the fare to Madrid?'

She turned and looked out across the green field. She felt strangely apathetic. Losing Terry didn't, somehow, seem to matter. It was the loss of integrity, the ignoble weakness of Terry that hurt her so badly. For this man, who had 'cut and run' and left her to face the music, was the one with whom she had always kept faith. She said:

'He's right over one thing. I'll never break up our marriage for any reason whatsoever.'

'Do you mean,' said Quentin incredulously, 'that if he makes a go of things in Madrid and asks you to go out to him, *you'll go?*'

She clasped her hands together in her lap so tightly that it was painful. She felt terribly tired – too tired to fight much more.

She said:

'Yes. Terry's a queer person. In his way, he is truly fond of me.'

'Well, you wouldn't think so!' exploded Quentin.

'All the same, I think he is, and I know he needs me and that one day he'll find that out, and then I must just try to help him. I am his wife.'

Quentin looked at the young girl with something of awe. She was so strong, this little gentle creature, he reflected. So very determined to do the right thing. Even now she wouldn't so much as consider the possibility of a permanent break with Terry. Yet Quentin knew that she loved *him*. He had seen it in her eyes when he walked towards her just now in the station yard. He saw it again as she turned her face towards him and held out her hand for her letter. He gritted his teeth and said:

'I daren't allow myself to say what I really think of that husband of yours. But this I do state here and now: Swanlake is your home for as long as you want it. My mother and I will take care of you.'

For one blinding moment of human weakness, she turned to him, gripped one of his arms with her desperate hands and clung to it as though she were drowning. She kissed his coat sleeve. He could almost feel the warmth of her lips in that passionate impulsive caress. His arms went around her and he muttered:

'Oh my darling, if things could be different ... if only they could be different for us two!'

She did not answer. She was struggling with her tears.

He added:

'But you've nothing to fear from me, you know that, my darling. I'll remain your friend. And you just go on being my little cook – will you?'

Then she said quietly:

'No, Quentin, I'm leaving Swanlake today.'

20

The look on his face was one of such dismay that it was in itself a compliment.

'*Leaving Swanlake?*' he repeated. 'Why? What for?'

Her fingers twisted nervously over the bag in her lap.

'I … oh … it's so difficult … the whole thing is frightful … I don't know where to begin.'

'Well, you know me, Fern. I am a plain-spoken man. No frills, please. Let's have it.'

'Yesterday,' she began in a small miserable voice, 'your mother found out something about me.'

He interrupted:

'Do you mean about *us?*'

'No. I daren't think what she would have said if she had found *that* out. It's about my father.'

'You said it was about *you,*' Quentin corrected her.

'Oh, you're so quick! But naturally, as your mother said, it concerned me because

I am his daughter.'

'You're speaking Greek. I speak plain English. Out with it, lass...'

Here was the north-country man, decisive, blunt, impossible to deceive. She adored him for it.

She said:

'My father's name is Bernard Wendell.'

That certainly was a small bombshell. As it exploded it shook Q.D. considerably. He could hardly believe his own ears. He stared at the girl whom he loved and whom he called 'the little cook', his eyes incredulous.

'You! Wendell's *daughter*.'

Then she began to tell him the whole story, calmly. He heard it from the beginning. He knew, of course, quite a bit more about the firm than Fern did. And he had always had a vague idea that the senior partner was culpable rather than the other man. He had died a month ago. The whole affair was in the hands of the law now, and they were still trying to find Bernard Wendell.

He heard how in the beginning Fern and her young husband had decided to take a living-in domestic job and thus relieve the financial tension; how they had sold their home and everything in it. Barely enough was left to keep Mrs Wendell, who was now living in obscurity on a small income that came from her side of the family. He heard how Fern had seen the advertisement that Miss Porter put in the paper after the Howards left; and how totally ignorant Fern had been of the fact that the Doreys were in any way connected with her father.

'You can imagine what I felt when I heard that Daddy's firm owed *you* so much money,' Fern finished in a choked voice. 'I was absolutely horrified when it all came out. Yours was the last house I would have come to work in under such circumstances.'

'By golly!' exclaimed Q.D., using his favourite expression. *'By golly!'*

Fern put her face in her hands.

'I can only ask you to forgive me. It's put you in an awful position. You couldn't possibly want to love the daughter of a man who you think has tried to ruin you, although...' she added with a flash of the old spirit, 'I know Daddy will one day prove his innocence.'

Then she felt Quentin's firm fingers taking her hands away from her face. He turned her round to him. He was not looking angry. He was smiling. The most tender, curiously sad smile she had ever seen on that hard face. So much tenderness combined with so much power, she thought. It was always astonishing to her. He was like a diamond of many facets. But, unlike the diamond, there was so much softness too.

He said:

'My poor dear little girl. What a mix-up for you. What a hell of a state you must be in!'

She could not speak but her lips trembled, and her eyes widened with astonishment. No reproaches? No condemnation? Only that kindly thought for her.

'I'll never forgive my mother for what she's done to you today,' he added in a low voice. 'I know she's got a rough edge on her tongue and that she's a die-hard ... doesn't take to young people very easily. A bit jealous of your success at Swanlake, in her funny way. But you've been a miracle of understanding and tolerance. You didn't deserve what she gave you. I never thought she'd be quite so cruel.'

Now Fern rose in defence of Mrs Dorey.

'It was such a shock for her, Quentin. She was thinking of you when she blamed Daddy about your loss of money, and she was quite right when she said that, in a way, Terry and I came to you under false pretences. We both knew we were capable of doing our respective jobs, but I suppose in a fashion we *did* "fake" our references. I mean, both the people Miss Porter spoke to have known us for years, but it was rather mean of us to let Miss Porter think we had been in *service* with them.'

Q.D. shook his head at her.

'Being generous to my mother, aren't you?'

'But it *was* wrong of us!'

'Look here, Fern, personally I don't mind whether you had another job before this one or not. I must be frank with you and say I've never cared for Barrett, but he's done his job up to a point, as best he could. But you've been a *marvel.* You've done more for me than you'll ever know – quite apart from your cooking.'

Her face flushed. She was on the verge of tears again.

'But I *am* Bernard Wendell's daughter.'

'So what? For a crime we're not even sure your father committed, are you to be penalised? What nonsense! I can think of nothing that would be more unjust. Q.D. prides himself on having a sense of justice and I've stuck to that throughout my whole business career.'

'You're not only just, you're … terribly,

terribly good and kind,' she whispered. 'I do so wish you hadn't had such bad luck through Daddy.'

'Never mind, I happen to love *you*.'

She shook her head swiftly as though to imply he must not say it. He made no movement to touch her, but he added:

'I'm not having you turned out of Swanlake just because you're Wendell's daughter. That's definite.'

She gave him a startled look.

'I can't stay. Not only because of that ... but because of ... the other thing between us. Now that my husband has seen fit to go abroad without me ... I can't stay on at Swanlake alone. It would be impossible. You must see that.'

He didn't want to see it. His whole being revolted against the idea of losing this girl who had become so precious to him. He knew that they could not be together in the way he wanted ... that she wouldn't break her promises to her husband ... but he had counted on her staying on at the Manor so that he could see her sometimes and feel that she was there in the background. He had learned to count on her. He burst out quite angrily:

'Well – it's very selfish of you to go! What

am I going to do without my little cook? Do you want to condemn me to a series of rotten housekeepers and a badly-run house again? My mother's a good soul but you know she can't organise parties in the way you do. She's never had to. We lived simply and hardly ever had formal dinners when my father was alive. *You* have taught us so many things. Life's been quite different since you came to Swanlake. Don't leave us, Fern, please.'

'My darling,' she said, involuntarily, 'you know I don't want to go. The thought of leaving you and Swanlake breaks my heart, quite apart from the fact that I hate to make things uncomfortable for you again. But I'll try and find you somebody... I'll search London until I do find you a good couple. You've got to have a chauffeur to replace Terry, anyhow.'

Quentin dragged his gaze from her beloved face to the fields and the tall elms beside them. To his amazement he felt an acute unhappiness.

'Your mother wouldn't want me to stay, although she did suggest that I should,' Fern continued.

'Oh, did she!' said Quentin grimly. 'Well, she's a bit late with her suggestion. I tell you

I won't find it easy to forgive her for what she's done.'

'Quentin, she can't possibly know how much I mean to you, and I must remind you again … it would be so awkward for me to stay on without my husband.'

'You mean you think I'd try to make love to you again,' said Quentin with a bitter laugh.

She said nothing, then raised her head and gave him the ghost of a smile.

'Maybe *I'd* try to make love to *you!* I'm not all that strong-minded but I must try to keep faith with Terry.'

'Even though he's ratted on you?'

'He hasn't really. Anyhow, I must keep faith for as long as he says he wants me to. He wants me to wait for him and he is trying to do this job abroad for both of us. I admit he's acting in rather a queer way, but sometimes I don't think Terry's quite like other men – he *is* a bit odd. *Very* egotistical. I don't think he realises how much misery he causes.'

'So you really mean to leave Swanlake?' said Quentin in a hollow tone.

'I must,' said Fern.

He suddenly turned and shouted:

'You can't leave without giving me a week's

notice. I'll dock your salary. I'll lock you in your flat. Oh, my *God!'*

And now it was the Big Man's turn to break down; his turn to hide his working face in his hands, almost appalled at the power this slip of a girl had over him.

Immediately Fern put out both hands and, as she had done before, clung to his arm and pressed her cheek to his shoulder. Now she was crying unashamedly.

'Darling, darling Q.D. You're so very sweet. I do so love you, and thank you, *thank you* for loving me.'

He turned and took her in his arms and hid his face against her warm neck. His voice broke as he said:

'I love you as I never thought it possible to love a woman. I'd give my soul to be able to marry you and I can't bear to lose you even as a friend. Something will go right out of my life if you leave me.'

'It'll go out of mine too, dear, dear Quentin.'

'That you should give your loyalty and courage to that juvenile delinquent Barrett who has never seemed to me to be even ordinarily *adult* ... that *kills* me! I wouldn't mind so much if I thought he'd take care of you, but for you to wait for him, and work, alone… Fern darling, must it be?'

She nodded. Her tears dried. She had to swallow several times convulsively before she could speak calmly. This brief hour in the car with Quentin had forged an even stronger chain between them. It could never break. Whatever happened in the future, he would be for ever in her heart as her ideal man; but she knew it was best for her to go away as quickly as possible so that she should not even be tempted to betray Terry.

It might be quite easy to divorce him. No doubt he wouldn't be faithful to her out there in Madrid. If she went to a lawyer she could have Terry followed and possibly get all the evidence she needed. Fern personally adhered to a principle that was a firm rule for Roman Catholics – even though she, herself, belonged to the Church of England. She did *not* believe in divorce. She would never agree to one.

'A promise is for ever,' she said those words not for the first time to Quentin, and repeated them again. 'A promise is for ever, otherwise it's not worth making. And I promised to take Terry for better or for worse.'

Q.D. the Big Man – ruthless in business – undefeated in most ways – felt very humble now as he lifted one of Fern's small hands and dropped a kiss into the palm.

'You're a good girl, Fern, and by golly that's an understatement.'

'We must go,' she said ... she laughed shakily. 'I've got to cook dinner.'

'For the last time,' he said gloomily.

She nodded and felt herself shivering, despite the fact that the day was warm.

'I'm going to tell my mother how I feel about you,' Quentin said suddenly and firmly.

'No, no, for heaven's sake, don't do that.'

'Why not? I'm proud of it and I want her to know that you're my chosen woman, and that if I can't have you I'll never marry Greta or any other woman she throws at my head.'

'Don't hurt her unnecessarily,' Fern begged. 'It can't do any good, and it'll only distress her.'

'Why the hell should you worry about that? She's treated you pretty shabbily.'

'Quentin, I don't want to come between you and your mother. That *would* upset me. You two are devoted at heart, even if you don't understand each other's ways.'

'But I'd like her to *know*,' Quentin argued, his forehead puckered, and he ran his fingers through the thick upspringing hair with the flecks of grey that made him look so much older than he was. With yearning she looked at that vital, greying hair, but she shook her head.

'No, don't let's tell her, please. It would only cause more trouble for you and widen the breach. Let me just go away quietly, please, Quentin.'

'If that's the way you want it.'

'I do.'

'So I've got to sit back and think of you standing up to life alone, and trying to make the best of it.'

'I'll try to find a job where I could have my mother with me, perhaps.'

She said those words more to comfort him than with any hope that such a job could be found. Besides, Mummy would never want to leave Aunt Pamela now. She had been uprooted from her home once; better to leave her where she was.

'Look,' said Quentin, his voice suddenly harsh, 'this is scarcely a moment for a money discussion. But you know how ruddy rich I am. Can't I be allowed to use some of my money in the way I want and make you secure? I can't abide the thought of you having to go on earning your living as a cook.'

She knew he meant well and kindly, and she was not going to feel insulted by his offer, but her deep sense of humour brought laughter, suddenly, into her eyes. She said:

'Darling, what a hypocrite you are! You just *adored* me cooking for you. Why shouldn't I cook for someone else?'

He tried to laugh with her, but humour was far from him. Through his teeth, he said:

'Because that would be different.'

'Yes, it'll be different,' she nodded sadly.

'Won't you even let me see you sometimes? Does it have to be a complete break?'

She took a long time to answer.

'Wouldn't it be better? We're so ... we love each other so much. It might be difficult for us to meet just as friends.'

'Well, that won't stop me phoning you for a talk, and asking how you are,' he growled.

'All right. I shall probably stay with my aunt for a bit,' she said. But that, too, she knew wasn't true. She wouldn't get a room in Aunt Pamela's small house. No ... she would have to find another domestic job quickly. Thank goodness it wouldn't be difficult, with her qualifications.

She tried to joke again.

'Will you give me a good reference, please,

Mr Dorey?' she asked meekly.

'Don't,' he said, 'I can only take *so* much.'

She sighed and switched on the engine. She would drive him home now. She said:

'Please, Quentin – we must not tell your mother about *us*. And I want you to know now, so that you don't bring up the subject again, that I'll accept my rightful wages, but you won't be allowed to do anything more for me. I don't care how rich you are.'

'Okay,' he said with a heavy frown.

As Fern drove off in the direction of Cuckendean, he lapsed into a silence which she did not try to break. The less said between them now the better, she decided. Tomorrow she must write to the hotel in Madrid and tell that hopeless husband of hers that she would accept his plan; and wish him luck in his new job. She would also tell him that she would join him the moment he found that he could send for her.

She felt an almost desperate wish now to get away as far as possible from Swanlake and Q.D., and from the searing pain of her hopeless love for him.

21

The conversation between Q.D. and his mother was short and sharp, and one of the most antagonistic the two had ever had.

The moment she saw her son's face as he entered the library, Mrs Dorey knew that he had already heard the news. She had not seen the staff car come in with Quentin, nor did she know about the disappearance of young Barrett. But that cold fury in Q.'s light grey eyes – those tightly-compressed lips – reminded her painfully of unhappy moments with his father – when old Q.D. suddenly lost patience and temper with her.

'So you've got the little cook out of the house at last, Mother!' were young Q.D.'s first words, and he slapped the evening paper on to his desk, sat down, and began to slit open the envelopes of the morning's mail which he had not yet seen.

If ever Nell Dorey quaked, it was now. She remained seated in her chair, bent over the tapestry work she was engaged upon. The fingers that held the needle trembled.

She said:

'Oh! So Mrs Barrett has had her say first, has she?'

'If you mean, has Mrs Barrett told me that you asked her to leave because she happens to be Bernard Wendell's daughter – yes.'

Mrs Dorey cleared her throat. She didn't like the tone of young Q.'s voice. She knew she had only herself to blame but she tried to adopt a superior manner.

'Can you blame me for that?'

And she tossed her head upwards. But now she met the full accusing glance of her son's strangely magnetic eyes.

He said:

'You had no right to sack that girl without consulting me. I engaged her and her husband.'

'But Bernard Wendell tried to *ruin* you!'

'You haven't got your facts right, Mother. First of all, he *didn't* try to ruin *me*. The money that I and several others placed with the firm was misappropriated – yes – and Wendell made things look black for himself by doing the vanishing trick. But I have no reason to suppose that either he or the other chap tried to ruin me in particular. They had back luck with their own investments, the poor fools. I should say the firm as a whole has shown an astonishing lack of foresight and acumen rather than been guilty of a deliberate attempt to defraud their clients.'

Mrs Dorey gave a nervous laugh.

'You choose suddenly to be very charitable to the Wendells.'

'And you have chosen to be extraordinarily uncharitable, Mother. You hit a young, helpless girl when she was down. Fern has nobody in the world except a sick mother and a totally unreliable husband to lean on. She had a good job and a nice home here and she enjoyed cooking for our parties. You have chucked her out. All I can say is – I'm ashamed of you.'

Mrs Dorey's face went brick-red. She knew that she had been ashamed of herself ever since she spoke so cruelly to Mrs Barrett. But she did not like to hear her son say so.

And her quick ear had caught the use of that Christian name *'Fern'*. She snapped:

'I think you've grown a lot too attached to that young woman, if you ask *me*.'

This was the moment when Quentin Dorey found it a difficult task to keep his promise to Fern not to tell his mother how he really did feel about her. Frustrated, wretched, suffering as he had never thought it possible to do, he wanted badly to let his mother know that he loved Fern Barrett. Yes, that it was *the woman he loved* whom she was driving from his home.

But he remembered Fern's gentle, kindly appeal to him not to hurt his mother gratuitously. Well – as their love could never come out into the open, she was right. What good would there be in shouting it aloud?

He felt in need of a strong whisky, got up and poured it out. He was generally so cool, so capable of dealing with trouble in the world of finance. But this, the most important emotional crisis of his whole life, was beyond him. He only knew that the thing he most prized and wanted was slipping out of his grasp.

He spoke harshly:

'I don't intend to answer you, beyond saying that I respect and admire Mrs Barrett about as much as I despise her husband.'

'Why are you so down on *him* all of a sudden?' asked Mrs Dorey, anxious to switch the focus from Fern.

Leaning against the edge of his desk, sipping his whisky, Quentin told her what young Barrett had done.

Mrs Dorey looked as solemn as she felt

now. The whole thing was getting a little beyond *her*. She was even beginning to feel sorry for the girl.

She felt still worse when she heard Quentin add that he considered that, all the way along, the innocent deception Fern had practised on them as to her true identity could be forgiven her, because she had no idea that the Doreys were personally involved in the Wendell crash.

'Oh dear,' exclaimed Mrs Dorey, dropping her needlework, 'I don't know what to say. I know you're very angry. I don't want this to come between us, Quentin. You really mustn't feel so deeply for Mrs Barrett ... although I admit she's been hard done by, so far as her husband is concerned. I never did trust his handsome face.'

'What's done is done,' said Quentin curtly, 'and the last thing Mrs Barrett wants is for her dismissal to make bad blood between us, Mother. But I hope before she goes you'll make it plain to her that she isn't being *dismissed* but that she is leaving of her own accord, with a double salary, and our thanks for all that she has done since she's been here. And you'll give her a first-rate personal reference, if and when she wants one.'

Mrs Dorey writhed a little. But she was not really lacking either justice or decent feeling. She might dislike Mrs Barrett, but she was beginning to do more than regret the part she had played in driving her from Swanlake. She began to mutter:

'Dear, dear, what a carry-on! I don't know what we'll do. Good servants are impossible to find down here. She's been very excellent at her job.'

Quentin gave a harsh laugh and drained his glass.

'You've put it mildly, my dear mother. It'll be a long time before we sit down again to any meals like we've had lately. But to hell with food. It's her loyal service I shall miss. She never let us down – not once – in any thing or in any way.'

Mrs Dorey got up and walked to her son's side.

'Now listen, Q. dear, stop being angry with your poor old mother. Remember she's only just risen from a bed of sickness.'

Quentin calmed down. His lips relaxed into a faint smile as he looked at the wily old woman.

'That's right. Work the sympathy-stop. But I *am* cross with you, Mother. By golly, I am!'

She put a hand on his shoulder.

311

'I've been too hasty. I admit it. I was so taken aback when I was told who she was. Look here – I'll go and ask her to stay. I'll make amends.'

'Better not. She *can't* stay here now she's alone. We'll have to find another couple. I need a chauffeur, and at once!'

'Oh dear!' said Mrs Dorey. 'Maybe we'd better send a wire to Greta's mother to tell her to postpone their visit over here.'

'Seeing as how you'll have nobody in the kitchen after tonight, I agree,' said Quentin shortly.

'Well, I'll go into the kitchen and tell Mrs Barrett how sorry I really am,' said Mrs Dorey, trying to get back into her son's good books, 'and I'll sympathise with her about her husband.'

Quentin did not stop her. What did it matter what 'old Mum' did or said? He knew that Fern would go. By this time tomorrow the house would seem as empty as the grave. No amount of munificence from his mother could keep Fern, his heart's darling, at Swanlake now. It was all too late.

He sat down heavily, put his elbows on the top of his desk and hid a white, tired face in his hands.

What was said between Fern and his

mother he never knew, except that the old lady came back looking extremely ashamed of herself and remained subdued for the rest of the evening.

Quentin only saw Fern once more before she left.

Early the next morning, before anybody else was up, he hung around the garage like a love-sick boy, waiting, until she appeared.

She came down the little iron staircase looking very pale, with dark circles around her lovely eyes, which suggested a sleepless night.

He went forward to meet her.

'My dear,' he said, 'my dear, I had to see you and thank you for everything once more, and tell you how desperately sorry I am that you're leaving us.'

Fern could not speak for a moment, but put out a hand and let him hold it.

She had been crying half the night. They were two very unhappy people, standing there, in the golden light of the warm September morning. But there was nothing more to say. Everything had already been said. All Fern could do was to hold tightly on to her own emotions and try to comfort *him*.

'Don't worry about me, Quentin,' she

said, 'I'll be all right. And I promise to write and let you know what happens to me. Yes, I'll write occasionally. Really, I will.'

'Thank you, darling,' he said under his breath, 'stick to that promise, won't you? Otherwise, I'll worry myself sick.'

'I'll leave my aunt's address in Highgate on a card on my desk,' she said.

'My mother is sorry now for what she did, Fern.'

'Yes, she said so. She was very generous, as I know what it cost her to make such an apology.'

'Oh *God* – to see you go – it murders me – I'm just a weakling about it – I can hardly take it!' he groaned.

'Oh yes, you can,' said Fern with a wry smile. 'Q.D. can take anything.'

'You think more of me than I think of myself, my lass,' he said with a strong Lancashire accent that suddenly brought the light of pure tenderness into her eyes. Somehow the sight of the big gruff fellow – the big tycoon with all his wealth and success – standing there, looking like a miserable school-boy – moved her deeply.

But the time for shedding tears was over. She put his hand swiftly against her cheek, dropped it and ran away from him. Half-way across the courtyard she looked back over her shoulders:

'I won't be leaving until after lunch. I told Mrs Dorey I'd make a nice supper dish that Maureen can heat up for you tonight.'

That simple and typical act of kindness on the part of his 'little cook', acting in the capacity in which she had come to Swanlake, was almost too much for Quentin.

'Oh damn, *damn!*' He uttered the words aloud. He did not go straight into the house but walked blindly through the kitchen garden into the orchard and down into the woods where he could be alone.

He had a lot of business to do today. He must get himself into the state to do it. He was positively appalled by his own weakness.

For Fern, more goodbyes, this time to the staff, had to be said and some sort of garbled explanation given for her abrupt departure. Then there were 'scenes'. Mrs Hatton sniffed into her handkerchief. Maureen burst into loud sobs, protesting that she had never been fonder of anybody than Mrs Barrett and that *she'd* leave, too, and go back to Ireland. Whereupon Fern said:

'Don't you dare, Maureen. You just stay with Rosie and Jim and look after Mr and

Mrs Dorey.'

By the time Hatton had driven Fern to the station (the gardener himself was depressed by her sudden departure), the lovely afternoon had clouded. A faint drizzle started. Fern left Swanlake in an autumnal mist – like the one that had settled over her own life, Fern thought. She could neither see nor think clearly. Even the goodbye with Mrs Dorey had been emotional. The old woman had apologised again and gone so far as to ask Fern to return if ever the occasion arose. But of course Fern knew she would never go back – *never*. It was best that she should not see Quentin again.

Now to try and think about the man to whom she was still married. She had written Terry a long letter telling him that she would like to go out to Madrid as soon as possible and help him to remake his life and start his new career. It would be awful, having to leave Mummy in England and *him* ... but better that she should be with Terry now, and so preserve the ultimate integrity.

She was in a state of daze, and almost too tired to think by the time a taxi had deposited her and her luggage at Aunt Pamela's house in Highgate. She could hardly see out of her eyes. She felt as though she had been uprooted by a violent storm – torn out of her natural surroundings and landed in a strange place. Swanlake had become her true home. To be anywhere else felt all wrong.

Her aunt opened the door to her. It was dark outside. Lights had been switched on in the hall. This was a small modern house; nothing special about it, but it was attractively decorated. Aunt Pamela had the family good taste, and it was full of the nice family furniture.

Miss Pamela Jarvis was older than her sister Mrs Wendell, but both had that delicate pink-and-white prettiness; white hair and a *petite* figure. When Aunt Pam saw her niece's slender figure, she gave a little scream and flung up both hands.

'My *dear!* You've come at exactly the right moment.'

Fern blinked at her with tired eyes, but tried to laugh.

'What sort of right moment? There've been so many wrong ones lately, Aunty Pam!'

'*Just you look who's here,*' said Aunt Pamela in a strange voice and flung open the drawing-room door.

Fern dropped the two suit-cases she was

carrying. Pulling off her gloves, she walked into the welcoming warmth of Aunt Pamela's well-lighted sitting-room.

But she did not look at her mother sitting by the fire. She only saw the tall, gaunt-looking man, standing facing her. A man whose clothes hung on him because he had lost so much weight ... a man with eyes that had once been as blue as her own, but were now dull and fading with age. He looked deadly tired and ill. But Fern's heart turned over at the sight of him. Joy and amazement drained the colour from her cheeks. It was her turn to scream.

'Daddy! *Daddy!*' And the next moment she was caught and held in her father's arms.

22

For the next few moments Fern was in a complete daze. Half laughing, half crying, she kept repeating *'Daddy'* and hugging the tall man with the cadaverous face which she scarcely recognised. It was obvious that worry and loss of appetite had turned her poor father from the fine, well-set-up, ruddy-faced man whom she remembered, into this 'shadow'. Her heart ached for him.

But Bernard Wendell's eyes were not unhappy and his smile was as jolly as Fern ever remembered it.

Aunt Pam left the little family alone. Mr Wendell sat on a sofa with an arm around his wife's shoulder. His daughter sat on a stool at his feet. At last Fern heard the truth – the facts that would be told tomorrow to those concerned with the collapse of the firm of Boyd-Gillingham, Price & Wendell.

Mrs Wendell had already heard it. She looked, Fern thought, a new woman and younger by ten years, wearing one of the old pretty dresses which she had packed away for so long, holding fast to the hand of the man in whom she had never ceased to believe.

'In many ways I think I've been a fool,' Bernard Wendell said with a deep sigh, 'but I acted on the spur of the moment and once having done the "vanishing trick" – I couldn't turn back.'

'But what *did* you do, Daddy,' asked Fern, 'why *did* you vanish?'

'It's all very tricky, my darling.' He sighed again and ruffled her hair. Bernard Wendell was a man who loved his wife and daughter above all things. It was for their sakes even more than for his own honour that he had taken the drastic step which he now explained to Fern.

'I swear to you on my sacred oath, as a husband and a father, that what I am going to tell you is the truth,' he began quietly.

Here Mrs Wendell broke in:

'You've no need to swear to us, Bernard darling. Fern and I *know* you.'

The muscles of the man's cheeks worked. He cleared his throat. It was no easy thing for him to express the gratitude he felt towards these two people who had continued to believe in him even when things looked blackest.

For some time, he said, he had suspected his partner, Boyd-Gillingham, of appropriating clients' money. But he could not be sure. Quite suddenly the storm broke over their heads and the awful news leaked out. 'Old B.G.', as he called his former partner, was dead. *De mortuis nil nisi bonum* – but the truth must be told, now, if at all. B.G. had been secretly gambling. Even though times were good and it might have been thought that no one could make such ghastly errors of judgment – B.G. had made them. He had failed to double his money. He had been influenced by certain business friends who were themselves not entirely 'straight', but there was no need to go into that, Mr Wendell said. It had no direct bearing on his own story. It just happened to be a fact that the wrong sort of contacts had caused B.G.'s downfall.

Having lost a great deal of money, he had also lost his head and begun to dive into yet deeper waters. He gambled furiously. He gained a little, but lost it – far more in the long run than he could recover. It was then that big sums of money were involved, including a huge property investment fund and the personal capital of one very big business man (whose name, Mr Wendell added, need not come into it). This man had been one of the chief victims.

Here, Fern coloured and her breath quickened. She felt that it must be Quentin Dorey to whom her father referred. But for the moment she remained silent, hanging on her father's words.

The story continued. Wendell finally approached his partner and accused him of misappropriation of funds. The senior partner dithered and blustered but finally broke down. He admitted that ruin faced the firm. He wept like a baby, uttering futile apologies, even threatening suicide. Finally he told Bernard that he was a very sick man – in fact, under sentence of death from his doctors. That was the truth, for he had died not long afterwards but he had not saved the day first, Mr Wendell remarked a trifle bitterly.

Bernard Wendell went home on the day of the flare-up between the partners – Fern wouldn't remember because she was not there – but her mother remembered only too well that night when he had looked so ghastly. He had told her that business was bad but that he did not wish to discuss it. But that night, Wendell had to face all the issues alone. Examining the case from every angle he could see that total ruin faced himself as well as his partner. Boyd-Gillingham had alarmed and shocked Bernard by stating categorically that he did not intend to take the whole blame and that he, Bernard, must carry part of the burden.

That, Bernard Wendell told his family now, had seemed outrageously unfair, not only to himself but to everyone. Thinking things over, he saw that his own personal assets were not even a quarter enough to cover the losses incurred by B.G. Within the next forty-eight hours all the big clients involved would demand a statement and their money back, and the storm would break. Wendell had to act quickly. He decided to take measures which might at the time have seemed totally wrong but which had since proved right.

He got out of the country before anybody knew anything or could stop him. He feared to give any explanations to his family in case they might be involved in a court examination under oath. So he left only a note begging them to trust in him.

He had a cousin living in Philadelphia, an American who was once at Oxford with Mr Wendell and always remained in close touch with him. Fern knew the said cousin well –

Martin Van Dwight – a blood relation on her paternal grandmother's side. Old Mrs Wendell had been an American.

Martin Dwight was a millionaire. He was the chairman of one of the biggest banks in Philadelphia. He had often visited England and was devoted to the Wendell family. He was also Fern's godfather.

'I knew,' Mr Wendell continued his story, 'that if anybody on earth could help me, it would be Martin. But I could not write or cable in such a serious contingency. I had to see Martin in person.'

Van Dwight was one of those millionaires who happen to be as generous as they are rich, and was in the habit of giving away huge sums of money. He had so much money that, as he often told his English cousin, he really did not know what to do with it. He had no children and he had hinted that he intended to leave at least half his fortune to his English relations – naming Fern in particular.

'Oh, Daddy. I didn't know that,' broke in Fern breathlessly.

'But I had the feeling that it would be Cousin Martin to whom your father would appeal,' put in Mrs Wendell.

Mr Wendell continued:

This was the one time when he needed Martin's money. He felt that if he went out and told him the truth, Van Dwight would advise and help save the family from disgrace; perhaps even imprisonment that awaited Bernard.

'I told Martin,' said Mr Wendell, 'that I had been entirely ignorant of the facts, but helped to invest the money entrusted to the firm, and that most of it was at the time swallowed up in a certain big property deal that failed to go through because of the firm's collapse. Boyd-Gillingham, Price and Wendell could not begin to fulfil their vast obligations. So much was bought on margin. I had thought the money entirely safe and never dreamed that B.G. was juggling with it like a maniac.'

So Bernard flew to Philadelphia. He meant to return almost at once with the anticipated help of his cousin. But by a stroke of appalling luck, from Wendell's point of view, he arrived over there to find that the Dwights were away for three months touring the Far East – a holiday which the millionaire had long promised his wife.

There had been nothing for Bernard to do but stay hidden in a mountain lodge owned by the Dwight family, where Martin's secretary, who knew Bernard, safe-guarded him; reading the English papers in despair, knowing that there was a hue and cry out for him; learning, finally, of his crazy partner's death and chafing against the loss of time.

Only a fortnight ago, the Dwights returned to Philadelphia and Martin heard his cousin's tale of woe.

'The dear good fellow immediately offered to put things right and although I wasn't keen on taking the money, I knew that I would be a fool not to do so,' said Wendell. 'What was fifty or even a hundred thousand pounds to a man of millions? Most of it is going to be left to Fern anyhow, so you might as well have some of it now, as Dwight said.'

Mr Wendell now sighed and smoothed his daughter's head.

'So you see, my darling, I have had to appropriate *your* funds,' he said, a wan smile lighting up his haggard face.

She leaned her cheek against his knee and hugged him.

'Daddy, Daddy, who cares about Martin's dollars or *any old money* so long as you can put things right and prove your innocence.'

'Bless you, darling, that's what I'm here to do. I've got the money. I can settle the debts. And I intend to brief the finest counsel available to prove that I had no hand in B.G.'s crime.'

'*Crime* is an ugly word, Bernard,' said Mrs Wendell in a low tone.

'Nevertheless,' said Fern's father, 'using other people's money that has been entrusted to one, is criminal in the eyes of the law. Now I intend to clear my name, which I think I can well do with the help of the staff, particularly my good clerk, Herbert Watkins. Incidentally, have you heard what's happened to Watkins?'

Mother and daughter exchanged glances.

'We've never heard a word from him,' said Mrs Wendell.

'Oh well, we'll soon trace him. I expect the poor boy was stricken by the belief that I must have been hand in glove with B.G. I think he had quite a lot of respect for me once.'

'And he will again,' said Fern firmly, 'everybody will, Daddy.'

The man bent over the girl's bright brown head, and when he spoke it was with deep emotion.

'The way you two have kept faith with me

327

through all this awful business makes all the difference to my world,' he said. 'I couldn't even send you a proper explanation or tell you where I was, or what I was doing, in case my letters got into others hands.'

It broke his heart, he added, to find his wife living in Aunt Pam's little house – to hear that their own beautiful home had been sold – and that Fern was having to earn her living as a *cook*.

'I'll never forgive myself,' he groaned.

'But it wasn't your fault, my darling,' protested his wife.

'And I adore cooking,' put in Fern brightly.

'I want to hear more about you, darling,' said Mr Wendell. He got up and walked to the fireplace, knocked his pipe against the fender then began to fill it again.

Fern looked from him to her mother and then down at the floor. Now all the excitement was fading, she began to remember her own personal tragedy.

'Oh, don't let's talk about me tonight,' she said nervously.

'Where is Terry?'

She had expected that question. She thought it best to answer truthfully.

'In a job in Madrid.'

'*Madrid?*' echoed both the Wendells.

'You never told me, darling,' put in her mother.

Fern bit her lip.

'It … it's only just happened.'

'Has anything gone wrong between you two?' asked her father quickly.

She grimaced. She knew she could pull the wool over Mummy's eyes but never over Daddy's. He was far too perceptive.

'Oh well, I suppose you'd better know,' she sighed. 'We haven't been getting on too well lately. Terry couldn't find what he liked in England and he was offered this job in Spain. He's supposed to be sending for me when he's made good.'

Mr Wendell forgot all the harassing affairs that had been filling his mind and his life throughout the summer. He turned his full attention upon his cherished daughter. He knew his Fern. He knew that whatever went wrong with her marriage, it wouldn't be *her* fault. She had always been a child of integrity and strong character. Strongest of them all, he thought sadly. And he had never liked his son-in-law nor wished Fern to enter into that marriage. After the wedding, he remembered telling her mother that it would never last. Terence was unstable even though charming. Fern was infatuated. And it would be Terry who would break it up.

Fern's own story was finally dragged from her. The Wendells discussed it unhappily, realising that all their worst fears had come home to roost. But they were not prepared for the next confession that tumbled out from Fern.

Fern loved her parents to such an extent that she had no secrets from them. As a family they were united and could only exist in an atmosphere of mutual confidence. She decided to tell them about the man for whom she had been working, and her deep feeling for him.

'He's a wonderful, wonderful person even though he's not what Mummy would call "top drawer". But he has all the qualities Daddy admires most in a man and I just feel *utterly* safe with him. After I discovered that Terry was fooling around with that girl in the village and my disillusionment set in, I'm afraid it wasn't long before I had to own I was in love with my employer. But as you know, Mummy and Daddy, I do not believe in divorce any more than you do and I told *him* so. I've just got to try and stick to Terry and make a go of things. That's why I've left Swanlake Manor.'

'My poor little girl,' said Mr Wendell, 'I never dreamed while I was over there in the States that you were going through such a shocking time. What is this chap's name?'

Then Fern looked up at her father, and gave a short laugh.

'Daddy, this will shake you, I'm afraid. His name is Quentin Dorey.'

Mr Wendell almost dropped his pipe. He swung round and faced Fern, his thin face flushing.

'Dorey! Q.D., the financier?'

'Yes, Daddy.'

'Good God!' exclaimed Mr Wendell. 'B.G.s famous client whose affairs I handled when he went sick.'

'Yes.'

'And he knows who *you* are?'

'Yes.'

'And it didn't make any difference?'

'He didn't know for a long time. His mother found out. Then he said it made no difference at all.'

'Oh, dear!' said Mrs Wendell, whose exclamations of distress were never much stronger than that. She was not a violent person. But Bernard Wendell exploded.

'Good God!' he exclaimed again. 'What an unfortunate coincidence. To have fallen for

Q.D. – the great Q.D. – and he feels the same for you? And you can do nothing about it?'

Fern rose and turned her face from her parents. Her lips were trembling. The sickness of her own grief descended again upon her, crushing her.

'No – it's all over. I'm not going to see him again.'

Mrs Wendell got up and walked to her daughter.

'You've worked so hard, darling, and you've been so brave and so good to me – I wish this hadn't happened to you,' she said brokenly.

The next moment, mother and daughter were weeping in each other's arms. Mr Wendell stood by in silent distress. He had met Dorey and spoken to him and admired the quick, decisive business methods of the man. Everybody in the City knew Q.D. by name. He had an excellent reputation. What an unfortunate coincidence that *he* should be the man whom little Fern had grown to love. A hopeless affair – from every point of view. Mr Wendell couldn't bear the thought of Fern's deep hurt. As for his son-in-law – he would like to wring that young imbecile's neck, he thought angrily.

Aunt Pam came in to announce a meal. The Wendells pulled themselves together and a temporary veil was drawn over the tragedies. For Vivien Wendell, at least, it was a wonderful thing to have her husband back with her and to know that he had the means to settle all the debts B.G. had left behind him and to be reinstated as an honoured member of the Stock Exchange.

Fern was the one who felt unhappy during that reunion supper, even if she didn't look it. Thankful though she was to see her father, she was haunted continually by the memory of Quentin and Swanlake, and her loss. She felt utterly heartbroken and lonely – even more lonely because she seemed to stand outside the circle of happiness that surrounded her parents. They held hands tonight like young lovers instead of old, staid married people.

'That's how my darling Q.D. and I might have become if we were married,' Fern thought dismally.

When she went to bed in the little room at the top of the house where Aunt Pam had put up a camp bed for her – it was to cry bitterly and to wonder how she was going to bear permanent separation from Quentin.

23

One dull wet evening in October, Quentin Dorey and his mother sat finishing dinner. It was a Saturday, otherwise Q.D. would have stayed in London. He could hardly bear Swanlake these days. They were going through a dismal patch of weather, too. The grounds of Swanlake Manor were sodden. Jim Hatton was grumbling because he hadn't been able to get on with the big border and had to spend most of the day working in his greenhouses.

Mrs Dorey suffered from rheumatism and even a touch of arthritis, which was making her quite lame.

Tonight Quentin looked as he felt – thoroughly disgruntled.

He was well enough in health but in mind he had never been less cheerful. He had even felt, lately, that some of his mental powers had diminished because he had neither the vigour nor heart to put into the big financial deals which used to mean so much to him. As he often told himself, nothing meant very much to him these days. The house had been like a tomb since his 'little cook' left. As he had anticipated, the whole place had suffered once she departed. He had found a very capable chauffeur to replace young Barrett (which hadn't been difficult, Quentin thought wryly), but from the domestic angle nothing had been right in the house since Fern went away. Even his mother admitted that. Reluctantly she also admitted that she herself often missed Mrs Barrett. She wished she had been nicer to the girl.

But it was too late. And now they had a new cook – quite hopeless, Quentin thought angrily, as he left half his flavourless meal untasted. She couldn't cook. When he *thought* of Fern's lovely entrées and soufflés and those meals at which she had worked so hard – he groaned. He hadn't dared to ask business acquaintances down here lately. As for the Paulsons, he had forbidden his mother to invite Greta or her mother over from Sweden.

'I don't intend ever again to be shoved into the arms of your goddaughter, and as our present cook can do little more than serve up overdone beef and watery cabbage, we won't have *any* house guests,' Quentin announced.

With unusual meekness, Nell Dorey con-
curred with this. She felt no more content
than her son. Life at Swanlake had changed
completely. She had even begun to suspect
that her son was in love with Fern Barrett. It
stood out a mile. No need for her friend,
Enid, to suggest it. She *knew*. Poor Q. was
pining – yes, quite obviously pining for Mrs
Barrett. Mrs Dorey deplored the fact but
faced up to it. Sometimes she clung to the
old pathetic hope that he might eventually
turn to Greta. But deep down in her
mother's heart she wished that Quentin
could be happy again even if it meant Fern
coming back. She could not bear to see him
so changed, so gloomy. He worked twice as
hard as usual with less result. He took a
fortnight's holiday but came back in the
middle of it, physically rested but with his
mind still in a turmoil.

One weekend, he arrived at the Manor
with an evening paper and threw it down
triumphantly in front of his mother.

'Read that and you'll see that all the
unkind things you said about Bernard
Wendell had no foundation, my dear Mum,'
he said.

Nell Dorey put on her glasses and waded
with some astonishment through a long

article headed: BERNARD WENDELL RETURNS. It was followed by the story – embroidered by the Press, of course – of his disappearance and why he had gone and how he had paid back every penny of the money the firm owed the clients. It stated also that Mr Wendell was now fully in a position to clear his own name.

'There'll be a public inquiry, but Wendell has plenty of backers – his own staff and people who knew him,' said Quentin. 'There isn't a slur on the fellow's name. He vanished because he wanted to be given the chance to get the money. He knew that if he stayed here to face the music they'd break him before he could do anything about it.'

'So you'll get all your own money back?' Mrs Dorey exclaimed, and had been gratified when he answered:

'I will.'

But Mrs Dorey was not prepared for his next remark.

'So you see, you owe young Fern a further apology,' he had added bitterly. 'She ought never to have been dismissed.'

Following that renewed reproach, Mrs Dorey came to the definite decision that her son was, indeed, in love with Mrs Barrett. But she thought it best to say nothing.

She had her own worries – small but galling. Maureen had left, stating openly that she could not get on with the new cook, and that she wished Mrs Barrett had never left. Mrs Hatton came up to work as usual – she was the faithful one – but the whole place had lost that look of shining order that had existed when Mrs Barrett was in charge. Mrs Dorey had to hand it to Fern that she had been 'one in a thousand'.

Suddenly tonight, for the first time for many long weeks, Mrs Dorey felt an urge to mention the girl to her son.

'You know I gave Mrs Barrett a good reference when that Lady what's-her-name phoned from Guildford – I forget her name; have you by any chance heard yourself how Mrs Barrett is getting on and what has happened to young Barrett?'

Quentin got up from the table. His face was granite hard, his eyes expressionless. He betrayed nothing of the emotion that Fern's name roused in him. He said:

'I have phoned Mrs Barrett twice. Each time she says she is well and that, as far as she knows, Barrett is getting on with this job in Madrid but that he has not yet made any move to send for her.'

'I hope the poor girl's all right. At least

she's got her father back.'

'Yes, she sees her parents quite regularly. They have taken a furnished flat in London for the time being.'

Mrs Dorey cleared her throat, took a humble look at her son's face and added:

'I must say I think Lady Whatever-her-name – is lucky to have Fern.'

Then Quentin gave a harsh laugh.

'That's a masterly understatement,' he said and walked out of the room.

Mrs Dorey drummed her fingers on the dinner table and sighed.

'Oh dear,' she thought. 'Oh, *dear*, what a pity it all is.'

And she was vastly surprised to find how much she wished that the door would open and that Fern's trim young figure would appear instead of the new housekeeper's portly one, and that she could hear that rather sweet and charming voice ask them if they had 'enjoyed the meal'. 'Really,' thought Mrs Dorey, 'I shall have to get rid of this new female and find another cook or Q. will *starve!*'

In the library, Quentin sat at his desk trying to concentrate on a business letter which he had brought down from the office. He did not care a damn about the dinner, he thought savagely, that was a *detail*. It was not to have *her* here any longer that wounded him. Not to be able to go and ask her all the questions that she usually answered so expertly. Not to be able to draw that adorable young figure into his arms and tell her how much he loved her. It was intolerable.

Tonight, he considered selling the Manor – selling everything up ... breaking away from his mother ... going to the other side of the world.

But what good would that be? To whichever part of the world you went, you couldn't escape from memories. You carried your own private personal heaven or hell with you. The last time he had phoned Fern she had answered all his anxious questions about herself guardedly. She had assured him that she was well and extremely busy – which helped.

'Do you ever give me a thought, lass?' he had asked in the Lancashire dialect that came easily to him when he was most moved.

'You know I do,' she had replied.

Now he knew that he dreaded the day when he would phone her only to hear that she was just about to go out to Madrid. It would be grim – to have to imagine her back in the arms of that young jackanapes. She hadn't been too happy about him, she said. His letters were sketchy, and she admitted she had a strong suspicion that he was involved with some Spanish girl whose name kept cropping up even in the occasional notes he wrote home. Someone called Nina, the daughter of the proprietor of the hotel in which he was living.

Terry seemed to have a special liking for that sort of girl, Fern had told Quentin with a laugh which did not deceive Q.D. It had a bitter edge to it. But the moment he suggested that she did something about her marriage, Fern had cut him short.

'Don't let's discuss that, Quentin dear,' she had begged.

'Then promise you'll look after yourself and let me know if you really need me,' he said.

Now he unlocked the drawer of his desk and took out a letter that Fern had written. She had kept her promise to write. This was the one she had sent last week. She told him that she had been for a month now with Sir Brian and Lady Lockover. In a cook-housekeeper's position which she had found a week after leaving Swanlake.

The Lockovers are quite young and charming and have five children. There's a German girl living in and two 'staggered' dailies to help, as well as a nurse for the twins who are three. It's quite an amusing household and they are frightfully nice to me and appreciative of my cooking. I did that Brazilian sweet that you and your friends liked so much when it was Lady Lockover's birthday party the other night ... it was a huge success...

Here Q.D. tightened his lips and half shut his eyes. Dear, darling Fern. His little cook. *His.* Not the Lockovers. *Damn them!* He would always feel that Fern was his, even though she remained married to that boy in Madrid.

He continued to read the letter. She wrote in detail and somehow it brought her nearer to him.

I miss Swanlake terribly. But then I shall never feel again about any job as I felt about chez-vous, as you can understand. But you would like this place. It's part Tudor and part of it earlier still – all stone-built and quite magnificent. Brian Lockover, whose name you probably know in the world of finance, is a company

342

director. He is mad about horses. Everybody here rides, including all the children. They keep a groom and three ponies and money is no object, and I'm very comfortable with two beautiful rooms of my own in what they call the 'Round Tower'. Fascinating circular rooms which I think must at one time or other have been part of a Norman structure. Very thick walls and narrow windows. I have my own bathroom and central heating, and in a way I suppose it's all more luxurious than my little flat as at Swanlake. They treat me as part of the family, too, and I often have lunch with Elizabeth Lockover and the children. In fact, I went to school with one of Lady Lockover's cousins.

But what wouldn't I give to find myself back in my flat at Swanlake? How are the darling swans? Will you give them a piece of bread from me when you next go down to see them?...

Here Quentin's fingers tightened on the sheet of paper so closely written in a firm, neat hand. So she *did* miss him. Life wasn't the same for her any more than it was for him. He knew that. He knew that true, loyal little heart of hers.

The letter continued with a description of the garden of Fern's present home, Heron

Hall. How much she missed Jim Hatton, she said. The head gardener at Heron Hall wasn't a patch on Jim. The herbaceous border would never have the show they used to have at Swanlake. But she loved the children. There were two boys at a prep school, who would be home for the Christmas holidays. Then there was Vanessa, age seven, a darling little girl who went to day-school in Guildford. And the adorable twins, Charles and James, with whom she was great friends. Fern told Quentin how happy she was about her father, too – and how his Counsel was quite positive he could restore his client's prestige completely. It was a great happiness for her being able to visit both parents, and see them living together again, enjoying some of their former comforts. But, Fern added, Daddy did not intend to spend one dollar more of Cousin Martin's money than was necessary in order to repay the firm's debts and restore his own reputation. After that he hoped to get back to work in Throgmorton Street and support his own family.

Quentin finished reading Fern's letter, folded it and locked it up again. He found himself wishing vainly that he could have been the one to finance Bernard Wendell.

Anything, in order to feel that *he* personally was doing something for Fern. What hit Q.D. hardest was the knowledge that not only was he separated from Fern but not of the slightest use to her. But what he could and did do was to write a personal letter to Fern's father, congratulating him on his return and bright prospects and telling him that if ever he was re-established on the Stock Exchange, he, Q.D., would at once place as much business as possible in his hands. To this came an instant reply, stressing Bernard Wendell's warm gratitude and thanks.

'*When all this is over I hope we shall meet again,*' he had ended.

That would be something, Q.D. thought ... even to become friends with Fern's father. But it was the thin end of the wedge and possibly Fern would deplore it. She insisted that she did not want to risk meeting him, herself.

Quentin was in his office that following Monday when the call came through which was to change the whole direction of his life – and Fern's.

Miss Porter put it through.

'An urgent personal call for you, Mr Dorey, from Mrs Barrett.'

That name was sufficient to excite and surprise Quentin. It was so thoroughly unlike Fern to telephone him at the office, and in the middle of the morning, too.

Once he heard her voice he knew that something serious had happened; it was trembling and unlike her own.

'Quentin, dear, forgive me – are you very involved or can I speak to you?'

He was deeply involved – two people waiting next door to see him, and an important meeting before lunch and he was already late – but what did that matter?

'What's happened, darling? Tell me...' He used the endearment automatically.

'It's Terry...'

'Yes. Well–?'

'Oh, Quentin ... he ... he's *dead*...'

Q.D.'s pulses jerked in a crazy way. He caught his breath. Then he said:

'How ... why ... when?'

She told him – in a state of acute nervous agitation, choking back her tears. It was not that she felt any deep sorrow. She was no hypocrite, she said, but she was shocked and she had once been very fond of Terence. He had been her husband – her first love. Quentin understood. Sudden death, and a violent one, had befallen the handsome, irresponsible young man. Shocking enough – even for someone less kind-hearted and loyal than Fern.

It had all happened three days ago.

The hotel in Madrid had telephoned her. She had received the call down in Guildford. It informed her that *Señor* Barrett had been involved in a fatal fight and was dead. Fern flew to Madrid at once. Sir Brian Lockover had been wonderful and given her every help. He had personally seen her on to the plane. She reached the Spanish hotel to find chaos – police, newspaper reporters; and the manager in custody, accused of Terry's manslaughter; his family weeping and wailing.

Everyone showed Fern kindness and sympathy, however. It was not her fault, they said, but the young English *Señor's* folly. He had been pursuing the hotel proprietor's beautiful brown-eyed daughter, Nina. He had been warned to leave the girl alone. She was only seventeen and her father knew that the *Señor* was married. One night Terry had drunk too much wine and – as Fern now told Quentin – she knew how unstable he could be when he had too much to drink. He was discovered by the Spanish director in Nina's bedroom. A scuffle followed. The outraged father had meant only to teach the boy a lesson, but he had a stiletto in his hand and the sharp blade pierced the heart of the drunken Englishman. Terry died in an ambulance on the way to hospital.

Quentin drew a deep breath as she finished her story.

'Good God!' he ejaculated.

'Can you believe it, Quentin … Terry … knifed … *dead*…?'

Quentin thought of his good-looking former chauffeur, with his uniform cap at a rakish angle on his fair head and his ingratiating smile. He muttered that he couldn't believe it. It was too terrible.

'Yes. *Terrible*. All that charm, all his potential good – finished. And to end in such a ghastly way … through his own folly.'

'My poor Fern – what can I do?'

'Nothing. It's all over. They buried him out there yesterday. I've just come home. Not to Guildford. I'm in London with my parents. The Lockovers understand. I can't go back – at present, anyhow.'

Suddenly a crazy excitement welled up into Quentin Dorey's heart. He said:

'Fern … my dear, dear little Fern … when I leave the office this evening, can I come and see you?'

A hesitation, then came her low voice.

'Not tonight, Quentin dear. You understand? I'm … suffering a bit from shock. I've got a frightful headache. And I've got a lot to see to and think over. Terry has an uncle somewhere – I must try to contact him. And put the announcement in the papers, too. So many things to do. Daddy's helping me.'

'When can I see you?' asked Quentin.

'Perhaps the day after tomorrow. I'll ring you again.'

'Promise?'

Her reply came now in a richer, closer voice:

'Oh, Quentin … my dear … yes … you *know* that I will.'

He hung up the receiver, reached for a cigar and lit it, his fingers shaking, his face flushed. But in his eyes there lay a new look of hope – a mad, joyous hope that flooded his whole soul and temporarily ejected all other thought from his brain.

He suddenly reached out a hand, pressed the buzzer and spoke to his secretary.

'Get my mother on the phone,' he commanded.

Very soon that good lady down at Swanlake

was hearing the news and facing her own final defeat – even if it was one tinged with maternal happiness for Q.

'I want you to know this instant, Mum,' he said in a strangely excited voice that she had never before heard from him, 'that now Fern is free I shall wait a suitable time and then ask her to marry me. Just accept it, and don't let us have any recriminations.'

Mrs Dorey made no recriminations. She really had reached a point when she did not know whether to be glad or sorry.

But it was a good many weeks and months before that all-important question could be put by Quentin to Terence Barrett's widow. Then it seemed only a short time before Quentin Dorey was able to realise his life's greatest ambition: not only find his personal heaven but lay his world at Fern's feet and help her to rediscover hers.

It was on the first day of June – nearly nine months later – that Fern and Quentin were married, very quietly at a little church in Chelsea near the flat in which the Wendells now lived. After the reception they drove in Quentin's Rolls Royce down to Swanlake.

By mutual wish, they were spending the first two nights of their married life at the

Manor. Afterwards they were to fly to America where Q.D. was going to combine his honeymoon with one or two big business dates; and spend a few days with Fern's cousin, Martin Dwight, in the mountain lodge where Mr Wendell had been sheltered during his awful crisis ... then come home *via* Canada, which both Quentin and Fern wanted to see. But Fern, in particular, asked for those first two days in her beloved Swanlake.

'It will be so magical – to be there again and with Q.D. as my own adored husband instead of my employer,' she said.

'And for me,' he had said, 'it will be equally thrilling, my dear, to be in my house with my wife, instead of my little cook.'

'As *well as...*' she corrected him. 'I intend to cook for us during the forty-eight hours we are there, my darling.'

Mrs Dorey made the gesture of her life – swallowed her disappointment over her goddaughter and attended the wedding. Fern expected no emotion nor, indeed, any display of affection from the tall, gaunt, north-country woman who had brought Quentin into the world. But Quentin knew his mother. Under that harsh exterior there really beat a heart, and Nell Dorey arrived in London with the firm decision to rise above her own wishes and welcome Fern into the family.

This, for Q.'s sake alone, as she told herself. She had never seen him look so well; so blissfully happy. She could not bear to dampen his spirits by raising any kind of objection to the marriage; besides which, the old lady knew perfectly well that, if she did so, she could not only antagonise him but lose him altogether. So she paid Fern the compliment of buying a new dress and hat for the occasion and softening those hard features of hers into a smile which became a real one, in the vestry, when she bent to kiss Fern.

'Be happy, my dear, and I hope you'll let me see something of you and Q. in the future,' she said.

Fern kept back her own impulsive longing to hug her newly-made mother-in-law, and pressed her hand.

'You know we shall always welcome you, Mrs Dorey.'

'I may say,' Mrs Dorey added, in a low voice, half-grudging the compliment she was about to pay, 'that Q. told me you, yourself, suggested I should go on living at the Manor, and after all my hastiness I think that was very magnanimous of you. But, as you know, I have already left and am staying with my friend, Enid. But as I told her, I think you're a fine girl and I'm sure you'll make Q. a very good wife.'

Quentin, an arm about his bride's shoulders, looked with twinkling, kindly eyes at his mother.

'Good for you, Mum. That's made my day,' he said.

Mrs Dorey returned to her pew, sniffing into her handkerchief. It had been a considerable wrench for her, leaving Swanlake and the life she had led so long with her only son, and knowing that she must surrender her domain to Fern.

But she knew that it was her duty to allow the young couple to live alone. And, if nothing else, Nell Dorey was a woman who had always done her duty.

Because of the recent fatality of the bride's first husband, the wedding was a very quiet one – attended only by close relatives. One school-friend of Fern's and the 'best man', a barrister who had known Q.D. for many years.

After an equally quiet wedding-breakfast at the Connaught Hotel, Quentin and Fern drove away in the famous Rolls, leaving at least two extremely happy people behind them – Fern's parents, who could not have been more delighted to see their beloved child so happy at last.

Mr Wendell followed the car out of sight and turned to his wife.

'A very different affair from her last marriage, when we were both so apprehensive, Viv darling. It will be all right for her *this* time.'

'I think,' said Vivien Wendell with a happy sigh, 'that Q.D. is one of the nicest men I've ever met in my life. And I couldn't care less whether he always wears the right tie or not. Anyhow, Fern will soon put *that* right. He's a darling, the way he asks her advice all the time. He is so modest – that brilliant business man! And he worships her. He'll give her everything that she deserves.'

'I'm not sure that I altogether care for that battle-axe of a mother-in-law she's collected,' added Bernard Wendell with a grimace.

'Fern told me she was quite beastly to her to begin with but she's all right now. The old snob was so afraid at first that Fern was just a hired domestic, not good enough for her son. I think she's rather pleased now because we've produced a title or two in the family, and because *you* are "in the clear" again, my darling.'

'Well, as long as she doesn't go and live with them and wreck Fern's happiness—' began Mr Wendell.

'She won't,' broke in Vivien Wendell, who was a shrewd woman. 'She isn't that sort. Anyhow, I hear from Fern that Mrs Dorey has some friend or other called Enid, who is tired of living in the country, and the two old things are going to have a flat together in Worthing. That'll be just far enough away from Swanlake.'

24

It was a golden June day.

Quentin drove the car. As they moved swiftly and smoothly through the London traffic and on to the main Brighton road, Fern sat lost in a silence more eloquent than words. She could not even describe to herself what she was feeling at this moment. She had to keep looking at the thin gold circle on her left hand to assure herself that she really was married to Quentin.

'My little Mrs Q.D.' he had called her, after the wedding.

There was only one shadow over Fern's happiness; one 'haunt' that perhaps would not vanish entirely for a little while. The ghost of poor Terry was with her. How could it be otherwise, she thought, when his death was so recent?

She could not mourn him, but she could be, and was, deeply sorry for his wasted life and catastrophic end. He had brought it all down on himself. That was his tragedy. Her brow furrowed. She seemed to see him

sitting in Quentin's place at the wheel of this
very car ... poor handsome, ne'er-do-well
Terry. And once she had thought she could
never belong to anybody else. She shivered,
then cast the shadow from her mind. She
must try never to think of the past.

Today she was all Quentin's. Everything
was different. Utterly different. This love
went deeper than the mere passionate adoration of a young girl. What she was giving to
Quentin was the steadfast, enduring
emotion of an experienced woman. And
what Quentin was giving to her, she thought
tenderly, was something so much greater
and finer than poor Terry had ever given.
Integrity ... security ... *absolute* love.

Quentin turned to her with a quick, happy
smile. The Big Man looked a mere boy
today, she thought, despite the grey in his
hair. He wore a dark-grey suit and a red
carnation which gave him a debonair look.
She, herself, had been married in a flowered
yellow silk suit, beautifully tailored, under a
long coat of fine pale-yellow kid. A brimmed
hat of transparent lacy straw in the same
pale yellow colour, was pulled down over
her head. On the lapel of the coat there
sparkled an exceedingly beautiful emerald
and diamond brooch which was her

husband's wedding present to her. There had been many others.

She hadn't been able to stop Quentin from buying presents. As she told him, he had indulged in 'a perfect orgy' and it had become almost embarrassing. A diamond bracelet, real pearls, a crocodile travelling-bag, a sable jacket, a short white mink coat for the evening. Almost every day there came an offering. And there would be more to come, when they got to New York, he said. Fifth Avenue waited for his wife!

Fern could hardly believe that she was now married to a man who was virtually a millionaire; that this sort of lavish spending came naturally to Q.D., although, he maintained, he had never before known the joy of being able to buy presents for a woman he loved.

Fern was thrilled with all the lovely glamorous things, but it was Quentin, the man, whom she wanted and everything else fell into obscurity.

'Happy darling?' he asked her.

'No – wretched,' she grinned at him.

'Don't tease me. Tell me the truth. You don't know what I've been through lately; so afraid you might change your mind or postpone our wedding.'

'I think we should have waited longer,' she said frankly, 'but I know Terry wouldn't mind. He never was a man for convention, and really one shouldn't do things just because of what other people think. One should do just what one really thinks *oneself* is right.'

'And you do think it was right for us to get married today?'

She leaned close to his side.

'Absolutely, Quentin. I asked Elizabeth Lockover – she said she saw no object in our waiting the conventional year.'

'I like that fellow Brian Lockover. They must all stay with us one day. All the kids, too.'

'I'd love that.'

She thought affectionately of her former employers. They had been heart-broken to lose her but thrilled by her story. They invited her to go down to Heron Hall with her husband after they returned from their honeymoon.

Q.D. pressed a hand over Fern's knee.

'Mum behaved rather well today, didn't she?'

'Mum behaved very well. I think she and I will find some basis for friendship in the future.'

'I'm sure she'll grow to love you dearly, Fern. Incidentally, did you see Greta's telegram amongst the others?' he added, rather wryly.

'I did. I felt rather mean – snatching you away from her.'

'You didn't do that, darling. I was never hers. I've never belonged to any woman but you.'

'But I have one big rival.'

'Who?' he asked indignantly.

'Not "who" but "what". High finance. I'll lose you again and again to some big property deal.'

'I shall always enjoy my financial life, Fern darling, but if you needed me and I knew it, I'd break off negotiations for the biggest deal that was ever put through – even if it meant me losing it.'

Her eyes sparkled.

'I believe you would.'

Swanlake waited for them, dreaming, enchanted, in the warmth and languor of the warm summer afternoon. As they reached the wrought-iron gates, Quentin hooted. Out of the lodge immediately there emerged the figures of Jim Hatton, his wife, his old mother and their young family. They had been waiting for this moment. They all held roses. They came forward and threw the flowers into the car, Jim looking a trifle sheepish but grinning all over his brown face.

'Welcome home, Mr and Mrs Dorey.'

'Welcome,' repeated Rosie, and gazed with awe at the young, beautiful bride who, she thought, did not look nearly old enough to have been married *twice*. And it *was* a little 'awesome' to think that she – the little cook whom Rosie had worked with a year ago – was now the mistress of Swanlake Manor.

But Fern had her own way of thanking these loyal people. She got out of the car and kissed the two women and the children, and pressed Jim's big calloused hand.

'Thank you. It's marvellous to see you again – all of you.'

Mrs Hatton said, a trifle anxiously:

'I had a letter from the secretary to say that you didn't want me up at the house tonight, is that true … Mrs B. – I mean Mrs Dorey? Can't I help?'

'No thanks, Rosie,' smiled Fern.

'The new "daily", Rita, will come first thing in the morning if you want, to help with the breakfast–' began Rosie.

'I don't want her,' broke in Fern, 'honestly, Rosie – I don't want *anybody*. I want to manage myself. You can come in later in the day to clean, but until then I want to be alone with my husband…' (She used the word proudly.)

Q.D., feeling benevolent as a bridegroom should, threw a pound note into the palm of the Hatton's little boy, then the Rolls moved on.

'*Well!*' exclaimed Mrs Hatton, 'fancy not wanting any servants. *She's* going to cook Mr Dorey's dinner, herself.'

'Well, I don't reckon he'll come to any harm with *her* cooking – not like he would if you was going to do it, duckie,' said Jim, and laughed when his wife protested.

Once in the house, Quentin shut the door, took his wife in his arms and kissed her long and ardently.

'My God, I love you so much I don't know what to do,' he said.

'Darling, you look quite pale. Go and pour yourself out a whisky and soda,' she laughed.

'I need it, my darling. What are you going to do?'

'Get off this suit, find my overall and start the dinner. Rosie's supposed to have bought everything I ordered. I'm going to cook you a most *recherch*é wedding meal tonight, Mr Dorey.'

'But it's our *wedding* night, Fern. Oughtn't I to take you out?'

'So you prefer a restaurant to my cuisine, eh?'

His rugged face broke into a broad smile. He shook his head at her.

'Eh, my lass, tha's a caution.'

'Eh, lad,' she mimicked his dialect, 'tha's one thyself.'

'Rotten,' he said. 'Nobody but a Lancashire lass can speak my lingo as it should be spoken.'

Fern giggled and ran lightly up the familiar staircase. The house looked its best – full of Jim Hatton's most beautiful flowers in the amber shadows of the approaching evening.

Rosie – Fern knew it would be Rosie – had arranged quite a lovely vase full of mixed flowers and placed it on the dressing-table in the big double guest-room which had been prepared for bride and bridegroom.

This was to be Fern's future bedroom. She had always liked it better than any of the others. She approved of the décor – the powder-blue carpet, the white and silver floral paper, and the delightful white and silver brocaded curtains framing three tall windows which had a glorious view of the garden and lake.

She began to take off her smart clothes. Her fingers shook a little with excitement as she did so. What a thrill this was ... coming back here as Q.D.'s wife. This lovely house was *her* home now, as well as his. Someone else lived in the little flat across the courtyard. Smythe, the chauffeur who had supplanted Terry nearly a year ago, and Mrs Smythe who, Q. complained, cooked so badly. They had been given the day off. They wouldn't appear.

Quentin brought up some of the luggage. Fern had already opened a suit-case and pulled out one of her old white overalls. She was slipping into it when Quentin came in with the larger cases. He had taken off his coat and rolled up his shirt-sleeves. A newly-lit cigar was between his teeth. His hair was rough and he looked warm. He grinned at her, and she adored him. He dropped the cases, took the cigar from his mouth and laid it in an ash-tray. He came close to the slim, starry-eyed girl and looked at her long and hard.

'What's for supper, Mrs Dorey?' he asked.

'Wait and see.'

'Can I cook it with you?'

'Certainly not. You know I don't allow

anybody in my kitchen.'

'Can I *wash* it up, then?'

'The dish-washing machine will do most of it, but I might allow you to help me with the oddments.'

'Can I lay the table?'

'You wouldn't know how,' she jeered.

'Okay, I wouldn't. But *you* know everything. And *you* are *my* "everything". Everything that is good and true and fine. There's never been another girl like you.'

Her cheeks flamed. She laughed. He was glad to see how much better she looked than she used to do. Not so thin. Not so worried. And very, very beautiful, he thought, awe in his heart as he remembered that this was his own wife.

Suddenly embarrassed – feeling like a young girl who had never been married before – Fern turned from her husband's ardent gaze and walked to one of the windows. She leaned out, sniffing the sweet warm air.

'The swans are there. Come and look. We'll go down and feed them after supper.'

He said:

'I always liked this place. Now I shall never want to leave it. You'll have to push me to the office.'

She turned back to him. His 'little cook', he thought, in one of those old white overalls.

'Oh, my adorable Fern,' he whispered, and pulled her into his arms. 'What a day to remember – this day of our marriage.'

She pressed her happy face against his shoulder, her arms about his waist.

'Some husbands forget the date. Promise you won't.'

'I never will, my love.'

'Mr Dorey,' she said, and tossed back her head and laughed up at him, with brilliant blue eyes, 'I don't really know *what* you're doing up in my bedroom. It's most unseemly for you to act this way with the cook, and if you don't let me go, I'll never get that dinner started.'

'I don't really care all that much about the dinner, you know,' he said in a low voice, and took her in his arms.

And now between them there was no more laughter or badinage – or speaking; but only the deep sweet silence which is love.

The publishers hope that this book has given you enjoyable reading. Large Print Books are especially designed to be as easy to see and hold as possible. If you wish a complete list of our books please ask at your local library or write directly to:

Magna Large Print Books
Magna House, Long Preston,
Skipton, North Yorkshire.
BD23 4ND

This Large Print Book, for people
who cannot read normal print,
is published under the auspices of

THE ULVERSCROFT FOUNDATION

... we hope you have enjoyed this book.
Please think for a moment about those
who have worse eyesight than you ...
and are unable to even read or enjoy
Large Print without great difficulty.

You can help them by sending a
donation, large or small, to:

**The Ulverscroft Foundation,
1, The Green, Bradgate Road,
Anstey, Leicestershire, LE7 7FU,
England.**
or request a copy of our brochure for
more details.

The Foundation will use all donations
to assist those people who are visually
impaired and need special attention
with medical research, diagnosis
and treatment.

Thank you very much for your help.